UNVEILING THE COUNTERFEIT BRIDE

A STEAMY REGENCY HISTORICAL ROMANCE

AVA DEVLIN

Unveiling the Counterfeit Bride

The Silver Leaf Seductions - Book 2

Ava Devlin

Copyright © 2020 by Ava Devlin

All rights reserved. This book or any portion thereof

may not be reproduced or used in any manner whatsoever

without the express written permission of the publisher

except for the use of brief quotations in a book review.

Printed in the United States of America

First Printing, 2020

http://avadevlin.com

Contact the author at ava@avadevlin.com

Cover art by BZN Studio Designs

http://covers.bzndesignstudios.com

Copyediting by Claudette Cruz

https://www.theeditingsweetheart.com/

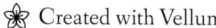 Created with Vellum

For Gemma and Noemie, who gave Serre Chevalier its magic.

BONUS MATERIAL

Flip to the end of the book for special bonus material, sent free to your inbox!

PROLOGUE

The tide was coming in.

It had been such a hopeful day at the start, sunny and calm on the water with laughter and hope for the years ahead echoing from the hull of the Atlas family's little boat. When they had seen the party waiting for them on the shore at Calais, it had seemed nothing in the world could rob them of the joy of their success.

And yet, Yves Monetier had learned long ago that ugly things could happen on beautiful days.

He had learned on that brisk autumn morning, when he'd been wrenched from his hiding place amongst the uniforms and rations by British soldiers, that beauty did not preclude horror. And he had learned on what seemed like the millionth day of his captivity in the dank and lightless cells of Dover Castle, when Mary Atlas had first come to visit him with hope of a return home, that lightless days sometimes hid the most brilliant joys of all.

Even so, knowing better as he did, it was hard to accept the bloom of blood that swirled into the sea foam as the water inched closer to the bodies lying on the rocks. It was impossible to believe that things had gone so badly so quickly.

He had thought his decades as a soldier had made him immune to shock like this, but perhaps the relative safety and predictability of these last three years, tucked in a prison cell, had made him forget how quickly life itself can be stolen from a man.

Or a woman.

Only a moment ago, there had been nine souls standing parlay on this beach, himself included. He knew he had been little more than cargo in this exchange, granted importance he did not rightly deserve on merit of his brother's standing in Paris.

It had been a simple enough deal struck between his brother's men and a British smuggling operation called the Silver Leaf Society. Release Yves from jail and return him to France and in return, a high-ranking British prisoner would be handed over to the Silver Leaf agents to be returned to his family in Britain.

The exchange had been immediately suspect. It wasn't only Jonathan Monetier standing in wait on the Calais shore, but two infantrymen and, bafflingly, Jonathan's twelve-year-old son, Charles. Once the prisoners had been swapped and Walter Atlas had begun to prepare to cast off back towards Britain, all hell had broken loose.

The infantrymen had been ordered to fire once their backs were turned. Both men died on impact. Yves would never know if his brother had intended to spare the woman and her baby, because the opportunity was never given. She had shoved the child into Yves's arms and charged Jonathan with a dirk she had hidden in her dress pockets.

Now, they were dead.

Only five souls remained on the beach: himself and the babe in his arms; the two grunt soldiers who had fired upon his British liberators; and his nephew, Charles, whose anguished cries over his father's lifeless body rang into the balmy summer breeze alongside the seagull song from above.

It felt unreal, as though he were not even inhabiting his own person, but rather observing this disaster unfurl from a distance, where all sounds were muted and movements slowed.

It would shame him, later, that hearing young Charles cry out like that hadn't spurred him to action. It would strike him cold that the infant girl in his arms was *not* crying. She was oblivious, gurgling and toying with the buttons on his coat, as though her entire world had not just shattered in front of her.

His brother's body was crumpled next to the woman's. Her bloodied blade glinted against the rays of sunlight, her hand still reaching for his throat, even in death.

Would God frown upon Yves for mourning her more than his own blood?

Mary Atlas had been a woman of honor, while Jonathan had never put much stock into ideas of altruism and nobility, even as a child. He had killed that woman's husband with the same chilly disregard, the same glee over his own power, that he'd used to knock birds from nests when they were young.

Jonathan's duplicity should not have surprised Yves. None of it should have. He must truly have lost the sharpness on the edges of his mind to think that his proud, arrogant older brother would have entertained a fair, albeit illicit exchange of prisoners with the enemy.

Walter Atlas and the British soldier whose exchange had been the price of his own freedom were crumpled near the boat, the water lapping at their clothes. Both men had died with their backs turned, thinking that their business was complete.

They had likely been happily planning what the hours to come might hold in store.

It was the lucky ones who never saw death coming.

"... the baby?" one of the infantrymen was saying, gesturing at the bundle Yves held. "Do you want us to handle it, sir?"

That was the push he had needed, the tumble from the suspended horror of the moment back to the cruel edge of reality.

"The child is mine," he said sharply, taking a step backward.

The two men exchanged a glance.

"An English baby, sir?" he asked, as though the chaos had addled Yves's brain.

"She is a child," Yves snapped, "and is as French as I am. The Atlas woman was only holding her because that is what women are prone to do. I would never have entrusted my daughter to that knife-wielding hysteric if I'd known her true nature!"

Before they could reflect too carefully on what he'd said, Yves marched around them and towards his nephew.

The boy had quieted, his keening cries reduced to little more than a whimper now. He was rocking on his heels next to his deceased father, his eyes fixed on his own shoes as the briny wind tousled his sandy brown hair.

"Charles," Yves said gently, drawing the boy's eyes up to meet his own, the same vibrant blue as his own. "Do you remember me, boy?"

He nodded, swiping at the tears on his cheeks in a flare of sudden embarrassment and scrambling to his feet. "Yes, Uncle," he replied, his voice fluting right on the edge of manhood. "Yes, of course. Papa was ... he was so happy that you were coming home. He was ... He was ..." The boy clamped his mouth shut, unable to say more.

"I know that, Charles. I know," Yves assured him. "We will have time to mourn soon, I promise. Right now, I need you to take your cousin for me and wait over by the rocks. I must ensure your father and the others are handled appropriately."

"Cousin?" the boy echoed, his eyes falling on the baby that Mary Atlas had pushed into his uncle's arms, moments before her death. "You have a baby?"

"I do indeed," Yves replied, carefully folding the girl into the boy's spindly embrace. "Much happened while I was captive. Now, please, take her to the rocks there on the far end of the beach. Such a little girl should not have to see such awful things. She needs a strong cousin like you to protect her."

The boy's shoulders straightened, his chin lifting with the acknowledgement that *he* was not the child here. "Yes, Uncle. I will protect her, of course," he swore, his grip on the girl becoming immediately more certain and steady.

With the baby held so carefully in his arms, young Charles could not catch the next tear that escaped. He marched down the beach with his back to the dead, that single tear glinting on his stoic face. He might be nearing manhood, but he was still far too young to have just experienced such horror. What in the name of God was Jonathan thinking, bringing the boy along for this?

Yves watched him go, drawing in a shaky breath before looking down at the bodies by his feet.

His brother was scowling even in death, his jaw set with the arrogant confidence that anything he ever chose to do must, by its very nature, be correct. He had died feeling justified, and looking down at him, Yves could feel nothing but anger, his sorrow reserved for those who had been hurt by this man's actions.

He turned his back to Jonathan and lowered himself to his knees, turning Mary Atlas onto her back as carefully as he could. Her mahogany curls caught in the wind, floating alongside the lovely curve of her cheek. Her pale eyes stared sightlessly into the sun.

He closed her eyelids and whispered an apology to her, hoping that somehow she could hear it. "You deserved so much more," he told her, folding her hands over her stomach. "I will pray for your soul. I will protect your daughter with my life. I am forever in your debt."

As though she could hear him, a shift in the clouds above cast a glimmering ray of sunlight onto a bit of metal around her throat. Yves reached forward without thinking. The pads of his fingers touched the golden locket, a sturdy oval embedded with a deep blue stone, and though he made no effort to remove it from her neck, the chain seemed to collapse of its own accord, releasing the necklace into his grip.

He stared down at it in stunned awe. A tremor of something he had not felt in many years seemed to pass from the trinket in his palm to the thumping of his heart. In that moment, he believed in something.

"Sir?" The voices were calling from his rear, boots sending pebbles and tufts of sand flying as his brother's lackeys trotted over to their dead master.

Yves pushed himself to standing and shoved the necklace into his pocket, turning and affixing the men with what he hoped was a stern countenance that brokered no argument. He was not like his brother, but they did not need to know it.

"If it please you, we're going to load up the bodies and scuttle the boat," the taller one said. "No one will know what happened here. We'll wrap up the captain and take him back with us to Paris, of course, with you and Master Charles alongside. We have a coach."

Yves nodded, too numb to argue, too broken to offer any other solution. Where else could he go, after all? He had nothing left here but memories of a life that had long ago ended.

These people deserved a proper burial. They deserved eternal rest on their home soil, in their own holy ground. Instead, they would be damned to the seafloor, cast into the abyss by their executioners. It was too nauseating a thought to truly ponder.

He made his way down the beach, averting his eyes from the stark reflection of the white coast opposite them. That was England. That was the past. If he looked over his shoulder one more time, he was certain he would shatter, and so the only option was to stay whole if he was going to protect that little girl.

He had to move forward, one step at a time. He had to decide to stay whole. One must decide these things, else the universe would dash a man against the rocks as surely as an unmanned ship.

He found his nephew exactly where he'd asked him to go, seated on the soft grass that lined the sand, the baby sleeping in his arms, seemingly perfectly content with her new family.

Young Charles was not crying anymore. He would soon learn how exhausting the activity of mourning could be.

Yves eased onto the ground next to him, listening to the roll of the waves.

"They are evil, aren't they?" the boy said, after a moment. "The English?"

The question startled him. "Why would you say that?" he asked. "They are just people, like we are."

"They imprisoned you." Charles frowned, digging his shoes deeper into the sand. "They took you away."

"Well, yes," Yves allowed, considering how that must seem to a child. "But I was in an enemy camp during a time of war. We French have imprisoned a great deal of Englishmen too."

"Papa said that's because they are evil. He said that if we let one English evildoer back to England, that we would be doing the world a great evil too, which is why we had to save you first, and then make sure to do the right thing."

For a solid minute, Yves was struck dumb. It did not seem to trouble his nephew, who blinked and returned to staring at the shoreline, where the white cliffs of Dover could be seen at the edge of the waves.

"Charles, your father was wrong. He was wrong, and it cost him his life." Yves sighed, damning his brother silently for conditioning a child to believe such things. "Evil did not cause this. What happened here today was a travesty for all of us, and it was the result of a betrayal of trust. Your father struck a deal, but did not keep up his end of the bargain."

Charles looked as though he might argue, but instead quickly turned his head, pressing his lips together in an attempt to hide his misery. He appeared to ponder this perspective, turning the thought over in his head, sharp edges and all. When he spoke again, his voice was small and uncertain, careful with each word as he said it. "Father said they wished us dead, and they killed him. But you are saying it is because he killed some of them first."

Yves managed to nod, but could not trust himself to speak. Even before those years in prison, he did not think himself equipped to explain such things. He had never been good with children.

Silence did not please young Charles, who frowned, rocking the sleeping baby in his arms. As quickly as this weighty subject had been drawn, it was dismissed, the boy apparently deciding to banish it completely for the time being.

He gave a long look to the girl in his arms, his eyes brightening when she yawned, her wide little mouth a halo of pale pink where the nubs of brand new teeth had begun to grow. He leaned down and dropped a kiss on her fuzzy forehead, wispy auburn curls coiling in haphazard strands of new growth.

When Charles turned back to Yves, he had managed a weak smile. "What is her name?" he asked, a hint of hope in his voice. "My cousin."

Yves did not know the baby's name, truth be told. It had never arisen on his journey across the Channel, and he had not been gallant enough to ask. He knew only that she was distressed, perhaps with the colic or struggling with those burgeoning teeth, and Mary Atlas had thought it best to bring her along for what should have been an errand of only a few hours. Walter Atlas had teased his wife about how she always found excuses to keep the baby near, no matter how improbable the situation.

This poor child had lost everything today.

She would need a name.

"I named her for your grand-mere," Yves said, his mother's face floating into his memory at the thought of parents and children. "Do you know what her Christian name was?"

"Isabelle," Charles answered with a nod of approval. "That is a good name."

"Yes, it is," Yves agreed, allowing himself to sigh. He dropped a hand across his nephew's narrow shoulders and looked down into the child's sleeping face. "My daughter's name is Isabelle."

CHAPTER 1

wenty Years Later

Isabelle Monetier had been having the most marvelous dream.

It was always disappointing waking up from a properly wonderful dream, like being clapped back to reality from the utterly fantastical before you could even rightly appreciate the magic.

As she roused, her warm, hazel eyes blinking open against the shafts of sunlight gleaming in from the breaks in the trees, her memories of sitting on a throne made of stars and crystal immediately began to fade. Spectacular vistas blurred, and wisps of nonsensical context evaporated quicker than she could chase them.

That was the grand injustice of dreams. One never knew when she was having one, and upon waking, she would rarely remember more than a vague and dull imprint of the ordeal. Was it not a tragic waste of life's most incredible experiences?

Isabelle was of the mind that dreams fully remembered would likely tarnish the real world so harshly that people would never wish to be awake again. Perhaps that was why they must be forgotten.

It must have been the stars in the dream that reminded her of her true life, and the hours that had passed since she'd decided to lie in the grass next to the brook and close her eyes for a moment. And remembering that the world existed could not be abided in the land of dreams, so she had been expelled.

Yes, she had known better, and no, she had not learned her lesson. At least, once she managed to pull herself together enough to open her eyes, the sun was still in the sky. She hadn't vanished until after dark again, even if the sun was heading quickly towards the horizon.

She huffed, shoving herself up to sitting and attempting to quickly pull the twigs and leaves from her loose mass of auburn hair, which had curled into a tangle that twined down to her ribs, embedded with greenery like some forest sprite.

Papa would scold her for certain, but at least she had picked enough dandelion for dinner before she'd drifted off! Her basket was overflowing with jagged green leaves, and if she hurried back to the house, there would be time for them to soak before it was time to eat.

Evidently, her loyal dog had grown tired of waiting for her to rise and had made for home without her. She must have slept for quite some time if the little devil had covered so much ground without her.

She gathered her skirt up into a knot at her knees to allow for easier movement and twisted her hair over her shoulder in an effort to disguise the mess she'd made of it. She swiped up her basket of greens and made haste out of the little glade.

It was a short climb into the open valley, and then a sprint across the meadow back to the house. This time of year, a firm breeze and the scent of wild strawberries charged the air, like sparks of sugar-touched electricity. The heady sweetness was so much that Isabelle often thought that the sunset's colors were merely reflecting the scents of early summer, spun of butterscotch and fruit with fresh cream.

The grass grew long on the incline to the main road. Isabelle loved the tall summer grass, tickling at her calves as she ran, and the wild freedom of the weeds and traveling flowers that found their way onto their side of the valley. It only took half an hour by foot to pass into the walled city at the center of the valley, but their little enclave just beyond the walls may as well have been an entire world of its own.

The village of St. Chaffrey was little more than a tight clutch of half-timbered houses and a single, tall clock tower, with whatever nature's whims decided up on to adorn it, be it climbing vines, icicles, or a heavy coat of dusty spring pollen.

In the winter, snow glazed the whole of the valley in thick sheets of icing, dusting that old clock tower and the citadel on the hill with sparkling silence. It had a beauty, of course, but Isabelle much preferred the summer, when the snow had retreated only to the tips of the mountains that hugged Serre Chevalier in their protective embrace, and rather than frost, the houses were overtaken by morning glory vines, winding their way up to heaven, culled only to protect the explosions of delicious tomatoes, eggplants, and melon that grew on the community trellises.

Birdsong and butterflies were the signatures of summer, when the coolness of the brook and the warmth of the natural springs could both be pleasant and enjoyed without risking frostbite.

It was the perfect time to show her cousin Charles how beautiful and welcoming the valley was compared to his busy, sterile townhouse in Paris. Of course, if she was late with the dandelion and the first thing Charles saw upon arriving was her being scolded, it would rather take away from her smugness at Serre Chevalier's undeniable superiority.

He would preen and snivel and point out that in Paris, one did not have to go pick their own salad greens for dinner. And Isabelle would agree. Wasn't that exactly the point, after all? Things never taste half so wonderful after a week on a vegetable cart. Everyone knows that!

She grinned to herself, skipping as she ran.

He would say that being surrounded by all these mountains made him feel like he was trapped in the bottom of a sugar bowl, and she would respond that there was no sweeter place to be.

Sniping with Charles was also one of the things that made summer so delicious. He'd show up every year, starched and buttoned and talking of war and business and court, but it would only be a day or two before he was dressing for comfort and eating grapes right off the vine. No one could resist the allure of the valley for long.

When they were younger and Charles would return to the capital with wrinkled clothes and sun-browned skin that made the bright blue of his eyes shine in stark contrast to his person, his distraught mother would have to start the process of civilizing him all over again. There was always a very short, very terse letter to her father about it, but of course, come the following summer, Charles had managed to convince his mother to permit yet another visit, with an inevitable outcome.

Now he was a man grown, and all of that nonsense regarding pleading and permission from his mother was unnecessary. Yet he still managed to come to them once a year, completely devoid of *joie de vivre* until the country could revive him.

It was all right. Isabelle never grew bored of the transformation.

As she approached the drive, she could see from a distance that her cousin had indeed arrived, and was engaged in conversation with her father. Both men looked so still and serious from where she stood, as though a reunion once per year were a somber affair rather than a cause for joy.

Isabelle would have none of it. She called out a greeting as she skipped her way over the heavy stones lining the drive, covering the ground between them in short and efficient order.

Her father's demeanor shifted immediately. Yves Monetier straightened, leaning more freely on his wooden cane, and greeted the arrival of his daughter with an affectionate smile and shake of the head. "You are late, Isabelle. And you've gnarled your hair."

"I'm sorry, Papa," she said, leaning forward to give him a kiss on the cheek as her fingers sought out the debris in her hair that had given her away. "I lost track of the time, but look, I got the greens for dinner!"

Yves took the basket from her, peering under the cloth at the quantity she'd gathered and giving a begrudging nod of approval. "I thought you'd wandered off to the Libertine again and had forgotten us completely."

"Oh, Papa, don't be so dramatic. The sun is still up!"

"Barely," put in Charles, giving her one of his stiff Parisian bows as though she were some courtier on official business and not his dearest cousin. "It is good to see you, Isabelle."

"Is it?" She grinned, giving him a quick jab in the ribs and using his moment of reflexive reaction to catch him in a quick embrace. "I can never be sure!"

"Let's go inside. These greens need to soak if we're going to eat them before they wilt. I'll see if the roast is on."

Despite his leg, Yves was still spry enough to be the first up the steps and back into the house, and eager enough for his dinner that he made no qualms about his speed. He was still talking, mentioning something about what cheeses were in the larder to the cadence of his cane thumping the wooden slats as he vanished from view, leaving the two younger people in his wake as the door swung ajar behind him.

"What's this about you going to the Libertine? Surely not by yourself, Isabelle!" Charles said with a frown, gesturing that she should enter the house ahead of him.

"Well, of course not," she said with a laugh. "Who goes to a public house and finds herself alone? Oh, stop grimacing like that. It's unbecoming. Plenty of girls from the valley go to the Libertine, Charles. We discuss how we plan to reshape the world. That *is* what we've been fighting for all this time, isn't it, Citizen? That's certainly what we're told we're fighting for."

Charles was incredulous. "Who was fighting for young ladies to fraternize in taverns?"

Isabelle lifted her chin, fixing him with her sparkling hazel gaze. "Liberté, égalité, fraternité," she recited, punctuating each word with feeling. "How could it mean anything else? *Fraternize* is quite literally in the mantra, right next to *equality*, I remind you, no matter how your compatriots flubbed giving women the vote!"

"All right, enough," he grumbled, holding his hands up in defeat, though clearly still unable to shrug off his visage of disapproval. "I simply worry about you alone around a bunch of men and spirits."

"Oh, please." She grinned, nudging the front door shut behind them and leading him into the sitting room. "Every man in the valley knows Papa, and as such, no man in the valley even considers it. It's downright dispiriting sometimes, really. I think they all imagine he would chase them down with his cane and show them just how strong he became in that English prison."

Charles collapsed into the chair nearest to him at that, dropping his face into his hands so that all Isabelle could see was the nut-brown hair on top of his head. "How is it that I've been here for less than an hour and I am already exhausted?" he muttered into his hands.

"Oh, don't fret," Isabelle replied, taking a seat opposite him on the settee. She uncoiled her hair and began to run her fingers through it, depositing twigs and dry leaves and the odd blade of grass onto the table in front of her for disposal. Secretly, she hoped she stumbled upon a bug, as to give Charles a true start. Alas, it seemed she must settle for the enjoyment of seeing him so quickly defeated. "It just means that you'll shed that awful facade faster this year than ever before. I'm thrilled. Honestly."

He peeked up at her between the cracks in his fingers and gave a weary laugh. "Yes, Cousin," he allowed. "I believe that you are."

As was tradition, the first summer dinner of the remaining Monetiers was served outdoors, in the soft grass of the back garden, glowing under a dome of twilight.

Charles recounted the news from Paris, which was not half so boring as Isabelle thought it might be, particularly regarding all the political intrigue surrounding the ever-changing landscape of war. He also mentioned that his mother was flourishing in Empress Josephine's coterie, and was just as insufferable as she'd ever been, which was no surprise to any of them.

"She has declared to me, as though the decision was always hers alone, that it is time for me to marry," Charles said with a roll of his eyes and a healthy swig of his wine. "I suppose I should be grateful that she did not say to whom I must immediately cleave myself, and trusts that I might choose wisely."

"Oh?" Isabelle said curiously. "And have you?"

"I've an inkling," he replied, though he did not sound particularly pleased nor enthusiastic about said inkling.

Yves frowned, using the edge of his fork to divide the remainder of his dinner. "Let us only talk of happy news tonight," he said with uncharacteristic brusqueness. "Perhaps Isabelle can tell us of her afternoon in the meadow, making flower crowns from the dandelions whilst storing the remainder of the forest floor in her hair."

Something about her father's demeanor unsettled Isabelle. However, he was right. Feelings even inching towards unhappiness were not appropriate for tonight. She must put such musings out of her mind until at least the morrow, so she put on an easy smile and allowed the subject to be changed. "Oh, dandelions are no good for flower chains, Papa," she said airily. "You'll want daisies for that. I shall teach you."

"Will you?" Charles chuckled, cracking perhaps his first smile of the summer. "I think Yves would look very well in a crown of daisies."

"You should both learn," Isabelle replied. "These are necessary skills for the enjoyment of the season. *Everyone* looks well in flowers, even my dog."

"Yes, where *is* Goliath?" Charles said, looking around as though the creature might suddenly burst from the grass in a grand entrance. "I haven't seen him all day."

"Oh, he wandered off in the glade," Isabelle said with a careless flick of her hand. "He is probably in Chantemerle visiting his many mistresses tonight. He will return at dawn, famished and whining and remorseful. I shall take him back, of course, and allow him to partake of my food and sleep in my lap, for I am only a girl, and Goliath is irresistible."

"Ah, what a life," Yves said wistfully, drawing laughter from his daughter and nephew.

A fragrant wind swept through the valley, still delightfully chilled from the snow-capped mountains from whence it had originated. The sun had set in full now, leaving them to their dessert by candlelight, serenaded by the chirping discourse of cicadas and laughter echoing out from one of the houses nearby.

Isabelle glanced up at the stars, winking out of hiding as the inky expanse of night overtook the sky, and for a moment she remembered that dream she was having back in the glade. Now, some hours later, the stars looked cold and a throne seemed lonely, no matter how prettily it sparkled.

The warmth of this table, with its sturdy wooden chairs and flickering candlelight, was superior to whatever her dream had concocted, she thought. Perhaps that's truly why we forget our dreams, for inevitably, they pale in comparison to the beautiful flaws of reality.

She smiled to herself, lifting her glass and committing this moment to her waking memory, where it would live forever in a halo of summer's dusk.

CHAPTER 2

*P*eter Applegate was not a patient man.

This trait often came as a surprise to others, in the rare occasions that they became aware of it.

Peter was a tall man, and as such, should have also been an imposing one. But, alas, he was also rather lanky and wore spectacles.

In a way, it was a relief to be precluded from shows of competitive masculinity. He knew very well that his bookish impulses and professorial appearance established an expectation of a quiet and mild persona, one he would never escape and was usually quite content to embody. He had come to believe it had provided him with a uniquely serene existence amongst his sex.

However, there were times ... times when the frustration of a situation simply pushed him past the boiling point and it all came flooding out in a rapid-fire rant that, more often than not, startled the other person so badly they either laughed or cried, and often never spoke to him again.

If his abrupt display of impatience had given Mathias Dempierre even the first hint of displeasure or surprise, Peter could not see it. The man whose ship they'd taken from England on clandestine business never seemed bothered by anything at all, which only made frustration in his presence all the more vexing.

Peter had been pacing the deck of the *Harpy* for the last two hours, repeatedly snatching up the brass looking glass and gazing off towards Marseille to ensure that it hadn't gone anywhere. All the while, the boat bobbed languidly in place, still several leagues out.

"What are we waiting for?" he demanded, turning to find Dempierre still carelessly reclined in his hammock, stripped down to his shirtsleeves, dangling a glass of chablis over the edge with the tips of his fingers.

The man was so infuriatingly blasé, so endlessly unaffected and unhurried, that Peter had wondered more than once how it might feel to strangle him or perhaps just briefly shove him overboard. Mathias even took his time smiling in amusement at Peter's harried state, the corners of his lips curling up like a cat's, punctuated with deep dimples, as he took his eyes from the sparkling sway of the water and turned them onto the other man.

"I already told you," Mathias replied, his voice as tranquil as the wake. "I am, shall we say, not particularly well loved in the Marseille ports. Once the guard changes, and a dear friend of mine with an enduring love for gold guineas takes up the post, we will be able to dock without hassle."

"Why does that not surprise me?" Peter sighed, collapsing

the telescope between his hands. "When does the guard change?"

"Soon," Mathias replied. "Now, if you could please step out of the light. I am attempting to be beset by a truly exquisite wave of *ennui,* and you are making it difficult to suffer, pacing so in my periphery."

Peter was too exasperated to respond. He dropped the looking glass into his coat pocket, pushing his spectacles back up into place on the bridge of his nose, and made an exit to the other side of the railing that likely contained a great deal more stomping than strictly necessary, especially considering that it went largely unnoticed.

There was no one else with whom to have a meaningful conversation on this blasted boat. They were over a week out from Dover, with only two deck hands, a cook, and Mathias himself serving as company in the *Harpy*'s cramped (though admittedly stylish) decks.

The sleeping situation had been particularly strange. Admittedly, Peter had never before attempted to navigate the physics of climbing into a hammock, much less managing to fall asleep in one. His legs simply did not fit, and it was not restful to lie with one's legs spread like a Christmas turkey awaiting stuffing. He attempted to find equilibrium with both feet planted onto the floor, opposite two sides of tenuously suspended cloth, but often once he began to doze off, his heels began to float downward and sent his toes skittering against the wooden floor.

It was, without a doubt, the least comfortable sleep he'd ever endured—including sleeping on public stagecoaches!

Dempierre, of course, had captain's quarters, complete with a real bed. No wonder he was always so at ease!

Peter told himself that this was the last time he would be caught up in one of Aunt Zelda's ridiculous schemes. He ignored the voice in his head that informed him that he had told himself this very thing, many times before.

After that business last year, in which he spent an agonizing month attempting to prevent the murder of one of his dearest friends, he had thought, surely, it was over. But he'd thought that too after every single forged document, every ridiculous caper, and every uncomfortable correspondence he'd been dragged into, all the while reminding his aunt that he had never offered nor become a member of her little operation.

Perhaps, more realistically, he would demand to know the full scope of what he was agreeing to before he began to agree to the Silver Leaf Society's requests. Yes, she'd just adore that.

He kicked at the dulled épée sword he'd left on this part of the deck and laughed mirthlessly at the thing, a gleaming reminder of how easily he bent to his aunt's will.

She had told him, following the events at Somerton last autumn, that she required his sword arm for an upcoming mission. Of course, he had taken her at face value, throwing himself into a rigorous routine of fencing lessons at Oxford that had been quite literally a painful learning experience.

Over the autumn and winter months, he'd been soundly thrashed into fighting shape by an unforgiving brute of an instructor, who left Peter's body knotted and bruised, if not somewhat more blessed in the way of muscle mass than it had previously been. The instructor insisted on training out of doors, even in the most brutal days of cold and wind.

The pain and frustration had seemed necessary at the time. After all, he had believed he was about to be tossed into a pit of swordplay, and he did not intend to find himself skewered at the end of someone else's blade.

And so, he had come to be a sufficient study at the art of slashing at other men with a sharpened stick. He had even come to enjoy the way his body ached afterward and the way his mind seemed to sharpen and silence in the midst of sparring.

It turned out she was being glib.

It was too embarrassing to even think about directly, but of course Zelda had never intended for Peter to partake in combat. How ridiculous for him to even consider it! Oh, how she'd laughed.

What'd she'd needed was his eye for detail and ability to restore old documents. These talents, performed by his "sword arm," could easily be twisted and applied to base forgery.

So he'd done all that parrying and jabbing and riposting for naught and had ended up, like always, next to a low-burning candle late into the night, crafting false documents, including their permit to dock in Marseille, which apparently could have been managed with a few gold guineas at the right hour of the day, courtesy of Mathias Dempierre.

Dempierre himself was only one of a handful of the most recent surprises his family had tossed at him. Evidently, Dempierre's entire family was involved with Zelda's precious Silver Leaf Society, and Mathias had been performing Silver Leaf smuggling runs to and from France since he was a teenager, with both goods and people as his cargo.

The Dempierres were old French blood, erstwhile nobility living in exile on British soil, and so perhaps for Mathias the meddlings of espionage felt somewhat more personal. He certainly seemed to bring up the revolution as often as it became even remotely relevant, and it was the only subject that seemed to spark some sort of fire in his languid demeanor.

Peter hadn't asked whether Mathias was involved with the Silver Leaf for reasons of personal justice or simply because his mother had been a founding member. He felt certain that if he attempted an earnest conversation about honor and morality with someone like Mathias, whose preening was more of an obvious priority than his principles, he would only be rewarded with lightly amused ridicule.

Well, whether she knew it or not, Zelda had presented Peter with a means to escape from his lifelong habit of plaguing himself with a never-ending barrage of thoughts, at least for an hour or two a day.

Exhausted and sweating and panting for breath, all while attempting the purely physical instinct of anticipating his instructor's next move, had given his mind a beautiful clarity. Gone were concerns over what else must be accomplished today, what he had failed to accomplish yesterday, what progress he was making in his current projects, what might be on the docket for tomorrow, and on and on. It was like unlocking a great tool for the art of living life, one that would have been very useful to have been given some twenty-five years earlier.

Still, he was fortunate to have discovered this trick at all, for he certainly would never have sought out fencing on his own accord. Now, he could not remember what life had been like without a physical outlet.

Having an épée to do drills with here on the deck had been the only thing keeping him sane since they set sail from the smugglers' cove hiding beneath an estate in Kent, Meridian House, of which his sister had recently become mistress by way of marriage. Nell was Mrs. Nathaniel Atlas now.

He likely should have started demanding answers about this mission as soon as he realized that one of the documents he was forging was a marriage license. He absolutely should have raised a ruckus when he was told to put his own name under the prospect of "groom," but he had known the futility of demanding anything from Zelda Smith, and so he had gone along with her instructions, for what else is there to keep one occupied in deep winter?

The marriage was a farce, of course, a means to smuggle a young girl from France to England without raising suspicions or sullying her reputation. The real problem was that this girl hadn't the faintest clue they were coming, nor was there any assurance that she would agree to being smuggled.

He sighed, slumping onto the deck with his back to the cabin wall and gazing out at the horizon. Perhaps his sister was right and he would enjoy things more if he simply decided to do so. For all that Nell was his twin, she couldn't have had a more different approach to navigating her life.

He admired and envied her reckless self-assuredness, truth

be told. He had never told her so, of course, for such flattery was simply not in the purview of being someone's brother. She probably knew anyway. She'd always been too damned intelligent for her own good.

She was pregnant now, deeply in love with that husband of hers, and glowing in the way of a woman who'd finally come into her own. It was a bittersweet thing for Peter, who had always thought that perhaps he and Nell would live out their lives in parallel, unmarried and devoted to their learning. Seeing Nell so blissfully happy, so completely settled, was a stark reminder of the expanse of life that unfurled ahead of him, filled with a great deal of time that he had never much contemplated filling.

At least his aunt's machinations would see him married for a time, even if it was by way of subterfuge and dishonesty. It was the safest way to get the girl safely out of France and back to England, where she belonged, where her family awaited her return with bated breath.

He tried to picture Isabelle Monetier, closing his eyes against the orange glow of the sun. Alice Atlas was her true name, the name she had been given at birth. Would she look like her brother, Nathaniel? He was tall and sharply angled, and had eyes that shifted as often as his political agendas did.

He attempted to conjure her, to put his brother-in-law's features onto a woman, but it was no good. She shifted into shadow as quickly as he could attempt to assign her this hair or that gown. Her elusive nature, slipping between the wickerwork of his mind as a shadow maiden, featureless and mysterious, fit well with the roll of the waves and the slosh of the sea.

It lulled him to sleep, where he dreamed of chasing a woman made of starlight, who ran with abandon through an endless sky.

~

THE WET THUNK of the *Harpy*'s hull meeting the dock was what brought Peter back to the waking world.

It had been a long-standing amusement of the Applegate family that Peter could remain asleep through just about anything. In this instance, he had slept through the order to begin sailing again, the sensation of the boat moving again, and anything else that might have occurred between their spot at sea and the full distance into Vieux Port.

The crewmen must have stepped over him repeatedly to get to their lines, drawing the sails down and steering the *Harpy* into a green and gray recess on the very outer edges of the port proper. A man was standing on the dock, hands on his hips, looking positively chuffed at their arrival.

Mathias did not waste time waiting for the boat to be secured, choosing instead to leverage himself off the railing of the ship and onto the dock with the confidence of a man who made a habit of such displays. His boots landed on the soggy wood of the dock with a sharp crack, making only the slightest interruption in his gait.

He had put his jacket back on, brass buttons gleaming in the low light as the sun set, teeth flashing in a wide grin as he embraced the man on the dock and launched into rapid conversation in French.

Peter did not feel the need to eavesdrop on their conversation or the imminent bribery that must occur, and so he made his way below deck to grab his bag of necessities for their journey inland, and stored his training épée in a safe nook opposite the crewmen's hammocks.

The two ship's hands and the cook were going to stay on board the boat while Mathias and Peter saw to their business, and Peter couldn't help but wonder whether or not the men took turns sleeping in the proper bed in the captain's quarters when the captain was out. He certainly would have, given the opportunity.

He shrugged into his own coat and made his way out onto the landing, waiting until there was a proper tether in place before he stepped off the ship.

"She's a good girl, the *Harpy*," Mathias said to Peter, clapping him on the back. "You'll miss her when we're sleeping on the road."

"Will I?" Peter muttered, without expectation of a response.

The wind was high, and there was a light mist in the air, mingling the spray of the ocean with the spritz of early-summer rain. It was a quick walk past the customs office and into the thoroughfare, and with the sun down, neither man attracted much attention from the passersby. Everyone there was huddled under their clothes with their heads down, feet shattering their own reflection in the damp cobbles as they shouldered their way through the mist.

It took only a few steps in such conditions for Peter to forsake his spectacles in favor of vision that was not streaked with foggy wetness. Like his sister, he knew he only truly needed them when reading, writing, or otherwise performing delicate work in close quarters, but, just as she did, he preferred to just leave them on. He felt rather naked without them.

"We will stay tonight with Pauline Olivier," Mathias explained, keeping a brisk pace as he led the way onto the Marseille streets in search of a hansom cab. "She is one of the original five, you know. The only one who did not opt to stay in England. Perhaps she will tell you scandalous things about your auntie."

"I would prefer to not know anything scandalous about my aunt, thank you," Peter replied, softly but with utter sincerity.

He had no doubt in his mind that the formidable, starched woman who had sent him on this caper got up to all manner of things of which he was happier in ignorance.

Mme. Olivier lived in a townhouse about a quarter hour from the ports, once they had secured transportation. There was still mist in the air, but the briny smell had given way to the earthier scent of garden rains, and through the haze, the warm light in the windows of the houses on the row seemed to pulse with glowing welcome to weary travelers.

The first thing that hit Peter upon entering the house was the smell of food. Proper, hot food that had been prepared by someone whose fingernails weren't constantly black and whose vocabulary likely extended beyond monosyllabic grunts. Was it heaven? It might as well have been.

"I hope she's made her honey bread," Mathias said wistfully, allowing a footman to take his sailor's coat with an easy roll of his shoulders and a deep inhalation of the fragrant air. "Do you like honey bread, Applegate?"

"I couldn't say."

"Oh, then I will insist some is made by breakfast, at the very least!" Mathias threw himself onto a nearby sofa as the mistress of the house was summoned, and watched Peter with amusement as he took polite care choosing his own seat and removing his spectacles from his shirt pocket to clean them. "You'll want it with a slathering of fresh butter and some preserves, if she has any. Absolute perfection. Say, how blind are you without those?"

"Not very," Peter replied, holding the circular frames up to the light with a squint to see if he'd effectively removed the smears. "But any improvement is worthwhile, I think."

Mathias nodded in seeming agreement, resting his head back against the pillows of the couch and allowing his eyelids to flicker shut. Evidently he was very comfortable in this house, though it was hard to say whether his comfort was the result of familiarity or his *laissez-faire* approach to the very concept of being alive.

Peter rather thought that spectacles or a cane or any other sort of minor inconvenience would sooner be dismissed by Mathias Dempierre in favor of simplicity at the cost of discomfort. It would give him more things to lazily complain about, which he did seem to enjoy, though his moaning lacked authenticity.

The Oliviers burst into the room with no announcement from the staff, producing their own fanfare in the boisterous exclamations of welcome.

Mathias had shot up from his reclining position to embrace the petite, round frame of Pauline Olivier before shifting over to give an equally warm embrace to the husband.

Peter pushed himself to his feet, uncertain what to do with himself as he watched this scene unfold, wrapped in a muddle of overly loud French affectations. It only took a moment, however, before Pauline Olivier spotted him and descended upon him with all the enthusiasm of a mother bear.

"Oh, you must be Peter! Welcome, welcome," she was crooning, taking him by the elbow and ushering him forward in the direction of the dining hall. "You have Zelda's look, you know. I can see her in your eyes. I can't believe how long it's been since I've seen the old girl. Here, watch your step, to the left!"

He had rarely been so overwhelmed in his life. English people simply did not excite this way!

Once he was seated, presented with a brimming glass of red wine, and captured within the sticky spider's web of conversation, some of the tension began to ease from him. Perhaps that was more the doing of the wine than the acclimation of such surroundings.

"So I am to take it that Zelda and Therese are speaking again?" Pauline was saying, exchanging a knowing look with her grinning husband. "Wonders never cease!"

"Zelda's intended heiress marrying Nathaniel Atlas rather made it impossible for them to continue the game of cutting silence, I believe," Mathias responded, sliding a plate laden with buttered honey bread across the table to Peter. "I don't suppose you know what caused the enmity in the first place?"

"Zelda never forgave Therese for getting married," Mr.

Olivier said with a chuckle. "Not a fan of men, that one, and rather possessive of Therese."

"It wasn't that she got married, Gerard," Pauline tsk-tsked, tapping one of her manicured fingernails on the embroidered tablecloth. "We all got married, and she didn't remain cross with us. Therese was different. She was Zelda's shadow, and no one expected her to use the Silver Leaf to bring that bore of a husband—no offense, Mathias—over to Dover from France during the war. It was a clear choice she made, wasn't it? A loud statement. She chose the husband over Zelda."

"Fascinating," Mathias murmured, his eyebrows raised. "I confess, on the basis of my existence, to be glad she chose the way she did. My mother is evidently more complex than I give her credit for."

"Therese Dempierre is an enigma, darling," Pauline assured him. "Make no mistake."

"Sight less scary than that Zelda, though," her husband commented, taking a healthy swig of his wine. "That one chills my blood."

"Oh, she's harmless," Pauline said without conviction, cutting her eyes to Peter as he audibly scoffed. "Now, you must tell me all about this business with Mary's missing daughter. You say she's been alive this entire time? Here in France?"

"In the Alps," Mathias confirmed. "We knew she had survived because we got incredibly vague letters from the man who took her in, which he never signed nor addressed. Atlas moving back into Meridian uncovered the information we needed to track her down. I do hope they are happy to see us."

Peter pressed his lips together, an unpleasant roll of realization tumbling through his stomach, far less pleasing than the honey bread. He had not known until this moment that they were not expected guests.

"Mm, apparently in the last letter, a vague mention of perhaps an impending proposal of marriage was made," Mathias continued, as though he were discussing plans for a Sunday picnic. "Of course, once she is married, she won't have nearly the freedom of movement she has now, and it's unlikely a husband would agree to having her smuggled over enemy lines to meet her true family, so we had to act in haste rather than what might have been otherwise tactful. God willing, we aren't too late."

"If I'd known she was only a few days' ride away from here, we would have taken the girl in. Isn't that right, Gerard?" She frowned. "I daresay Mary and Walter would have preferred Alice in the care of trusted friends."

"We never had children of our own," Gerard put in, giving his wife's hand a little squeeze. "How do you intend to spirit the girl past various authorities?"

"Peter here is a talented forger," Mathias informed them. "Oxford educated!"

"Are they teaching forgery at Oxford these days?" Gerard Olivier wondered with a wan smile.

"Restoration," Peter mumbled, knowing his cheeks were coloring at this revelation of his lack of ethics. "I work with medieval manuscripts, mostly."

"He did the most marvelous entry documents," Mathias put in. "I suppose Auntie Z didn't realize that coin works just as well. I intend to keep them, however. I expect one day they might come in handy. For the girl, he's done up her papers as Alice Applegate nee Atlas. Since we won't be returning to port in Dover, we need something seemly for the port authority in London. It will appear as though the two are returning from honeymoon on the Continent, and without record of the *Harpy* departing London with no woman on board, it will not raise any suspicion. We also have a French marriage license for Isabelle Monetier nee des Pommes if we are stopped en route between the Cote d'Azur and Marseille."

"Clever," Pauline said with a nod of approval. "You didn't want to be the husband, Mathias? Knowing her parents, she is likely a very pretty young woman."

"God, no." Mathias laughed, shaking his head. "I was not given the option, but I would have had to gently decline. The *Harpy* would not take kindly to me favoring other women on her decks."

"Hopeless," Pauline huffed. "Just hopeless."

"We have a strongbox in the study," her husband said, directing his words to Peter. "I rather think your documents will be safer here than in your things for a rather difficult journey. The mountains are not kind to travelers."

"Oh, I told Peter all about it. Red-eyed ibexes out for blood and packs of roving wolves hidden in the snowbanks! He's thrilled."

"Such nonsense!" Gerard chuckled.

"I do hope conditions are in our favor," Peter added. "The terrain is not ideal for speedy travel."

"Oh, I think once you see how beautiful it is, you'll not mind a few extra days," Pauline said reassuringly. "Let us put this talk of business away while we enjoy dessert, and we may pick it up again in the parlor afterward, hm?"

"Yes, madame," Mathias said with the slightest bow.

"Good." She beamed at them across the table and rang the little bell she kept at her side. "I do hope you boys enjoy chocolate."

CHAPTER 3

"Papa, you need a new hat," Isabelle said with a giggle, flicking the brim of her father's well-worn straw cap with her fingers. "This one is so threadbare, it hardly does anything at all."

"I like my hat," Yves replied with a sniff, his dignity unimpaired by the rays of sun that were beating down on him from above. "It's still a perfectly good hat."

"Papa, your hair is escaping the cap!" Isabelle laughed, reaching up to brush at wispy strands of silver-blond hair that stuck out from the loosened straw weave. She called ahead to her cousin, "Tell him, Charles!"

"I'll do no such thing," Charles called back absently, too focused on counting out coins to pay a street vendor to partake in family squabbling.

It was market day in Briancon, and now that they were settled into their summer routine, it was the perfect time to trek into the town as a unit and take advantage of local wares on display in the old citadel streets, each one cleaved in half by running water from the spring, flowing down to the ancient aqueducts that surrounded the city.

The trickle of the constantly running water was punctuated with grand echoes from the bells of the old church that sat at the top of the hill, wrapped in the voices of the townspeople as they chattered, joyously oblivious to the perfection around them.

Isabelle heaved a great sigh and turned her face up to the sun, delighting in the way it spread warmth from the tip of her nose to the very ends of her fingers. She would freckle, she knew, but truth be told, she always thought there was something charming about the modest spray of freckles that found their way across her nose in the warmer seasons.

"Unbelievable," Charles was muttering as he made his way back to them, a paper-wrapped parcel tucked under his arm. "It's as though they think I will pay whatever they ask because I am a visitor."

"Did you pay what they asked, Charles?" Isabelle asked without opening her eyes, knowing his only answer would be a frown.

"If you'd stop dressing like a Parisian, they'd stop charging you like one," Yves replied with a wry smile. "You know that."

"I shouldn't have to," Charles muttered, poorly stifling yet another huff of indignation. "What's next? A spot of luncheon perhaps? Is that little shop with the buckwheat crepes still around?"

"Mm." Isabelle sighed, blinking away the glow of the sun

and nodding in affirmation. "And the chevre will be fresh. That sounds perfect. Papa?"

"Oh, yes, whatever you two decide," Yves said, his eyes crinkling on the corners when he smiled at the two of them. "I am not nearly so fussy as either of you."

He will freckle too, she thought fondly as the breeze ruffled the escaped strands of her father's hair.

"It will be good to sit down for a while," Charles said, offering his arm to his cousin. "Perhaps this is the right time to talk about some things that your father and I have been discussing. I have been anxious to have out with it, but he has insisted on patience. Much as it pains me to delay things, he made a compelling argument for temperance."

"Well, it sounds as though you have already been discussing these things," Isabelle replied, casting a suspicious glance over her shoulder at her father. "Am I to understand that you've been planning something to do with me, although I have not been present?"

"Yes," Charles said, his tone conveying that he saw no issue at all in such a discussion. "It concerns all three of us, and our future as a family. I wished to speak of it the instant I arrived, but your father insisted I wait until we had a few days to adjust and enjoy one another's company first."

Isabelle did not reply, gesturing in the direction they must walk to get to the cafe with the buckwheat crepes and fresh goat's cheese. She did not know why she suddenly had a sinking feeling in her chest, as though a heavy rock had been dunked past her heart and came to settle, clattering and uneven, in her rib cage.

She did not know what aspect of her future could possibly have been discussed at length between her father and her cousin. What was there to decide? Everything was perfect as it was.

She blinked, startled by a pair of children splashing across the water recess and vanishing into a narrow alley between two vine-covered structures, their little wet footprints chasing them to their next destination. For just a moment, she thought she'd be better off following them than continuing on her current course towards some manner of somber discussion for which she certainly was not prepared.

They chose to dine on the terrace, under great cloth parasols that fluttered prettily in the alpine breeze. Isabelle made a show of sitting still and moving only to retrieve her wine glass as quickly as possible, so that neither man might see the nervous tremor that had worked its way through her bones. She smiled and made no comment when the cafe owner greeted them, giving her father a robust handshake and a smattering of gossip from the village main. She endured hearing about a stolen goat, a scandal of infidelity, and some nonsense about the mayor and his fascination with commissioning a statue of himself before the man mercifully realized he was rambling and cheerfully took his leave in favor of retrieving their food.

"What sort of man commissions a statue of *himself?*" Isabelle said with distaste. "Aren't monuments by nature meant to be tributes from the outside?"

"Hm," her father replied, sneaking a glance at Charles next to him. "If so, no one should tell the emperor thus. I believe he has already done the exact thing several times."

"There is no shame in greatness!" Charles retorted, his cheeks coloring. "If you wait for others to behave the way you want them to, you might spend your entire life unsatisfied. It is best to simply create the world you desire around you."

"Yes, well, he certainly has done that," Yves muttered, lifting his wine to his lips to disguise his amusement at his nephew's indignation.

"Is that what we've sat down to discuss?" Isabelle wondered with a teasing lilt. "Shall I be parceled off to Napoleon as his next sculptor? I must warn you both, I have no talent with the craft."

"Parceled off," Yves echoed with a grimace.

"Do you think you would enjoy Paris?" Charles asked, his gaze far more intent upon her face than the moment merited. "Could you find adventure in conquering a new horizon?"

Isabelle considered it, the Paris of her mind made up of inky lines and charcoal people from the likenesses she'd seen and smelling of smokestacks and perfume alongside the din of all the people. "Perhaps," she said after a moment, propping her chin on her hand. "I suppose it would very much depend on my purpose for being there, and what my day-to-day life might entail."

"You would be the wife of a *commandant*," Charles replied evenly, "with all the privileges such a station entails."

Her first instinct was to laugh, but the amusement died on her lips before even an expression of joviality could be assumed. "I expect you mean one of your colleagues, Charles," she said softly, "or are you referring to yourself?"

"Isabelle, it is a sensible match," Yves said, reaching across the table to brush his calloused fingers over her hand. "The two of you are well matched and have affection for one another already, and there is not much for a young woman in a place like this. The valley is where one rests and retires, after life has been thoroughly lived."

"I have affection for him as a sister does a brother!" Isabelle choked, jerking her hand back as her back went up against the chair. Her eyes sought her cousin's, though she found his expression unreadable, his eyes flat above a mild frown. "Charles, I know you feel the same. You have never once considered me in an amorous fashion!"

The very idea of it was stealing her breath from her lungs. It was unnatural! They were already family!

"Admittedly, I do not regard you in the way you describe," Charles confessed, folding his hands together on the table next to his neglected glass of wine. "Still, cousins historically make for happy marriages, and it is far more common than not for feelings of romantic love to develop after the vows, as a pair becomes settled into married life."

"Yes, but ... Charles." She squeezed her eyes shut, mortification creeping up into her cheeks, warmer than any blush born of the sunshine. "There are ... there are physical aspects to marriage ... that, I cannot ..."

Yves cleared his throat, pushing his own seat backward as he pushed himself to his seat. The interruption briefly severed the tension of the moment, with both his daughter and his nephew turning to him in silent askance.

"I have business to discuss with Jacques," he lied. "I shall leave you two in privacy to continue your conversation."

"Papa!" Isabelle huffed, ready to shoot to her feet and drag him back to sitting, but he was surprisingly swift for a man who used a cane, and he sidestepped her grip and vanished into the cafe before she could stop him.

She sank back into her chair with a sullen slump of defeat and reached for her glass, avoiding her cousin's eye.

"Isabelle, I would never force any such relations upon you," he whispered, obviously horrified that such a topic had been broached at all. "At a certain age, people must marry. It is simply how the world works! There is no woman in my life with whom I could imagine being tied to for all my days but you."

"Charles, you would grow to hate me in very short order," Isabelle said in a sigh. She pressed her fingers above her eyebrows, strands of her cherry-brown hair escaping from its braid and lashing her about the face as though her very being was aghast at the suggestion.

"I could never hate you," he protested.

"You love me because we see one another seldom, and in those moments, we remind each other that there are many ways to see the world," she said, pausing for a moment to seek the comfort of another gulp of wine. When she lowered the glass, she was pleased to see that he seemed to, at the very least, be listening to her attentively. "To be constantly bludgeoned with a vision that is not your own would only serve to foster resentment. We would be horribly matched, and I would no doubt humiliate you when expected to integrate with the wives of other important people! I have no introduction to court, no training in etiquette or Society. This is a mad idea!"

"Those things can be taught," he said with a dismissive shrug. "My primary concern is whether or not you would find a way to be happy. You are twenty-one years old, my love. Do you plan to live out your life as a spinster caring for an aging father?"

"Of course not." She looked away, an uncomfortable tug on the fringes of her mind.

The truth was that she knew her life would take her many places, the way one knows she has toes, even when she cannot see them, or that she enjoys the taste of grapes when none are available to taste. There had been an unspeakable but compelling knowledge there her whole life, a promise of something to come. She could not say that to Charles.

"Is there someone here that interests you?" he continued, undeterred by the way she winced at his prodding. "Have you a better option than me?"

"It is not about anyone being better than you!" She bit her lip, shaking her head as though to clear it from rash words and thoughts. "I simply know it is not right. And I believe you know it too. You are looking for a simple solution, a quick answer to a problem you do not want to toil to solve, and we would both suffer for that impulse."

He was quiet for a moment, considering her, his features cast into sharp relief by the lowering sun. "Do you recall that year that you took me to a lecture in the forest?" he asked softly. "Where a man from the Sorbonne had come to study an ancient altar."

"Of course I do. You fell asleep and began to snore while the man was talking!"

He chuckled, nodding and indulging in another sip of wine. "I did not mind accompanying you for something that did not appeal to me, because it was gratifying to be in your presence while you were so excited. That is what love is."

"No," Isabelle protested, perhaps a little more loudly than she needed to. "That is nonsensical. I would have much rather gone to that lecture with a friend from the village who would have enjoyed it the same as I did."

He blinked at her, surprise clear on his face, so she continued, uninterrupted.

"For example, no matter how well I love you, my dearest cousin, I would patently decline being dragged along to one of your military strategy sessions on the basis that I would be poor company due to a lack of investment. You would be better served in the company of a fellow officer."

"You are not understanding my point," he said, drawing his eyebrows together. "You are being contrary for the sake of it."

"Perhaps I am," Isabelle retorted, relieved to see her father emerging alongside a young man with their plates of food. "And you can do better than a contrarian wife, Charles. You are going to have to."

He sighed, shaking his head as the plates were deposited in front of them, fragrant and steaming. The line of his mouth communicated what he did not dare say aloud, but Isabelle knew that expression.

It meant that as far as Charles was concerned, the matter

was far from settled. It meant that, like always, an argument was only ever resolved once Charles got his way. Which meant this ridiculous prospect of marriage would need to be discussed again.

And again.

And again.

CHAPTER 4

The donkey's name was Hortensia, which was, in Peter's estimation, plenty enough reason to consider her exceptional.

Watching the old girl gracefully navigate the endless ups and downs of alpine terrain, clinging to rock faces with nigh fantastical balance, all while bearing the brunt of their belongings on her back, had ingratiated him well past the point of simple human-to-equine appreciation.

"You should see the goats up here," Mathias had said when Peter first commented on Hortensia's acrobatics. "You will see them midway up a sheer cliff face of a mountain, clinging to seemingly nothing at all, and licking salt from the rocks as though it were no matter to them, one way or the other."

There had only been a few goats so far, and from a distance, but with the looking glass from the *Harpy*, Peter had found that Mathias was indeed correct. The strangeness of France continued to outperform itself, though he told Hortensia in no uncertain terms that she remained the most impressive of the lot.

The first two nights had been spent at waypoints, sleeping in communal rooms at inns throughout Provence. Once they had reached the mountains, it became necessary to build fires and occasionally sleep on the road, as it was difficult to predict exactly how long it might take from one settlement to the next.

Mathias had attempted to teach Peter to read the map they were using, a jumble of topography and notations that clambered over one another into something that was somehow even less intelligible than the thousand-year-old meandering observations of Saxon monks which occupied Peter's days in Oxford.

In truth, the long and trying nature of this voyage had given him an appreciation of Dempierre's lackadaisical approach to the business of living one's life. His calm dismissal of seeming dangers and ability to defuse the suspicions of townspeople about their business had done them a great service.

That wasn't to say he didn't still often get the urge to throttle the other man. No, on the contrary, the relentless tendency to burst into song in particularly acoustic natural settings paired with his absolute refusal to acknowledge objective bad luck was enough for Peter to fantasize rather at length of finding ways to silence him.

Much like France itself, Mathias was an ongoing surprise to Peter, with a variety of connotations attached. He was beginning to realize that surprises made him rather uncomfortable.

For example, when Mathias had spontaneously begun praising Nell as a beauty and social success, Peter had been so disoriented that he had reacted with something akin to anger, as though this alien description of his sister must somehow be an attack on her honor.

"The first time I saw Mrs. Atlas, she was the most mysterious beauty on the ballroom floor," Mathias had insisted, raising his eyebrows in an attempt to enhance his appearance of sincerity. "It is only to be expected that two people so alike would marry one another. After all, Nathaniel clearly enjoys being the most attractive bloke in the room."

It had taken a whole day and a partial night for Peter to realize that Mathias was being genuine, and that his sister evidently had come into her own on a far more profound basis than he had previously realized. It put a pit in his stomach as he tried to sleep that night, filling him with the sharp and unforgiving feeling that she had left him behind on her ascent to happiness.

Perhaps this realization about surprises had begun the night she'd run off with her now husband. He would never forget the way *that* had felt, despite her very sensible letter explaining her rationale.

"If we keep going, we can reach the general region we're aiming for sometime after nightfall," Mathias was saying, holding that cryptic map out in front of him as though it paired up with the scenery on the horizon. "We'll just have to ride in the dark for a bit. I wager it's worth it if it means we get a proper bed tonight."

"Is that safe?" Peter asked with a frown, resisting the urge to peer over the head of his horse, past the confident gait of

Hortensia, and down the steep decline that crashed into the earth. "We're still on a mountain."

"Well, going down is safer than going up," Mathias told him, folding up the map and tucking it into his breast pocket. "And it's a full moon and clear skies. Should be all right. I've navigated safely with far less visibility, I assure you."

"Steering a ship is somewhat different than descending a cliff face," Peter replied, shifting in his saddle.

"Certainly true enough," Mathias allowed. "This is preferable. The cliff has the decency to stay still."

This argument was not one Peter would generally accept in silence, but it had become apparent that attempting to reason with Mathias Dempierre was only an exercise in exhausting himself and amusing the other. It was true that the rocks beneath them didn't shift and lunge like the waves at sea, but one couldn't simply follow the north star and expect to always find a path underfoot in terrain like this!

He told these things to himself, playacting the entire argument in his mind. This way, and only this way, was he certain to retain his composure and emerge victorious.

∽

It was, in fact, dark for quite some time before Peter and Mathias reached the base of the valley, lit all along the way by the two bobbing lanterns they'd suspended on either side of Hortensia's pack. Every time the glass clacked against the buckles on their luggage, Peter had to suppress the urge to cringe.

"And that's why Gigi ended up with all those birds,"

Mathias was saying, wrapping up an extremely long-winded explanation of why he'd fostered a lifelong fear of dogs. "She blamed me at first, of course, but now, well, my sister would hardly be herself without all those blasted birds. Do you have a pet, Applegate?"

Peter startled at this sudden pocket of expectant silence, wheeling around to look behind him as though one of his family members must have appeared to join in the conversation. "Uh, no. No," he said, clearing his throat as they veered off the mountain road and onto a dirt trail towards the lights of the town center. "I like animals, but we're not permitted to have them at the boarding house in Oxford, and I have lived there for so very long."

"My sister says it's unnatural for people to live without animal companions," Mathias said with a chuckle. "Perhaps if I come back with Hortensia on my arm, she'll change her tune."

"How would you put a donkey on your arm?" Peter wondered, but Mathias had already begun to hum, taking them the long way around the hill where the largest of the three settlements was situated.

Peter had noticed, as they had traveled, that there were signs in every French city that declared "all directions!" whilst pointing in only one direction. Occasionally there was another sign, pointing elsewhere, which announced, "other directions!" which only served to confuse the matter further.

It was still unclear to Peter what in the hell any of it meant, exactly, but Mathias seemed to know, and he was the navigator, after all. He supposed it was all appropriately French.

"Ah, this looks good," Mathias said, nodding towards a squat, rectangular building that sat between the two smaller villages nestled at the base of the hill. "Lodging and food, I think? Shall we check?"

"Please," Peter muttered, visions of a proper bed floating in his mind, as tempting as any siren at sea.

"*Le Libertine!*" Mathias read off the wooden sign as they drew near. "Ah, wonderful. I always did admire the libertines. Right fun bunch, they are. Or were? I'm not sure if any survived the war. Or the pox for that matter. In any event, stay here with our things and I will negotiate some repast and pillows, hm?"

Peter agreed, but Mathias vanished so quickly that it was unlikely he'd heard.

There was a burst of voices and light as he vanished inside, the door swinging shut behind him, and for a moment, the most deliciously perfect breeze swept down from the mountains and swirled through the dirt basin that made up the bottom of the valley.

Peter rubbed Hortensia's nose, leaning against the warm sturdiness of her body as he tipped his head back to take in the night sky.

It was clear here, crisp and bright under a full moon that shone just the slightest bit pink. A professor had told him once that every month's full moon has its own name, something special that only comes once a year. They were mostly animals from what he recalled; wolf moons and rabbit moons and so on. He wished he knew which one he was seeing tonight.

He had never lived anywhere with mountains. Even visiting the northern reaches of Britain did not come close to what he was seeing here tonight, surrounded on all sides by alpine giants, each with a spray of brilliantly bright stars seemingly bursting from their peaks.

It made him feel small, he realized, but in a lovely way, as though all of his worries and woes were irrelevant amidst the towering eternity of a place like this.

Mathias returned with a porter in tow to stable and store their things as they were invited within to rest and restore. Peter had little time to react before Hortensia was clanking away, lantern flames swinging on her haunches, and he was under Mathias's arm, being steered into a place a fair sight more lively than one would generally prefer after a long journey.

It was an explosion of music and the tang of beer and wine, all muddled together under the thrum of laughter and conversation. A fiddle player was sat on a small platform, one of her legs propped on a chair in front of her as she carved out the notes of a rousing reel, seemingly unconcerned with neither the visibility of her striped stockings nor the sliver of visible thigh that peeked out from under the ruffle of her skirt.

Peter found that there was a glass of beer in his hands, put there by forces unknown, and that he didn't mind the taste of the stuff at all. He also found, in short order, that he had lost Mathias to a buxom brunette, to whom the Frenchman was currently accosting with the full powers of his dimpled smile.

"Babette likes pretty men," said a female voice from his left.

"She always has. Your compatriot thinks he's a hunter, when really he is the prey."

He turned to find a young woman sipping a frothy ale, a half smile of amusement on her face as she watched the pair transition from shouted conversation to energetic dancing. "I hope your friend does not fall in love too easily," she said, turning her eyes up to meet Peter's. "Or else, I hope he recovers from a broken heart with haste."

It was too dark to make out the color of her eyes, with only a smattering of candlelight, heavily intersected by the shadows of the Libertine patrons who seemed incapable of sitting still. All Peter could tell for certain was that they sparkled.

She smiled, using those shadowed eyes to take the measure of him. He could make out her hair, a thick rope of fire-kissed brown braided over her shoulder. She was dressed like a revolutionary, with a wide leather belt bisecting a heavy linen skirt and a shirt that would have raised quite the scandal on the civilized side of the Channel. Still, Peter could not find complaint in the view he was offered of her shoulders, nor the suggestion of the shape beneath the billowy fabric.

"I do not know you," she observed, tilting her head. "Do I?"

"It is doubtful," he replied, shouting perhaps a little louder than was necessary to be heard over the din. "We only arrived tonight in the valley."

Her eyebrows lifted, lovely, lush arches over that mysteriously colorless sparkle. "A visitor! And with an accent, besides! You must tell me everything! Is that an English accent? Could it be?"

Peter was glad that it was too dark for the girl to see the color that rose to his cheeks. It was true that his French was far from perfect, at least when spoken. He could read and write it like a native, but unlike his sister, he had never put much time into practicing the oral tradition. What a sorry spy he would make!

"Is the pretty man English too?" she asked, undeterred by his embarrassment.

"He is afraid of dogs," Peter blurted, for reasons he would never be able to fathom. He immediately clamped his jaw shut, the heat on his face only rising.

Luckily, the girl seemed to find this outburst amusing, for she released a bright laugh and touched a hand to his arm. "I have a fine, great beast of a dog named Goliath," she said conspiratorially. "Shall I go fetch him?"

Peter gave a startled laugh, relief diffusing throughout his body as he raised his glass to his lips, hoping a sizable gulp would soothe the frayed edges of his nerves. "I am tempted, but I suppose that would be rather cruel," he confessed. "And your beast would likely scare our donkey anyhow."

"Oh, a donkey!" she said with a grin. "You *are* exotic."

He gave her a twisting half smile, bemused by her seeming familiarity and ease. It was not only the way she addressed him, as though they were old friends, but also her presence in an establishment such as this. He glanced over his shoulder at Mathias whispering into the brunette's ear, a hand resting comfortably on her hip, and had a moment of uncertain realization.

"Do you ... erm," he said, turning back to the girl, who was prettier every time he looked. "Is this your place of employment?"

"Am I a doxy, you mean?" she asked, her eyes widening with amused surprise. "I am not, sir. Are you?"

"W-What?" Peter stammered, wishing for all the world that he could simply melt into the floor now and cease to exist. "I did not mean to imply ... I thought, perhaps, you were a barmaid or ... or ..."

"Yes, or," she echoed, still grinning, as though such an insult were greatly amusing. "I'm afraid not. You are not in England tonight, where all women must be rigorously chaperoned from one sterile room to the next. 'Equality' is in the motto above the door, is it not? We are all brothers and sisters here."

Peter had sisters. This woman was nothing like any sister he'd ever known.

She gave his arm another pat and gestured towards a long, communal table that stretched from one end of the room to the other, inviting him to sit with her and perhaps to continue this talk of siblings and prostitutes until he was nothing more than a burnt-out husk of humiliation in spectacles.

"Tell me," she said, sliding onto the bench with the ease of one who had sat there many times before. "What brings someone like you to Serre Chevalier, particularly in the company of someone like him?"

Peter looked over his shoulder at Mathias once more, whose familiarity with the buxom Babette seemed more intimate by the second. He shook his head, easing himself into the seat across from his new acquaintance with a self-conscious grimace. "He was not my choice of companion," he confessed. "Though I certainly would never have made it so far without him."

"Are you an academic?" she asked, tapping her blunted fingernail against the wooden table. "You are, aren't you? I can always tell. Are you here for the ruins?"

"I am an academic, but I'm afraid my business here is rather more personal in nature," he said, considering how to frame his mission in a way that wouldn't sound as though he had arrived to kidnap some poor, unsuspecting Frenchwoman. "I am visiting a relation of my brother-in-law," he said slowly, approving each word before it could leave his mouth. "He wished to invite her to England to spend time with her family, but could not come himself due to prior obligations."

"He sounds like a shoddy relative, then, doesn't he?" she tsked. "Well, you should see the ruins anyway, since you're here. We've got plenty of Roman and medieval structures, and there's a pagan altar in the forest that dates back to the Iron Age."

"Truly?" He couldn't help leaning forward, his curiosity piqued in a sudden flash of bookish fervor. "Is it protected?"

"Only by the mountains and trees, which seem to have done a fine job thus far. Anyone in the valley can point you to the proper trail if you decide to go see it. It's rather grisly, with little egg-shaped hollows carved into the stone, where blood from sacrifices was collected."

"How many?" Peter asked, fascinated.

"Twelve, I believe," she answered, apparently just as

enthralled. "The fellow from the Sorbonne who came some years ago believed it perhaps coincided with an early understanding of the passage of time. Wouldn't that be fabulous? Another visited when I was little and said it was likely more to do with the moon and was a women's altar, but I could never make sense of that idea. Women surely weren't buying eggs by the dozen since the dawn of man, after all."

"Twelve would not line up with most of the women's rituals I've encountered either," he said, "though of course, most of the pagan practices I study are Celtic in origin. Unless perhaps it is to do with the star visibility here. Either way, I would certainly love to see it."

She was giving him a soft sort of smile, as though charmed by something more than his words.

"Have I said aught amiss?" he asked, remembering again how awkward he was.

"No," she replied. "It is just so very seldom that I hear any accent at all, and yours is very charming."

"Oh, well," he replied, awkwardness magnifying into a shroud of sudden bashfulness. "Not as charming as the pretty man, I'm sure."

She considered him for a moment, likely reflecting on this second clumsy exclamation he'd made of apparent envy. She tipped her head to the side, trailing her pinky finger into the lip of her ale, as though working through some internal deliberation before she next spoke.

"Would you like to go now?" she said after a moment, the sparkle of her eyes somehow more intense than they'd been a moment before. "I could take you."

"Into the forest?" he replied, aghast. "Alone?"

She giggled, biting down on her lip. "Are you afraid I will compromise you, sir? Or perhaps sacrifice you to the old gods?"

"Should you not be concerned about yourself?" he countered, bewilderment clear in his voice. "I am a strange man and you are a girl alone."

"I am a *woman* alone," she corrected. "And I was born here. I could vanish into the wood before you had a moment to act improperly, and you would never find your way out again. Besides, my loyal beast Goliath is always close at hand. It is a good night for it. It is bright."

He opened his mouth and then shut it again, not trusting himself to be sensible. Here was a beautiful girl—no, a beautiful *woman*—offering to take him to see something ancient and untouched and fascinating, alone by moonlight in an alpine forest.

Yes, he was exhausted from travel, but what sort of dolt would turn down such an opportunity? How *could* he?

He could practically hear Mathias in his mind, suggesting that perhaps she had a bit more planned than simply an educational hike, after all. He should not give it a second thought, but looking at her again, it was hard not to wonder how soft her skin might feel in his hands, how someone so brazen might taste ...

He gave his head another shake, forcing a cough as though to dislodge the flash of heat that had gone racing through him.

"Shall I borrow a lantern or two?" she asked expectantly, as though she knew he had no choice but to agree. "We can bring your donkey if you feel you need protection."

"All right then," he said weakly, with barely more than a nod before she'd flung her legs over the bench and vanished towards the bar. He realized that she likely hadn't even been able to hear him and had reacted to his nodding alone.

He stood, smoothing down his wrinkled clothes and quaffing the remainder of the ale in his glass. It was not often that he did anything impulsive, nor was it a familiar feeling to be so utterly at a disadvantage in every way. Still, when he saw the red flash of her skirt and the raised pair of lanterns in her hand from across the room, he found himself moving towards her anyway.

Was it against his better judgement? Perhaps.

Peter was rather of the mind that his internal system of judgement had never been prepared for such a scenario in the first place.

CHAPTER 5

*I*sabelle's heart was thundering.

On a base level, in the purely reasonable part of her mind, she knew she was being foolhardy. She had climbed out of her window some hours earlier intending to come to the Libertine, drink away her anxieties, and cry at the exceptionally comforting Babette Boulier, who was the owner's daughter and Isabelle's dear friend since childhood.

Usually when Isabelle was confronted with unpleasant but necessary stages of growing up, Babette would counsel her over the noise of the pub until some accord with acceptance had been met, at which point, Isabelle would wander home with her shoes in her hand, climb back through her window, and fall asleep, resigned to the inevitability of her future.

It was the only path forward she could fathom anymore.

Of course, from the very first, Babette had refused to play her role as the voice of reason. She had recoiled from the news of Charles's proposal and shouted a great many things that echoed Isabelle's own thoughts perfectly. It was all wrong, and no amount of ale was going to change that.

"Your father is too strict," she'd said, tossing her wealth of brown ringlets. "There are many men who would suit you better."

Who these men were, Babette would not say, just that most anyone would make a better match than stuffy, dignified cousin Charles. If he was looking for a wife, Babette had reasoned, why not meet some of the *other* eligible ladies in the valley, such as herself?

Isabelle had sighed and fussed and fretted while the two of them had attempted to find a silver lining to the whole mess. Charles was handsome enough, yes, but that did not take away her primordial distaste at the idea of him in any carnal context. Paris might indeed be a fun and fulfilling adventure, though Isabelle would not have chosen to infiltrate the capital via its tea rooms.

It was hopeless.

When the first of the two handsome strangers had walked through the door, a cocky smile complimenting his lightly stubbled jaw, the focus of their conversation had been utterly upended. Both had lapsed into appreciative silence to watch him stride over to the bar and negotiate a pair of keys for the evening.

That first man was the type of attractive that was only enhanced by the certainty that no one, least of all a red-blooded woman, could trust anyone who looked that way. He smiled at every woman in the room, winked at a fair few as he negotiated the terms of his room, and ordered drinks before walking back outside to retrieve his compatriot, slinging the keys to the inn rooms at his side like a beacon to interested parties.

The second man had not been nearly so afflicted with arrogant swagger, looking more concerned with finding a hot bath and a quiet bed than he did in the revelry of the Libertine. He had a mess of unstyled hair that fell over his brow in a careless flop, and round spectacles that caught the reflections of the candles that lined the top of the bar. He was tall and slender, dressed more sensibly for travel than the other gent, whose careless stylish flare had clearly been a consideration of his riding kit.

She couldn't help but smile, a twist of amusement working its way through her as he ducked out from under the other man's arm and looked down at the glass of ale in his hands as though it had been conjured there by some unspeakable black magic. This one was nothing like his friend, despite the sharp lines of his jaw and the attractive shape of his lips. How the two had ended up together was likely a very fine story indeed.

"You like the tall one?" Babette had whispered, casting a quick indicative look at the two men. "Go talk to him, while you still can. I shall distract the pirate."

"Pirate?" Isabelle had repeated with a laugh, but Babette was already gone, hips swaying as she reached her mark and wove her magic around that hapless stranger as only she could do. He followed her to an enclave opposite the stage, apparently transfixed with whatever she was saying to him, and of course, at that point, Isabelle had no choice but to follow through with approaching the other mysterious man.

After all, tonight could very well be her last chance to flirt with a stranger, especially in a place where strangers were so very, very unusual.

But, in fine Isabelle Monetier fashion, even her attempt at harmless banter had gotten well out of hand seemingly within seconds of greeting the fellow.

She didn't even know his name, but here she was, holding two lanterns over her head, ready to lead him into the woods, unaccompanied, in the dead of night. She knew it was mad. She knew if she told Babette, even her wildest friend would not approve of this particular venture.

If only she'd been telling the truth about Goliath. The useless creature was likely still snoring, jaw slack, with his head half covered by her knitted blanket, at the foot of her bed.

Rationale said that she could change her mind right now. Nothing said she couldn't. She could tell him the truth. She could say that she realized how silly this was. Or she could say nothing at all, and simply flee back to her house, leaving him confused in her wake. She could convince herself that none of this had ever happened and fall asleep safe and sound in her own bed, nursing a curl of hysterics in her chest at what she'd almost done.

But Charles was at the house. And Father. And a future she did not want.

So, instead, she stood perfectly still, waiting for the handsome English stranger in the round spectacles as he made his way through the crowd to her side, all the while, her heart hammering a wild cadence against her ribs, likely trying to escape and find a host with more sense.

She had never met an Englishman before. The only foreigners that ever passed through the valley were Italians and Swiss who lived near the border, and neither were prone to stop and socialize at the Libertine. The exoticism of the encounter only made it more alluring.

Charles had said himself that she should aspire to expand her horizons past the place of her birth, hadn't he? Of course he had meant to his own ends, but what about hers? What about her ends, hm? Charles never thought about that!

The Englishman reached her, giving a sheepish smile at how long it had taken him to shoulder through the crowd and taking the lanterns from her hand as she pushed the door open to lead them to the much quieter open space without.

"Ah, that's so much better," he said with a little sigh of relief. "It is lovely out here. I was admiring the night sky before I went in."

Isabelle looked up. The moon was so bright as to be almost glaring, drowning out the stars closest to it. From here, she could see Orion on the hunt, and on the other end of the sky, the vain queen Cassiopeia poised on her throne. Her father liked the stars too. He had taught her the shapes so well that she could not help but see them when she looked up.

"There we are," he said, as the flame caught in one of the lanterns, high and bright enough to share its heat with the other. A golden glow spread around him as he rose from a kneeling position and handed her one of them, a wry half smile still on his face. "Are you having second thoughts?"

She shook her head, raising the lantern high enough to shine its light on his face, the flames split into twins that danced merrily in reflection before his eyes. "Are you?"

"Oh, probably," he confessed with a sheepish shrug and a chuckle. "It is not often beautiful women attempt to lure me into the wilds. I daresay if it were, I'd have gone missing long ago."

She smiled, lowering the lantern and beckoning him towards the path into the forest, spinning on her heel so that he could not see the pleased smile that had spread across her face at the implication that she was beautiful. "Come along," she called. "It isn't far."

They walked in silence for a spell, the only sounds coming from their footsteps and the nocturnal life in the wood—the sounds of frogs and owls and such. It was a warm night, with a generous breeze coming in from the mountains, which whistled its way through the tree boughs above.

There was much she wanted to ask this stranger.

How did one travel between two countries at war, exactly? Was life in England really as stuffy and boring as she'd been led to believe? Perhaps most importantly, what did the valley look like to someone who had never seen it before? Was he enchanted, as she would believe any person must be, or underwhelmed, having seen many more places of superior beauty?

She could tell, however, that the allure of this venture came largely from its mystery. Her chattering at him like a nervous schoolgirl would do very little to enhance any element of fantasy for either of them. Instead, she glanced over her shoulder, and asked softly in her provincial accent, "Would you prefer we speak English?"

"Oh," he replied, genuine surprise in his tone. "If you like. Your English is likely a sight better than my French."

"Can you tell all that from a single sentence?" She giggled, slowing her pace so that he might draw up nearer to her side. "My father has always insisted on my fluency. He insists on a great many things, as I suppose parents are prone to do."

"Mine hardly notice my studies one way or the other," he replied. "Though I am in competition with many younger siblings for their attention."

"Oh, I haven't any!" Isabelle said, delighted. "Are you the eldest amongst them?"

"Afraid not. The title was wrested from me by way of a handful of minutes," he said, shaking his head on a laugh, as though the matter had irked him as a child. "My twin sister is technically the eldest, though I would like to think we are equals in the rank."

"A twin sister," Isabelle breathed. "How very unusual! I used to dream of what it must be like to have a twin, though I always imagined a copy of myself with whom to trade places and enact all manner of childish pranks. I confess, the idea is less appealing now, as I've come to rather enjoy being the only one of me."

"I don't mind it. Nell and I are similar in many ways. If we had been identical, perhaps one of us would have resisted the truth of our nature."

"And what nature is that?"

He considered it for a moment, his thumb sliding against the line of his jaw. "I suppose," he said finally, "that you might be skeptical if I claimed it was our irresistible nature. In truth, it is our bookishness. Neither of us could read until we were older than the average child, on account of our eyesight. Once the mystery was solved, we both dove into the world of books and learning like kings at a feast, and haven't come back up for air since."

"I might have believed you," she teased, nudging him with her shoulder, "had you said it was irresistibility. It is a curious thing to ponder, a brother and sister who share both a birthday and a spirit. You must be very close."

He nodded, a wistful expression on his face. "We always were, yes. She recently married and, I fear, has begun to surpass me in a great many ways as she has come into the full bloom of her womanhood. It is difficult to know how to feel when one is both happy beyond measure for a person he loves, but also mourning the things he has lost in her ascent to triumph."

"You miss her being yours completely," Isabelle said in understanding. "If I had a sibling, I might feel the same, watching her leave me behind for a brand new life."

"I cannot imagine your end of things, being an only child." He chuckled, his teeth, even and white, glinting in the moonlight. "Did you have no one to terrorize you, only to turn around and become a playmate not a moment later?"

She hesitated, a pang in her chest at those words. Here in the dark glade, the wind cloaking the sounds of their voices from any who might come upon them, engulfed in a gentle glow of light amongst moonlit darkness, somehow, it felt like the perfect place to give confession. After all, she would likely never see this man again.

"I have a cousin," she said carefully, "who has spent his summers here in the valley with us since I was a baby. I often think of him as a brother. I always have, but apparently he thinks of me as something more. I declined a marriage proposal, but no one seems to accept my no as a final answer. If this follows the pattern of every other thing I've resisted in my short life, then every day I will need to fight the battle anew, until, eventually, I must give in."

"What sort of man wishes to wed an unwilling woman?" He balked, halting in his stride, aghast. "Do your parents not protect you?"

"It isn't like that." Isabelle sighed, turning to face him where he'd stopped. "He would never force anything upon me. He is a gentle and good man, but stubborn and helplessly out of touch with what makes the heart beat. To him, this is sensible. We are fond of one another and he must marry, and it is as simple as that."

His lips were pressed together with disapproval, his weight shifting as though he wished there were a monster to slay on her behalf, so that he might resolve her woes.

"It isn't the worst fate," she continued, reaching forward to touch his fingers, where they gripped the lantern. "Many people are facing far more dire prospects tonight, and here I am, lamenting that a good man, who will give me a good life, wishes to secure my future. Please, pay me no mind. I feel guilty having burdened you with it."

"I am not burdened." He was looking at her hand on his, his voice low and quiet. "You do not need to justify your feelings of distress opposite the suffering of others. You are entitled to mourn for the happiness that was robbed of you. Never apologize for that."

She released a soft, sharp breath, those words striking her in the center of her chest with an unexpected force. She raised herself on her tiptoes, her hand still resting on his, and pressed her lips into his, her eyes fluttering shut.

She had kissed men before, of course, but never truly in earnest. Exchanging kisses meant a great many things here in the valley, and between friendly greetings and awkward youthful curiosity, she had allowed her lips to brush another's a handful of times. None of those times had felt like this.

He caught her around the waist, pulling her against his body as he tilted his head, savoring the gift she'd given him. It felt safe, anchored, and so intoxicating.

When he pulled away, she wanted to protest or perhaps to apologize yet again, though she was not even a little bit sorry. Mercifully, the way he was looking at her seemed approving, or at the very least, pleased.

She cleared her throat, pulling her hand away and turning on her heel. "It's just over the ridge there," she said, all too aware of the breathlessness in her own voice. "I will climb up first, and you may pass the lanterns to me before following."

"Gladly," he replied from behind her, a telltale grin in his voice that sent the blood rushing to her cheeks.

She set her lantern on the ground and gathered her skirt into her fist, hitching herself up and over the small earthen mound that had been established both to mark the location of the altar and to protect it from any wayward wood felling. He handed her the lanterns and vaulted himself over with apparent ease, still looking awfully pleased with himself.

She opened her mouth, intending to say something, anything that might defuse what she had done, but as soon as his eyes fell on the little stone table ahead of them, his expression took on an enchanted, dazed quality that seemed to have done the job for her.

Strangely, seeing him distracted from their kiss sent a wave of disappointment crashing over her, and as she followed his approach, she had to instruct herself rather sternly not to pout.

He set his lantern on the cusp of the altar and turned to take hers as well for the other end, providing them with a little dome of light with which to view this curiosity.

The man touched the egg-shaped indents, drawing his long, slender fingers over them, one by one, his expression one of utter reverence. Somehow, that only made her want to kiss him yet again.

"When I was a boy," he said softly, "I used to spend hours in the ruins 'round Winchester. They seemed impossibly old to me, but this ... this was ancient when the halls of Wessex breathed the first inkling of a united Britain. It was a grand old thing before Egypt and Rome."

"Yes," she replied, her heart fluttering at the thought of it. "I think about it sometimes, even in the village. The clock tower has been there since the twelfth century, and if I lean against it to enjoy an apple on an autumn day, I cannot help but wonder how many others have done that exact thing, too, just there, having sat in the same place. It makes one feel very small, does it not?"

"Do you think the one who made this felt small?" he asked, tossing her a sheepish smile, his hair falling across his brow. "Perhaps we are not so small as we think."

"Perhaps not, but I do not mind simply being one of the girls who ate an apple at the base of a medieval clock tower. There are far worse things to be than small."

He was watching her, his expression thoughtful, perhaps even admiring. "May I kiss you again?" he asked, as though asking permission to inconvenience her somehow.

She nodded, her breath caught in her throat, and this time, when he drew her against him, the softness of his kiss felt more indulgent, less urgent. She reached up to touch his hair, so fine and silky and wayward, and attempted to imprint this memory deep in her soul, so that she may conjure it until she was old and withered, no matter which direction her life took after this night.

She knew this stranger would leave the valley. If not tomorrow, then soon. Visitors never stayed long. Perhaps he might remember her too. She hoped he would.

He pulled back, his breath heavy and sweet, his thumbs rubbing circles into the sides of her waist. "You are remarkable," he breathed, blinking at her with eyes that shone in the moonlight. "Utterly remarkable."

She blushed, lowering her lashes to disguise how much pleasure those words brought her, and rested her head against his shoulder, breathing in the pine scent of his clothes. Perhaps he would spirit her away tonight, and they could live their lives as brigands, on the road.

It was a silly idea, but an endearing one.

"I do not even know your name," he whispered, resting his cheek against the top of her head.

"I do not know yours either," she replied with a little giggle. "Is that terrible?"

"My name is Peter," he told her, tilting her chin up to meet his eye. "Peter Applegate."

"*Enchanté*, Peter," she murmured, stroking the lines of his jaw as she leaned forward for one last kiss, stolen in this impossible evening. "I am Isabelle."

It took a moment to realize that he had stiffened, his posture suddenly rigid, his lips tight and unresponsive to her kiss. She pulled back, confusion in her eyes to see him gazing down at her with wide-eyed horror.

"What?" she demanded, pushing back to put some distance between them and dropping her hands on her hips. "What have I done?"

"Isabelle," he repeated, looking somewhat queasy. "Your surname wouldn't happen to be Monetier, would it?"

She startled, taking the smallest step back and catching her heel against the altar. She lost her balance, nearly toppling backward, but found that Peter Applegate had rushed forward to catch her, helping her ease to a seated position on a timeless piece of history.

"How did you know that?" she demanded, her voice dry. "Who are you?"

"Oh, God," he groaned, squeezing his eyes shut. "I do not even know where to begin. Isabelle ... Miss Monetier. I have come to the valley looking for *you*."

CHAPTER 6

Peter hadn't slept much.

Which was to say that he hadn't slept at all.

If Isabelle Monetier had gotten her way, they would have left the glade straight away and stormed an assault on her family home the likes of which would make the soldiers at the front line tremble in awe. It had been a very near thing, but somehow Peter had managed to convince her to wait until sunrise.

"I am sick to death of the machinations of men!" she had shouted, snatching up his lantern from the edge of the altar and thrusting it out at him in such a way that the candlelight swung and dazzled about her. "You said you were looking for *me*, Peter Applegate, not my father! Why should we require his presence for you to speak freely?"

He could see the resemblance to Nathaniel now, so clearly it was a marvel he hadn't recognized her immediately. She had the same sharp structure to her cheeks, the same carefully sculpted lips, but her eyes glittered with a fury he would wager Nathaniel Atlas had never allowed himself to display to another person.

She was magnificent. So much so that he did not trust himself to attempt to speak again as she swept around him, stomping her way out of the forest clearing with enough fury and speed that if he did not quickly gather his senses about him, he would be stranded there until the sun rose.

"What do the English want with me?" she ranted, in such a way that it was clear she did not expect an answer. From behind, the glow of her lamp had created a red-gold halo around her, one that remained undisturbed as she did not deign to turn around and acknowledge him. "What do any of you fool men want from me? I just want to be left in peace!"

"I am sorry," he mumbled, a ringing in his ears that was fit to knock him senseless any moment. How had he mucked this up so badly?

"Sorry?" she repeated, a dangerous note of laughter in her tone. She spun around and took three rapid steps backward, until she was nose to nose with him, her lantern held high alongside their faces. "What are you sorry for, Peter Applegate? For kissing me? For deceiving me? Or for telling me half a truth and refusing to disclose the other half?"

He blinked, somewhat abashed by his immediate physical impulse to pull her close to him again, distracted by the scent of her moon-touched skin and the flush in her cheeks. He was most certainly *not* sorry for having kissed her.

He took a shaky breath and took a step back, turning to the side in the hopes of regaining some of his sense. Another gust of mountain-chilled breeze brushing over him helped clear some of the smoke from his mind, some of the panic from his heart, but he had never been particularly handy at emotional confrontations like this.

"Isabelle," he said carefully, measuring every syllable lest he somehow make things worse. "If I had a full complement of information to give you, I would do so right now. The reason we require your father's presence is because he is the only person in the world who knows the missing parts to a half-told story."

She narrowed her eyes, considering this. "Why would you sail into enemy territory on behalf of a half-told story?"

"Because," he sighed, pressing his fingers into the bridge of his nose as he realized there was nothing more to that sentence. *Because my aunt told me to* was not the answer he wished to give her, even if it was the truth.

"Because," she repeated with a mirthless laugh. "Fine. *On y va*, back to the pub. Perhaps your pretty friend will give me the information I seek."

He clamped his jaw shut and shuffled after her, reminding himself that this was not the time to foster petty jealousy. Not every man was born with unseemly confidence and a charming smile. Indeed not. He hadn't been.

Once they had reached the Libertine, it had become apparent that Mathias had retired for the evening, much to the disappointment of the innkeeper's daughter. At least, she had seemed disappointed until Isabelle had completed whispering things into her ear, during which her demeanor had become markedly more icy until she had nothing left on her face but a glare.

"I will wake you at dawn," Isabelle said, tossing her thick, auburn braid over her shoulder. "I will sleep here with Babette. There is no time to waste."

"Won't your father be alarmed that you aren't home?" he had asked helplessly, watching her make for the staircase, the other girl's arm around her waist. She turned over her shoulder and threw him a withering look that reminded him of his lack of tact in bringing up her father yet again.

He had slumped off to the bar, where it was obvious that fostering the disfavor of those particular two young ladies was highly frowned upon in this place. He was overcharged for two glasses of ale and then forced himself to slump up the stairs and collapse into a hard, narrow cot in the hopes that a bit of intoxication would pull him into sleep.

However, his sister's nagging worries about how heavily he slept haunted him through the hours, insisting that if he dozed off, he might not wake until the next evening, thereby cementing the hatred of a woman he was pretty sure he had just fallen a little bit in love with. And so he stared at the ceiling, creating shapes that weren't there in the water stains and cracks, until a sharp rap at the door alerted him to the fact that the sun had crested the horizon.

Mathias was already downstairs, enjoying a steaming cup of coffee and the giggles of the innkeeper's daughter as though nothing at all was wrong in the world. When he spotted Peter descending the stairs like a beaten dog behind the bright-eyed and determined young woman he'd vanished with the night before, his flaxen eyebrows rose in surprised admiration.

Ah, what a joy it would have been if Peter might have

preserved this misunderstanding simply for the pleasure of surprising the unflappable Mathias Dempierre.

"Your friend made quite a mess," murmured the other woman, stroking Mathias's hair briefly before vanishing to attend to a groggy pair of regulars who had not moved from their seats since the night before.

"Hello there," Mathias said to Isabelle, flashing her his most devastating, dimpled smile. "Who might you be?"

"I am Isabelle Monetier," she snapped back, wiping the smile immediately from his face. "Who the devil are you?"

～

They walked to St. Chauffrey, opting to allow Hortensia to enjoy the lie-in that neither of them would get.

In a sliver of brightness around the discomfort of this entire situation, Mathias had been blissfully silent, seemingly stunned beyond glibness, for the entire walk. All of them were silent.

Isabelle led them to a half-timbered house on the edge of a wide and wild meadow. The property was surrounded by a wealth of summer crops, bright and multicolored and fragrant enough to make Peter's stomach rumble. If she heard, Isabelle did not acknowledge this, and silently allowed them in through the front door, motioning to a sitting room while she went to rouse her father. The house was still dark, and some fumbling around to find curtains to open provided a bit of muffled swearing in her absence.

Yves Monetier was hastened into the room, dazed and rubbing the sleep from his eyes by the sharp prodding of his impatient daughter. He was a man of middling years, with pale hair that was sticking up in a variety of sleep-induced directions, and laughter lines about his eyes and mouth that implied a much more cheerful general demeanor than the befuddled scowl he shot at the two men in his sitting room.

"I've never seen these people before in my life!" he exclaimed, turning to find his daughter drawn up to her full height, arms akimbo with her fingers tapping impatiently at her slim waist.

"They are English," she informed him, lifting her chin.

"Beg pardon?" Mathias gasped, making a move to go immediately to his feet.

Peter gripped him by the jacket and tugged him back to seating, choosing to stand instead in what he hoped was a deferential posture, rather than one that implied he was about to lose consciousness at any moment. "Monsieur Monetier," he said. "We are here on behalf of the Atlas family."

There was a long, pregnant pause during which Yves Monetier's face went rather slack. It was difficult to tell what he was feeling. Panic? Disbelief? Perhaps he was simply stunned, for in that moment, it truly did feel as though the very turning of the world met a hiccup.

This development seemed to finally soften Isabelle's rage. She dropped her stern pose and went to her father's side, touching his arm. "Papa?"

"The Atlases are dead," he choked, looking helplessly from Peter to Isabelle. "I saw them die."

"You saw Mary and Walter Atlas die," Peter said gently.

"Their son, Nathaniel, is still very much alive, and he has recently become aware that another Atlas yet survives."

"His sister," Mathias said pointedly, glancing at Isabelle. "Alice."

It was at this point that Yves Monetier began to tremble and made his way quickly to sit before his legs gave out beneath him. "How is this possible?" he whispered, more than once.

Isabelle was frowning, uncertain what to do with all of her indignation when the scene had unfolded so unpredictably. "Papa," she said gently, "do you need water? Do you need to lie down?"

She did not ask the questions that so obviously burned within her. She could not, with her father so toppled by this surprise.

"Shall I ask them to leave?" she said in a low voice, her tone thick with apology.

He shook his head, taking a trembling breath and looking up to meet her eyes. "My love," he said. "My sweet girl. There are things I did not tell you, because I thought they would only bring pain. I did not know anyone survived. I swear it."

She straightened, her expression creased with concern, and pointed at Peter. "You," she said in a tone that brokered no argument, "come with me."

"Where are you going?" Mathias demanded.

"We will put the kettle on and make my father something to eat," she said to him, beckoning Peter to her side. "You speak to my father. I will speak to Peter Applegate here, and perhaps afterwards, we may all sit down and have a coherent conversation about what is happening and how it involves me."

She did not wait for a response, taking Peter's elbow and nudging him in the direction of the house's kitchen, leaving Mathias and Yves Monetier behind to stare warily at one another.

The last thing Peter heard was Mathias suggesting that Yves might know his mother, Therese, to which Yves responded with a helpless groan.

He stood awkwardly while Isabelle knocked around the kitchen, filling a kettle and setting it to the flame and plucking eggs from a straw-lined basket near the larder. He watched her in something akin to awe as she set a breakfast in motion as though it were second nature to her.

He realized with an unpleasant start that he had never watched a meal come together like this before, and that despite his significant learning, he had nothing at all to offer as an assist.

"You should begin speaking," Isabelle said with her back to him, as fat began to crackle in a skillet. "I am at the end of my patience, Peter Applegate."

He hesitated, glancing around up at the wide, high ceiling above them, hung with an assortment of dried herbs. "Will your mother be joining us?" he heard himself asking, in rather a more tactful attempt at gleaning information than he would have expected from himself.

"My mother died when I was a babe in arms," she said. "My cousin is asleep upstairs, but he will not wake for another hour at least. There is no sense in continuing to delay my enlightenment."

"That is not what I am attempting to do," Peter said quickly. "What do you know of her?"

"My mother?" she asked with clear confusion, turning to look at him. "Only as much as my father did. She was an Englishwoman that assisted in his escape from a British prison. She did not survive to join us on this side of the Channel."

"Yes," Peter replied, genuinely surprised that she had this information. "Her name was Mary, and your father's name was Walter."

She paused, midway from turning back to attend the eggs. "My father's name is Yves. We've just come from the room where you met him."

"Your adoptive father," Peter said as gently as he could manage. "The man who sired you was Walter Atlas, Mary's husband."

She blinked at him and then laughed, a quick snorting sound that came with a shake of the head and the return of her attention to her eggs. "You've come here looking for a lost girl named Alice," she recited. "I heard your friend say so. I am afraid you have come to the wrong girl."

"Isabelle." He sighed, stepping forward but stopping himself from the urge to touch her, to take her soft shoulder in his hand and turn her around. "I wish that were true," he said, watching her transfer the hot eggs into a plate and douse the fire, just as the kettle began to scream. "But if we were in the wrong home, why did your father react the way he did?"

He saw the slightest break in her movements, a pause in the ritualistic grace of her hands as she arranged mugs and tea leaves on the counter. He heard her take a measured and deep gulp of air before resuming her task, as graceful and learned as a ballerina flitting through a *pas de deux*.

She did not look to him again as she moved, though she did speak. Her voice remained strangely bright as she instructed him to retrieve a loaf of bread from the pantry to his rear as she began to carry the prepared food out onto a sturdy wooden table in the adjoining room.

She avoided his eye, her expression frozen in a sort of determined placidity as she poured four cups of steaming tea and set about carving the bread into quarters, whilst instructing him as to where to locate the freshest butter and a set of wooden plates.

Mathias and Yves appeared in the dining room apparently without having been summoned, both seated somberly in their places when Peter returned from his given errands. Isabelle Monetier stood at the head of the table, her hand resting on the back of her chair as she motioned for Peter to find his seat.

She sat last, lifting a cup of tea to her lips with a measured control of her features that could only be the result of disguising a great tumult of emotion. Seeing her like this, Peter was confident that no one who had met her brother, Nathaniel, could deny the obvious relation.

There was a period of quiet, where the only sounds were forks on plates and the clinking of porcelain cups on saucers. They ate in unnatural silence, each of them fortifying themselves for the conversation that must follow.

When at last the eggs were consumed and the tea had run dry, Yves cleared his throat and reached across the table, dropping something small and solid from his fist onto the tabletop in front of his daughter. She looked down at the trinket, glimmering blue against the rays of early-morning sun, and reached forward to touch it.

"I was going to give this to you on your wedding day," Yves began, his voice weary with the secrets it had kept. "It was your mother's. She was wearing it on the day she died."

CHAPTER 7

Isabelle had no qualms about rousing Charles from his oblivious slumber by the most raucous means possible.

She did not knock, but rather slammed his door open, snatching a discarded shirt from the floor and throwing it at his face as he came up from his blankets in an alarmed stupor.

"I need you downstairs immediately," she had announced, ignoring his sounds of protest and offense. "You are the only person I am certain is not entirely insane right this moment, and I need you to weigh in on the nonsense currently unfolding below."

She hadn't waited for him to respond, whipping out of his room with the same energy she'd used to barge in and taking the stairs two at a time with her skirt in her fists until she'd reached the landing again. She went to the rear of the house and opened her bedroom, allowing Goliath to prance past in obvious offense at having been left alone all evening before she shooed him out the rear door to do his business while she attended to her own.

The only thing that gave her pause as she directed herself to return to the dining room was the sight of her own reflection, radiating so much emotion that for the slightest moment, she did not recognize herself.

She forced herself to take a breath, leaning back against the wall and letting her eyes flicker shut for a moment, counting the ticks of the hallway clock until she got to a full minute. She had never been given any reason to disguise her emotions before. She had never been blindsided with chaos like she had been during the last week, either.

While she'd sat at that table, listening to her father set the stage for what was certain to be the most upsetting event yet, she had done her level best to keep everything contained beneath the surface. It was easier than she had expected it to be, and the power of such deception was strangely intoxicating. Composure, it seemed, was far more frightening than any outburst, and seeing how much it unsettled her father, it had begun to unsettle her as well.

As soon as he had mentioned Charles's presence on the fatal day in question, it had given her the excuse she needed to leave the room. Walking past the doorframe had reignited her usual freedom of emotion, which now had resulted in her standing opposite herself, wondering who this wild-eyed woman was and who she was planning to hurt.

She shook her head, pressing the backs of her hands to her cheeks and summoning that unnatural calm she had displayed earlier. If her life was going to be upended this morning, yet again, she at least might attempt to retain some dignity during the ordeal.

When she rounded the corner to return to the dining room, it was in time to meet Charles on the staircase, rolling up his shirtsleeves and wearing a snit of an expression on his face. She did not speak, instead motioning for him to follow her and leading the way back into the most dour breakfast gathering the world had ever seen.

"Oh!" Charles exclaimed, clearly taken aback by the presence of strangers. "I did not realize we had company. I would've worn a waistcoat."

"Sit down!" Isabelle snapped, though she was pleased to hear that her voice sounded rather more stern than ragged. "These two men are envoys from England. Gentlemen, this is Commandant Charles Monetier, my cousin."

"Envoys from England?" Charles repeated in obvious bafflement. "What news? I am on leave for the summer season."

"They aren't here for you," Isabelle informed him. "They are here for me. It has nothing to do with the war."

It was a strange sort of pleasure, seeing someone other than herself lose their grasp on the reality existing around them. Charles demanded an explanation with a forcefulness that could not be ignored, which to her great pleasure, caused the other three men at the table to wince.

Yves released a long, beleaguered sigh, turning to his nephew with the amount of enthusiasm a man generally reserves for his own execution. "Charles," he began, "do you remember the day I returned from England? The day your father died?"

Charles startled, casting a quick sidelong flick of his eyes to the strangers before squaring his shoulders. "Of course I do," he replied. "Who could forget such a thing?"

"What do you remember?" Isabelle asked eagerly, finding her way back into her chair and leaning forward to meet her cousin's eyes. "Tell me what you remember."

"Uncle Yves had been captured some years prior," Charles said, shifting with obvious discomfort. "By the English, of course."

Isabelle felt her heart sink as her cousin laid out a scenario that was close enough to identical to the one her father had spun. She reached out to take the necklace that had been abandoned on the table, and when her cousin's eyes saw her fingers close around the blue stone, a light of realization seemed to spark behind his eyes, stopping his account mid-word.

"The baby wasn't yours," he said with a kind of wonder, turning to his uncle. "The baby belonged to that woman with the knife, the one who killed my father!"

"Your father turned his back on an honorable exchange and shot two men dead once he had his side of the barter," Yves said defensively. "You were a child, Charles. He told you what you needed to hear about good and evil so that you might witness murder and see it as just."

There was a long silence around the table, during which everyone present went to a great deal of effort to avoid the eyes of everyone else.

Finally, the blond man who had traveled here with Peter

cleared his throat, rapping his knuckles against the wood of the table as though to interrupt the awkwardness.

"Twenty years ago, it seems a great many people died without good reason," he said, cutting his eyes to Charles in a way that clearly conveyed an exclusion of Jonathan Monetier in this sentiment. "You did a noble thing, taking the child and raising her as your own. It is a thing I think very few men would have done."

"Papa?" Isabelle felt the hot prick of tears at the corners of her eyes as the last pillar that held up a plausible untruth to this story crumbled away.

"Isabelle, you are my daughter," Yves assured her gruffly. "Nothing can take that from either of us. I would have told you the truth if I had known you had any surviving family."

"You might have known if you'd given the Silver Leaf Society some means to communicate with you," Peter Applegate said with a raise of his eyebrows. "I have read the letters you sent to them. 'The babe is alive and well.' 'My daughter is thriving.' 'She will be happy.' 'She will soon marry.' You ensured that they could never reply to you. You did not even sign your name."

Yves glared at Peter. "You understand that such correspondence is rather sensitive at a time of war, I imagine. Identifying myself would be revealing the location of an English hostage, an innocent child who has no part in this conflict! I could not take the risk."

"I am not a child," she said calmly, drawing the attention of both men away from one another. "And, I daresay, I am hardly English."

"Agreed," Mathias muttered.

"We came on behalf of your brother," Peter said, his tone so much gentler when he spoke to her, his gaze so much kinder. "He has spent his entire life thinking you had perished with your parents. Upon learning of your survival, he is extremely eager to meet you. We have come with a means to smuggle you to England, if you so desire it."

She held up her hand to silence the immediate outrage that exploded from the Monetier men at this suggestion. She waited for them to quiet, tilting her head curiously at Peter Applegate. "Why did this brother not come himself?" she asked. "It seems rather convoluted to send others to bring me to him."

"Ah," Peter said, casting a nervous glance at a glowering Charles. "Nathaniel is a member of Parliament, which is currently in session. It would cost him his seat in the House of Commons to abandon his post now, and he did not wish to wait until the autumn to find you."

"He is also a sight more valuable to be taken prisoner than we are," Mathias put in cheerfully. "And I imagine he did not want to leave his wife behind with a child on the way."

"You expect us to hand Isabelle over to two men, *English* men, who are confessed criminals, and send her sailing into enemy territory?" Charles demanded, incredulous. "You cannot be serious."

"No one expects you to hand me over to anyone, Charles," Isabelle sniffed. "I am not a parcel. I shall have to decide this for myself."

"We can bring you back home, if that is your wish," Mathias

assured her. "You would not be obliged to remain in England, should you choose to come."

"If you do not," Peter said, "I encourage you to at least write to Nathaniel. His joy at your survival is sincere and deep, but he does not wish to disrupt your life."

This sentiment drew scoffs from both Isabelle and her father, but the sincerity in Peter's expression, the way his hand rested on the table, as though reaching for hers without taking liberties, calmed the thrashing of emotion inside of her. She wished that he had told her some of this in the forest the night before, when she might reach for his hand and lean into him for comfort without the prying eyes of others.

Then again, he was well reasoned in not attempting to convince her of something so outlandish without her father's input. Here in the aftermath, she had to admit that he'd made the right choice, despite her temper in its wake.

"I need to think," she decided, pushing herself back from the table and coming to her feet, which already itched to go running through the meadow, into the sheltered privacy of the woods. "I need to be alone."

She turned and left, without waiting for their reactions.

~

SHE WISHED that she could simply fall asleep and escape from the world for a while. It seemed to Isabelle that when one most needed the fantastical comfort of dreams, they were impossible to find.

Goliath had followed her as she ran from her home, from

these revelations about her origins. He had followed her all the way back to the stone altar in the woods, his little legs pumping with a determination that must have meant he sensed her distress. She had taken him into her lap and felt a tug at her heart when he rested his cheek on her knee, pressing his face down with a little extra force as though to say he loved her.

The emotions that had struck her this morning had all been strong and crippling, but damned if she could identify any of them by name. Now that the revelation had ended, she felt curiously numb, as though her entire being was overtaken by a loud hum of neutrality and emptiness. If she had truly come to the forest to think, she was failing spectacularly.

For a moment, at least, with her fingers buried in the soft fur of Goliath's scruff, she felt her mind clear a little.

The dog was only just a touch bigger than the woven handbasket Isabelle used to gather greens. He had been the smallest of his litter, often ignored and overpowered by his siblings. He hadn't let it stop him from thriving, burrowing under the bigger pups to knock his way to his mother's milk, refusing to perish on the plight of his size.

"Ought we to call him David?" her father had said, when she'd chosen him from the rancher's basket, already smitten.

And she had said no. He was no hero, no ideologue proving his point. He simply was mighty, and refused to be tamed, like the giant of Biblical fame. The first time she had said his name, Goliath had jumped from the ground nearly to her waist, as though he approved.

She looked down at him, curled in her lap, and felt some of

the brambled iron around her heart ease. His little head was shaped like a dimpled piece of fruit, with tiny incisors poking out from his lips when he lay on his side like this. He always knew when and how to provide just the right amount of love.

"Isabelle?" came a voice from her left, soft and uncertain as footsteps shuffled through the grassy terrain. "It is Peter. Peter Applegate?"

"I know who it is," she replied with a dry, humorless laugh. "You may come through. I am doing nothing of import."

He navigated through the overgrowth with a careful kind of grace, born more of frequent missteps, she imagined, than from a naturally elegant stride. Still, it drew her eye, watching him weave and sidestep the obstacles like an exceptionally practiced dancer, at ease in his own form. Watching him reminded her of how close she had been to him the night before, in this very place.

How far would she have taken their interlude, had fate not intervened? How impulsive had she been feeling, when the largest surprise in her life had been Charles and his thoughts of matrimony? Would she have lain with him, here on the soft grass near the stone?

She quickly broke her gaze from him, taking a sharp gulp of air and returning to the comforting visage of Goliath. It did not do to add more confusion to the already chaotic melange within her. Still, here, in this place, with him, she couldn't help but remember how it had felt to be pulled tightly against his lean body, and how soft his lips had been on hers.

He sat next to her, unspeaking, and for a breath of time they simply existed together in this place, serenaded by the wind in the lush overgrowth of summer leaves and the delicate snores of a loyal dog.

"Is this Goliath?" Peter asked eventually, though his voice remained gentle and undemanding. "He is mightier than even I expected."

"He is a force to be reckoned with," Isabelle agreed with a reluctant smile and a little sniff, which pulled the impulse to burst into tears deeper into her, where it might be contained. "How did you know I was here?"

"I didn't," he confessed. "I simply hoped. Your father is searching a stream bed near your house while Mathias and your cousin attempt to verbally joust one another to death. I imagine if he knew I'd found you, your cousin would run me through with steel instead of metaphor."

"Charles is very protective of me." She frowned, lifting the hand that sat between them and unfurling her fingers around Mary Atlas's necklace, its vibrant blue stone seemingly glowing against her palm. "He should not be. Our parents killed one another. He loathes the English."

"I think perhaps that does not apply to you," Peter answered, his silver-gray eyes falling to the stone in her hand. "He wishes to accompany you to England, but he also knows such a thing is impossible. If we were to delay our departure, I might be able to draw up mock papers for a chaperone, but it would take time, and said chaperone could not be nearly so high profile as your cousin."

"My father cannot come either," Isabelle said, knowing as soon as the words left her mouth that it was true. "I could not bear to see the hurt in his eyes at the implication that my true family has been elsewhere all along. I do not know how I am expected to behave now, Peter. I don't even know my own name."

"People choose their names all the time. They always have, since antiquity."

She finally turned to look at him, if only to shoot him a glance of skepticism, which made him chuckle, despite the weight of the current conversation.

"The apostle Paul was born Saul," he said, lifting one finger. "Caligula of Rome was actually named Gaius. He chose to be called by his childhood nickname, all the way to his throne and death, and so that is how he is remembered."

She considered this, a glimmer of amusement threatening to burst through her comfortable numbness. Quietly, she said to him, "Alice Atlas is an awful name. It sounds like someone with a lisp stumbling over their classroom reading."

He did laugh at that, restraint seemingly cracked enough that he pulled a smile from her too. "Never tell your brother," he said, "but I could not agree more. Isabelle Monetier is a far superior name."

"Mary," she mused, tilting her hand to show Peter the necklace. "My mother's name was Mary. Why have I never asked her name before?"

"That is a beautiful necklace," he said, rather than answer. "It is a symbol of the mother you did not have a chance to know. One who loved you enough to put you in the arms of a good man before she risked her own life."

"It is a locket." Isabelle held it out to him so that he could lift it from her palm, the thin, metal chain grazing against her palm like a whisper of a more joyous touch. "I cannot get it open."

"Perhaps there is something of Walter Atlas inside," Peter replied with a frown, turning the trinket onto its side to inspect the seam. "That would explain why your father did not give it to you sooner."

"Perhaps." She sighed, leaning her head back against the cool and solid stone. "None of that matters now."

"It looks like it got stepped on," Peter said, inspecting the flat gleam of unpolished metal on the back. "You see, there is a protrusion here, at the lip of the opening."

She nodded. "If there are miniatures inside, they are likely long eroded anyway. I want to wear it, but I have felt some strange fear of putting it on, as though the moment I do, I have accepted that this is reality and there is no turning back."

He loosened the chain and held the ends of the necklace up, offering to place it around her neck. "There is never any turning back," he said to her, waiting until she nodded to lean forward and secure the clasp. "My aunt used to say to us all the time that the only path worth taking is the one that goes forward."

She pulled her braid through the necklace, allowing it to rest heavy and cool on her breastbone. She touched it tentatively, as though she expected to be zapped with some bolt of lightning at any moment, but it was only a necklace, she realized, and there was more than one path she might choose which went forward.

"That is a very unusual stone," Peter said, as though to

relieve her of the obligation to respond. His long, elegant fingers brushed over the opaque and heavy setting in the locket, coming ever so close to touching her flesh without doing so. "Lapis lazuli isn't found in England or on the Continent. It is mined far to the East by Arab jewelers and artisans, worn by royals and priestesses as a sign of their status. I have only ever seen it in displays at the University museum of artifacts from the ancient world."

"I wonder how she came by it," Isabelle said, her voice perhaps a bit breathier than it should have been. "What do you know of her, Peter? How came you to be involved in this business?" A sudden, horrifying thought popped into her mind, and quickly she demanded, "Are we related?"

"No!" he said loudly and abruptly, startling Goliath enough to make him yap and leap from Isabelle's lap in indignation. "No, absolutely not," he said again, with an apologetically lower volume.

Goliath gave him a short bark of reproach and settled into the soft grass between the two of them, apparently quick to forgive and eager to return to his nap.

Peter heaved a sigh, adjusting his spectacles as he considered how he might explain. "It is all rather tangled. The Silver Leaf Society is and was an operation put into motion to reunite families torn apart by the war. For over two decades, the Silver Leaf has borne refugees and exiles and even some prisoners across the Channel, amassing a cache of smuggled goods to use for bargaining and to keep the operation funded and active.

"My aunt is currently the head of this organization, and as

such, occasionally requests my assistance with matters of great import."

She blinked at him, uncertain how exactly one responds to an operation of human smuggling, benevolent as it may sound. The fact that it was headed by a woman was a point of interest she must remember to investigate at a more appropriate time.

"The Silver Leaf Society had five founders, one of whom was your mother, Mary," he continued. "It was her work that liberated your father from the prison below Dover Castle and returned him to French soil."

"In exchange for a British prisoner," Isabelle said, nodding. "So I understand, she was then betrayed by my uncle Jonathan and the three Britons died on the beach."

"Yes." He paused, and then awkwardly added, "I am sorry."

"As am I." She turned to him, pulling her legs up under her skirt and looking hard into his eyes. "I have many more questions, Peter Applegate," she said, clutching at the exotic blue stone around her neck. "I hope you will answer them on our journey to England."

"I will endeavor to tell you all I know," he swore, earnest and hopeful. "When we get to London, my aunt and Mathias's mother can likely answer a great many more questions about your mother. Your father's sister-in-law still lives as well, and her son, Kit, who is your cousin."

"And I am to have a niece or nephew as well," she said in wonderment. "Isn't that what you said? My brother's wife is expecting?"

Peter's expression softened, a wistful look coming over his

face. "I cannot believe Nell is expecting a child. It seems so unreal."

"Nell," Isabelle repeated. "Your sister, Nell?"

"Oh. Yes." He shook his head, running his fingers through his hair. "I told you it was tangled. My sister is your brother's wife. When they wed, they returned to your ancestral home in Dover and uncovered the information necessary to finally find you."

"So we *are* family," she said, a teasing lilt in her voice. "You liar."

"We most certainly are *not* related," he said defensively, his volume coming up again. "There is a difference!"

"Is there?" she wondered, if only to watch a flush of red spread over his cheeks until she couldn't repress a giggle anymore.

How wondrous it was, to be able to laugh right now, with all that was happening. Every little thing felt unreal, but somehow it had gone from a weight, crushing her from throat to gut, to simply an aura of surreal uncertainty, something less painful, for the moment, if still very confusing.

"I do not want a chaperone," she said, which to her delight made the blush spread down to his jaw. "Are we to pose as relatives? I should like to see these forged papers. From where will we sail?"

"Erm," he sputtered, shifting his posture a little and clearing his throat. "Mathias has a boat docked in Marseille. We are to pose as man and wife," he said, in a fit of what must have been truly exquisite discomfort. "Until we arrive in London."

She bit her lip, torn between the desire to tease him further and to sensibly plan this madness of a journey.

"So we will be sharing a bed?" she said, opting for mischief. She felt she had earned it, and he was rather adorable when flustered.

"No, of course ... no," he managed, unable to resist a flick of his eyes down to her lips, as though the memories of their embrace had been toppled onto him like a sudden storm. "We will ensure your reputation is safe and protected throughout the journey."

"I haven't a reputation," she replied with a quirk of her lips. "Alice Atlas is a clean slate, is she not? A truly pure bride for any man."

"I thought you did not want to be married," Peter pointed out, exasperation beginning to tinge his voice.

"I did not want to be married to Charles," she said, pushing herself to her feet and clicking her tongue to wake Goliath. She offered her hand to Peter, who accepted it as he scrambled to stand as well. "I don't mind so much the idea of being married to *you*."

It was strangely gratifying, the way his mouth sagged slightly open, their hands clasped as he found his footing a mere breath away from her. Last night, he had seemed like a fleeting fantasy, a thing to remember when she was resigned to her life in a dispassionate marriage. She wanted to kiss him again, and if things had not changed so very much, she would have, with free abandon, right there in the sunlit glade.

Instead, she held on to the idea that, at the very least, she had one ally to be by her side as she embarked on this adventure, this lunatic upheaval of all she'd ever known.

She beckoned with a crook of her finger and led man and dog through her well-worn footpath back to the open valley, where now she must speak to her father and placate her cousin; where she must pack her belongings and say her farewells. This was the path to the future, the one that led forward, and now that she had stepped onto it, she must begin to make decisions on how this adventure would unfold.

CHAPTER 8

The first thing Peter noticed upon returning to the Monetier home was that Mathias had been decked squarely in the face.

Naturally, he seemed unbothered by it, nursing the swell of his eyebrow with a bit of wet cloth while he admired the collection of maps Yves Monetier had in the study. Yves himself was frowning, but seemed otherwise unharmed, which led Peter to determine that the conspicuously absent Charles Monetier had been the one to strike Mathias.

He rather resented that he had missed it.

"What happened here?" Isabelle demanded, righting an overturned table ornament as she spoke.

"Madam, I'm sorry to tell you this, but your cousin is rather unstable," Mathias said casually. "Bloke flew off and attacked me right in the middle of explaining the logistics of transporting you to England to your father here. I think he was enraged by the prospect of a false marriage."

Yves cleared his throat, raising an eyebrow at Mathias that made the younger man sprout a sheepish smile.

"I also may have taunted him about the survival of my family, once he recognized my surname," he added with a shrug. "Can't stamp out every titled family's line, no matter how many toddlers daddy beheaded."

"Good lord, Mathias!" Peter burst out, no longer wishing he had been present.

"Well, it's true," Mathias shot back, raising his eyebrows. "The crime of being born noble was a death sentence, no matter how innocent you were. I used to have uncles, aunts, and cousins, you know. Now I just have my parents and Gigi and the blasted birds."

"Dempierre," Isabelle muttered, passing around Peter to find a seat at her father's side on the cold hearth. "I am surprised you would come back here."

"Well, I do like going to the places I'm prohibited, truth be told," he replied jovially. "As evidenced by the lengthy apology I issued to your father about an hour ago."

"He ate my cherry tomatoes," Yves grumbled. "Right off the bush."

"Mathias, you are worse than a child," Peter groaned, sinking into an empty armchair. "Mr. Monetier, I apologize on my friend's behalf. I hope he did not ruin your harvest."

"Only my dinner," Yves replied, with what looked like a smile of amusement twitching at his lips. "Friend, is he? The two of you are odd companions."

"Yes," said Peter, as Mathias replied brightly, "Whatever do you mean?"

"Where is Charles?" Isabelle cut in, impatience in her voice. "Papa, where did he go? I fear he might do something rash if he wishes to prevent my leaving. You know how he can get."

"He won't," Yves assured her with a pat on her knee. "At least, that wasn't his aim when he stormed out of here. I imagine he is just clearing his head and cooling his temper before he attempts to interact any further with our ... erm ... guests. As far as future behavior is concerned, I fear you are correct. We will have to convince him not to interfere."

She grimaced, clearly less than optimistic about this prospect.

It gave Yves pause, his eyes finding the necklace around her throat and his expression softening as he searched her eyes for some sign of how things had changed. "Are you all right, my darling girl?"

"I am as well as I can be, Papa," she replied, resting her hand on top of his with a weary weight. "I think it will take time for me to truly come to anything resembling a full understanding of everything that has been revealed here today. If I go through a period of anger, I hope you will forgive me. At the moment, I feel rather numb and overwhelmed."

He heaved a sigh and nodded. "You are entitled to anger. The truth is that I did not put effort into searching for any relatives you might still have because by the time I got you home, I did not want to ever give you up. After three years in the dark, huddled in a dank, stone cell, you were the first beam of light to warm me, and that feeling only grew. I am sorry that I did not tell you the truth sooner."

"Were you never going to tell her?" Peter asked curiously, drawing expressions of obvious intrusion from both father and daughter. He shifted, an awkwardness coming over him as he attempted to explain the question. "I only mean that I see the kindness in it, if she truly had no one left, to carry the burden of such awful knowledge for the both of you."

"That is true," Isabelle said softly. "There was no perfect answer, Papa. We all just do the best we can."

"But you knew Mary and Walter Atlas, did you not?" Mathias said with a curious tilt of his head. "Certainly through unusual circumstances, but you did know them."

Yves nodded, his expression grim. "Mary and your mother, Therese, were the ones who negotiated my release from Dover Castle, courtesy of a great deal of bribery in the form of smuggled goods. I recovered my health for some time at La Falaise under the care of a doctor requisitioned by Lady Dempierre, until I was strong enough to travel. My interactions with Mary Atlas were limited, mostly related to the logistics of seeing me home and a few comforting stories of prisoners she had already successfully smuggled back to Calais."

"You were captured in battle?" Peter asked, as politely as he could, considering that he was speaking to the enemy.

"I was a quartermaster," Yves explained on a sigh. "Perhaps the easiest person to target in an empty camp, next to the cook. It was a stupid mistake, an ambush, and because of who my brother was, I was presumed to command quite a large ransom.

"It only goes to show that they did not know as much about my brother as they thought they did. He would never pay a ransom, and as we all learned to our sorrow, he would not even stand for being on equal footing at a parlay. Domination was the only thing Jonathan understood."

Isabelle was frowning, idly fingering the locket around her neck. "You have not said such things to Charles, I hope," she said to her father. "If our roles were reversed, I would be devastated."

"Of course I haven't," Yves assured her. "His mother likely has canonized her late husband with elaborately embellished tales of Jon's heroism, while I'm certain Charles has heard his fair share of stories that are not quite so gallant from the officers who knew his father."

The slap of the front door being slammed shut startled all of them, heads swinging around guiltily as Charles Monetier returned to the house. Peter felt a wave of relief, having pictured a great many things the man might have done to foil their plans to whisk off his prospective bride, many of which would have landed both Mathias and himself in a French jail cell.

He appeared in the doorway, his expression grim and his knuckles bruised, his neat brown hair in disarray from the wind. He looked only to Isabelle, as though the rest of them were not present at all, and stated rather than asked, "You have decided to go."

"I have," she replied softly, coming to her feet with the grace of a dancer, that long skirt of hers flowing like water around her legs. She crossed the room with brisk, light steps, her warm, hazel eyes illuminated by the low afternoon light spilling in from the open window.

Charles did not move to greet her, but he did not draw away

when she laid a comforting hand on his shoulder, a gesture which seemed to deflate him of all outrage he had remaining as his eyes fell to meet hers.

For a moment, they seemed to communicate in silence, as those who have known each other for a very long time sometimes do.

Peter was reminded again of Nell, and he wondered how he would feel if one day, someone had shown up and told her that she wasn't his sister after all. It was a thought so alien that he could not truly get it to find shape in his mind, much less imagine how he might react in such a situation.

"I will come back," she said. "This is my home, and you are my family. Regardless, if I have a brother still living, who has been searching for me, I feel I owe it both to myself and to him to meet. This may be my only opportunity to ever do so."

"Isabelle," he said, his words strained, "you must see the danger in embarking off to the unknown with two strange men. How do we even know they are telling the truth?"

"They are," Yves said, rising from where he sat and crossing his arms over his chest. "They are telling the truth. I can attest to that."

"No harm will come to Miss Monetier on the road," Peter said to Charles, drawing the other man's cutting gaze with a snapping immediacy. "Both Mathias and I are committed to protecting her. You know our names and where we live. You are a man of immense power. If harm came to your cousin through this venture, I have no doubt you would successfully enact a revenge that both Mathias and I would very much rather avoid."

"Pretty words," he said dismissively, waving his hand. "I must accompany you at least as far as Marseille."

"No you mustn't," Isabelle returned immediately. "Charles, you have to let me do this on my own. This is the one time every year when you do not have to bark orders and wrap yourself in starch and steel. Stay here. Enjoy beauty and peace. Please. I could not bear to take it away from you."

He looked as though he was about to retort, a firm and formidable argument brimming just behind his lips. Something about her expression withered those words before they could form, causing his shoulders to sag and his head to shake in exasperation.

It was hard not to feel a pang of jealousy at how casually she touched him, and how easily he calmed at her behest. It was easy to see why he would wish to take her to wife. In just a day, he had seen her embody many skills which would make life pleasant at her side, even if their marriage lacked a carnal passion in favor of a familial fondness.

He knew he couldn't begrudge Charles Monetier for proposing to her, but he did anyway.

Any man would be lucky to have her.

"I would like to go over the details of these forged marriage papers before you set off," Yves said, breaking through the silence before his nephew might recover any of his discontent. "Let us come to an agreement about the rules and perimeters of this venture, and we will all feel happier once it is in motion."

"Splendid idea, Papa," Isabelle agreed, her face brightening. "Let us discuss over luncheon, perhaps? I think all of this difficulty will look a little smoother with good food and a glass of wine."

"Agreed," Mathias put in, clapping his hands together in anticipation of the coming meal.

"Agreed," echoed Peter, more concerned with the temptations of Isabelle Monetier than any French gourmet.

Charles Monetier scowled, but in the end, he did mutter, "Oh, fine!"

And that was that.

CHAPTER 9

The hardest part of leaving was being told that she could not say goodbye to anyone outside of her household, unless she was willing to lie. And though she knew she ought not confide in anyone, she couldn't help but go to Babette, who had been her friend for as long as she could remember, in the hopes that the other girl would do as she always did, and convince Isabelle that all would end well, because it must.

"What will your father tell people?" Babette had asked, her eyes wide and voice hushed. "Charles is allowing this?"

It was a comfort in the following days, as Serre Chevalier grew smaller in their wake, that not once had Babette asked who Isabelle truly was. She had not questioned her identity in any way, and that small kindness had brought to the surface a torrent of tears and emotion that Isabelle had not trusted herself to feel prior to that moment.

The answers were simple ones. Papa would say that Isabelle

was staying with a lady of breeding in a nearby city to refine her talents and make introductions to polite Society. Charles, if he had his way, would most certainly *not* allow it, but mercifully was not the arbiter of Isabelle's life, as he may well have become should these strangers have arrived any later than they did.

She had lain in Babette's rooms, tears soaking into her friend's skirts while her hair was stroked and a loving murmur of encouragement guided her through the initial wave of feeling. When she had come through it, her eyes puffy and sore, it felt a little like the aftermath of a baptism, as though she now had permission to begin anew.

It had long been like this between them. Neither girl had a mother to soothe and encourage her, and so in a way, they had learned to play this part for one another when the time called for it, through childhood mishaps and adolescent heartbreaks and the burgeoning fears of what life may be as young adulthood settled onto both of them.

Once Isabelle had finished her episode of crying, Babette had left to fetch some toasted bread and jam to eat on the floor of her bedroom, like they had as children. As adults, this treat was paired with a crisp summer wine and less concern over being caught before the crumbs could be swept away.

"I envy you, of course," Babette had said later with a wistful sigh and a glance out her window, as though she might flit through it off on her own adventure. "I fear I will never in my life leave the valley."

Isabelle had her knees drawn up to her chest, her back to

the wall opposite her friend. From this spot, Babette was glowing under the shaft of sunlight streaming in from without. "There are worse places to live out one's life," she replied. "I have spent much of my life fearing the opposite, and that nothing will ever be quite as good as home."

It was true. She had told her father and her cousin and even the new and intriguing Peter Applegate that she was open to the idea of exploration, that of course one day she had intended to venture out into the world. She had told herself the same thing, many times, but the secret reality of her heart was that these thoughts of foreign destinations and unfamiliar surroundings often filled her chest with knots of worry and uncertainty.

She had always considered herself a part of the valley, and had no idea who she might be outside of it.

"You should stay tonight," Babette told her, spreading her favorite plum preserves in an exacting, thin layer over her toast as a means of pointedly not observing the embarrassing distress on Isabelle's face. "I will beg off of working tonight and we can go in the morning to get you packed."

"I cannot," Isabelle replied sadly. She shook herself, remembering how finite this moment was, and took a moment to memorize the vision of Babette and her toast, marigold skirts spread in a pool around her legs on the floor of her little room, her dark curls pinned in a haphazard mess to her head as the summer afternoon breeze gave the occasional gust of charitable wind through the tiny window that sat high above her bed. "We must leave at daybreak so that my Papa can accompany us to Aix en Provence, under the guise of depositing me at the household of a Society matron, and still have enough time to get home again in decent time. This way, all may observe the veracity of the circumstances of my departure."

"And then he will leave you alone to travel onward with those two men," Babette said with a glint in her eye. "How excited you must be. Such freedom to misbehave!"

"I have no plans of misbehaving, at least not in the way you are thinking," Isabelle said with a twist of her lips. "Nor do I think either man would risk the proposition, considering their encounters with my family on French soil nor their accounts of the one that awaits me abroad."

"Well, it's not often the woman's plan anyway," she said dismissively. "Besides, they are both handsome and must certainly both possess some manner of roguishness to have been sent on such an errand. The fair one absolutely knows his way around despoiling maidens and the like."

"Does he, now?" Isabelle said with a lift of one auburn eyebrow. "What did you get up to after I left?"

"I'll tell if you do," Babette replied with a flutter of her dark lashes.

And so, in the comfort of familiarity, framed by the influence of this new unknown, Isabelle spent her final afternoon in the valley, allowing her fears and trepidation to give way to excitement as she confessed to moonlit kisses with a captivating stranger on a night when all seemed possible.

∽

Isabelle was not typically an early riser, and on the odd occasion when she was roused near sunrise, it was often due to some obligation or other which prevented her from appreciating just how spectacular this time of day could be.

With their horses saddled and the donkey loaded up with essential items, the four of them had ridden out towards the mountain path just as the shimmer of pink across the mountain faces began to slide into a brighter orange. From here, there was no horizon on which to watch the sun crest from nothingness to the touch of land. Instead, it was the peaks of the mountains, who could see much farther than the tiny people on the ground, which reflected the colors of the dawn, as though the nature of their very stone shifted and shone in homage to the sky.

It was beautiful enough to silence them all as they scaled the winding medieval road that would take them to the old Roman paths out of the Alpine landscape and into Provence, which Yves insisted was nothing more than rolling hills, all in vibrant purple this time of year, as lavender came into bloom.

"When we get to Aix tomorrow, we will have a grand luncheon to send you on your way," Yves said to Isabelle with an encouraging smile from the saddle of his mount. "I have always found a good meal to be the best way to begin any venture."

"We'll have another grand meal in Marseille, for certain," Mathias added, "and you may ask all manner of questions to the Oliviers about your English family. Your mother and Mme. Olivier were dear friends."

"Oh," Isabelle replied, surprised to be confronted so early in this journey with answers to her questions. She lifted her hand to stroke the cool blue stone around her neck, attempting to picture this woman who had been her mother, to fashion her an accented English voice and perhaps a fine floral scent. All she had managed to conjure thus far was a vague impression of a woman, standing very far away, across a thrashing, stormy ocean that separated them from one another.

In her mind, her mother was just a figure on a rocky outcrop, so far away that all she could make out was the whipping of a dress in the wind. The dress was white. Her mind had decided on that much, at least.

Of her true father, no one had mentioned much of anything. Peter and Mathias explained that it was her mother who founded the Silver Leaf Society and that their connections to the Atlas family were through her alone. Yves had described him as tall and handsome, and of having eyes much like her own and a booming voice that was quick to laugh and soothing when he had held her bundled body as an infant, but he too had mostly interacted with Mary Atlas, whilst Walter worked in the background to assist his wife's clandestine ventures.

What a singular man he must have been, she thought, to allow himself to play a supporting role to a powerful wife. Most men would balk at such an idea. She glanced at the three men she rode with: the independent and opinionated man who had raised her; the irreverent and mischievous smuggler; and the starry-eyed scholar, who was driven by an insatiable hunger to see and learn, to understand.

Her gaze settled on Peter, taking in the easy way he rode, as though he had been introduced to the saddle at a very young age. He had not spoken much since they set out, his attention caught by the new vista found around every bend on the road. He was an unassuming man, she reckoned, with his hair blowing unstyled in the breeze and the careless wrinkling of his shirt. She might have thought him shy and perhaps even insecure if she hadn't met him as she had, as an impulsive stranger with no ties to his business with the Silver Leaf.

Perhaps he was both of these things, but he had not hesitated to kiss her. He had not held her with the weak and uncertain grip of a man who doubted himself. The man he was when he had run his fingers over that ancient altar in the dark forest was intense and crackled with confidence and energy and passion.

Where did that man go during the day? In the sunlight, Peter often chose to lapse into silence, allowing his brash and gregarious companion to ensure that all the light available shone on him alone, allowing Peter to observe and ruminate in near invisibility.

As though her thoughts had been spoken aloud, he turned, meeting her eyes as light glinted off the frames of his spectacles with a curious raise of his brows.

She blushed, immediately lowering her gaze to the mane of her horse, her heart suddenly rapping against her ribs like an insistent caller at the door. Still, she could not resist looking up once more, just to see if he had noticed her staring.

He most assuredly had, for he was still watching her, and gave her a small, secretive smile that she could not help returning, warmth flooding from the tops of her ears to the tips of her fingers. It was such a small, strange thing to spark such a deep thrill, but for the remainder of the ride towards

Aix en Provence, she found herself trying to catch his eye, and every time she succeeded, she got another burst of that giddy, childish pleasure, watching his lips curve into a little smile as her own bloomed across her face, both of them looking away before they could be observed.

CHAPTER 10

Aix en Provence was a city of fountains, with a floral scent that wafted through the air, courtesy of its many lavender fields, and the feel of a much smaller town, where people lingered to greet one another rather than bustling on with the necessities of their days.

Isabelle and Yves had finished their luncheon and wandered afield from the cafe where the group had eaten. From Peter's vantage point at the outdoor table, opposite Mathias, he could see them seated on the grass a stone's throw away while she seemed to be instructing her father on how to braid two daisies together. The sun, glinting bronze-red off the top of her dark hair, was mesmerizing.

"Do I need to be concerned?" Mathias asked, his tone easy and casual, though his gaze seemed to carry a bit more weight as it startled Peter out of his reverie.

"I think you'd rather benefit from the occasional concern, yes," Peter replied, stabbing at one of the lingering berries on his empty dessert plate while avoiding the other man's eye.

It was no use, however, as he could still feel the other's appraising stare upon him, making his skin prickle and itch with sudden embarrassment.

"Your brother-in-law is an amicable man," Mathias commented, leaning back in his chair and crossing his arms over his chest. "Still, somehow, I imagine it might be terrifying to cross him."

Peter grimaced, silently agreeing with this. Nathaniel Atlas was an incredibly contained person, but there was a simmering intensity under his easy charm that suggested many things that simply were not for the public eye. Atlas had, after all, run off with Nell in the dead of night, in pursuit of a dangerous thief, and his reasons for that behavior were still not entirely clear to Peter, for he was certain that the man's obvious affection for Nell had developed somewhat after the fact.

Perhaps, considering the circumstances, he would not be opposed to Peter's interest in Isabelle, despite his meager financial status and ongoing tenure as an academic. Peter knew before even completing the thought in his mind that he would be opposed, for certain. The sister of a Member of Parliament, rescued after twenty years of estrangement, does not wed a pauper with ink stains on his fingers and cobwebs in his coffers.

He gave an unhappy sigh and stole another glance at her, laughter echoing across the meadow as she situated a crown of flowers on her father's head, using her fingers to pull strands of hair through so that it settled into place above his ears.

Looking at the two of them, one could easily believe that he had sired her. Their complexions were both rosy and freckled in the sunlight, and while his hair was a pale yellow, shot through with gray and hers was that lush cherry brown, in profile, they had similar noses, similar chins.

He couldn't help but feel a pang of sympathy for the shade of Walter Atlas, though perhaps, if his spirit lingered, it was relieved that Isabelle had grown to womanhood in a loving home, blossoming into such an enchanting young woman.

"Christ," Mathias muttered. "You've seen pretty women before, Applegate. Come to your senses."

"Of course I've seen pretty women before," Peter snapped, cutting his eyes to Mathias with a glare. "I don't know what you're implying, but I ..."

Mathias waved his hand, batting off what were certain to be dishonest proclamations from the other man. "God knows in any other situation I would encourage this," he said, lowering his voice. "This is perhaps the one situation in the world where I cannot. The girl obviously returns your doting gazes, and you're wound up tighter than a war drum, but *you know who she is!*"

"I'm not going to ... to attempt to ... to compromise ... that is to say to attempt to ... *despoil* her," Peter managed, awkwardness and distaste clogging each word in his throat before he could get it out. "I have nothing but respect and admiration for Miss Monetier."

"Miss Atlas, you mean," Mathias corrected, the glint in his eye the only thing that did not appear completely at ease. "You will be posing as her husband. She obviously has taken a shine to you. There will likely be temptations on the remainder of this journey that you have not foreseen, especially once her chaperone is gone. French girls are not raised like English misses, as I'm sure you have noticed. You must keep your head firmly on your shoulders."

"My head isn't going anywhere," Peter said with a sniff. "I don't know where you got the idea that I'm some sort of cad."

Dempierre's face blossomed into that slow, feline smile, his cheeks dimpling at Peter's discomfort. "You never did tell me how you came to find her the night *before* we were set to go looking."

"No," Peter agreed with a frown. "I did not."

This only made the other man chuckle, because if there was one thing Mathias Dempierre could do, it was to find amusement in anything. He had even managed to laugh at his own humiliation early that morning, when the mighty Goliath had been trotted out, after much agonizing over having to travel with a large, frightening, protective cur.

While Mathias still seemed somewhat wary of the little ball of fur and teeth, he had immediately realized the joke that had been played upon him. Rather than react with anything resembling a humbled disposition, he had continued to play the frightened hunter, set upon by a tiger, much to the amusement of all three Monetiers.

Almost on cue, Hortensia let out a bray from where she was tethered at the rear of the cafe. She daintily lifted one of her legs, holding it pointed and bent as Goliath zoomed around beneath her, evidently delighted by all the tall grass and this new, docile creature to whom he had been so recently introduced.

Isabelle seemed unbothered by the risk of the little beast getting kicked or stepped on, and so all Peter could do was watch with latent anxiety as the two creatures got acquainted.

"I went looking for you that night," Mathias was saying, though his eyes had followed Peter's to the antics of dog and donkey. "I have it on good authority that you are much more fun when you've had a few drinks, and I wanted to see for myself."

Peter scoffed. "Did my sister tell you that?" he asked, wondering when in the blazes of hell he had ever gotten sauced in front of Nell.

"Secondhand," he confirmed. "She heard it from an old school chum of yours, apparently, and was rather curious as to what version of you people had met that she had not."

Peter heaved an annoyed sigh. "Alex Somers," he said with a shake of his head. "Without a doubt. He made it his mission in my first year at Oxford to coax me out of the library and into the pub. I was browbeaten into revelry."

"Wonderful! Sounds like my type of chap."

"Yes, I rather think the two of you would get along famously," Peter allowed, unable to mask a little frown. He liked the carefree and irreverent Alex Somers a great deal, despite their differences in disposition. And it was true that he had enjoyed Oxford significantly more once he had allowed Somers to drag him out and ply him with lager.

So why did Mathias irk him so? Thinking about it, he realized that Nell rather liked Dempierre and had no real fondness for Somers. How strange. Usually, the two were of a mind on the character of others. Perhaps Nell had been browbeaten into liking Mathias outside of Peter's purview, and that was the way of such men.

So lost was he in this train of thought that he startled when Yves Monetier spoke, suddenly right next to him and sliding into his chair with his crown of daisies ruffling in the wind. "I have gone over both sets of marriage documents," he was telling them, "and have added my signature. I put them in the oilskin on your ass's back. I rather hope that one day she has a bit more fanfare if she weds properly."

Isabelle had gone to beg for scraps for Goliath within the cafe, the dog waiting eagerly at the bottom of the patio steps, his little tail thumping rapidly against the grassy ground. It was, Peter realized, the last time for quite a while that father and daughter would be together.

"Are you headed back into the valley tonight?" he asked.

"Yes. I have a spot of business in Mont Genevre that I can attend to en route, which will save me a trip later in the summer," Yves replied. "Though now that we are here, I wish I were staying on. I never thought anything would make me wish to return to England again."

"I would say I know the feeling well," Mathias replied, "but of course, I do not. Exile is nothing like imprisonment. If you did return, it would be a much more pleasant experience, I assure you."

"I do not wish to delay you, particularly when forging documentation is required. Perhaps, if Isabelle decides to stay on for a while, you might come retrieve me and smuggle me out next spring, hm? I should like to meet this Nathaniel and thank him for the sacrifice his parents made."

Peter and Mathias exchanged a look. It was impossible to imagine how Atlas might respond to such a thing, having spent the bulk of his life in search of revenge for this deeply misunderstood loss.

"Yes, perhaps I ought to phrase it differently," Yves said with a nod. "They certainly would not have made the venture if they had even mildly suspected its outcome."

"With due respect," Peter said carefully, "one must assume a certain degree of risk when embarking on criminal endeavors, no matter how well-intentioned."

"Said the forger to the fugitive, as a smuggler looked on," Mathias added cheerfully.

Yves gave a surprised bark of laughter, his shoulders seeming to relax at the unexpected levity.

"What are we laughing about?" Isabelle asked, descending from the cafe with a plate of scraps and a large lamb bone on a plate. She smiled brightly, first at her father and then at Peter, who flushed and hurriedly lowered his eyes to the table, as though this innocent glance had just confirmed everything Mathias had said earlier. "I do love a good jest."

She looked radiant, of course, in a sturdy riding kit of sky blue and white, her hair braided over her shoulder with a few strands loose and blowing around her cheeks. He'd like nothing more than to fully appreciate how she looked, without observation and judgement from without.

She passed into his periphery, calling to Goliath with her platter of morsels for him, and the little fellow trotted over with a gaiety in his step that sent his fluffy little backside up and down amidst the grass like a hopping rabbit until he reached his mistress.

"Mr. Dempierre here was just pointing out that we are a band of outlaws," Yves said to his daughter, watching her with the kind of abject appreciation that Peter was forcing himself to avoid. "Though of course, we do not aim to harm anyone."

"Like Robin Hood," Peter put in, thinking fondly of the tales.

"Well, he did rob some people," Mathias said with a furrowed brow. "I come by all of my illegal goods honestly, I'll have you know."

"Who is this Robin Hood?" Isabelle asked, depositing the empty plate on their table and settling back into her seat.

"A medieval highwayman of sorts," Peter answered, quashing the academic desire to deconstruct the historical accuracy of the tales before telling them, because he could not bear to dampen the sparkle in her eye. "He was said to steal from the elite and distributed their wealth amongst the poor and starving. There are many stories."

"Why don't you tell us one, young man?" Yves suggested, patting his daughter's hand as though to remind himself that she was still with him, in this moment, for just a little longer. "I would like to hear a story."

"Oh, yes, do," Mathias encouraged, seemingly genuinely pleased at the prospect. "That bit with the archery contest is my favorite. I do love a good ruse."

"All right," Peter said, finding himself grinning despite the strangeness looming about them on the cusp of this endeavor. He summoned the images of his childhood to mind, when he and his siblings would play a band of merry men in the small wooded area near Winchester, himself waving a tree branch triumphantly as the mythic hero. For a moment, he could almost smell the moss in the stream and hear Nell's laughter on the wind.

"Our story takes place during the Crusades," he began, "while a great king was abroad on his holy mission, and the kingdom of Britain was left with an empty throne..."

CHAPTER 11

*I*sabelle had always been quick to cry. Happiness, sentimentality, hope, and surprise were all as effective at drawing the sparkle of tears from her pretty hazel eyes as sadness and pain. So she knew her father bore no expectations that she might retain a stoic visage upon the moment of their goodbye, giving her the freedom to allow her emotions to flow honestly as she wept into his shoulder on a tight, tight embrace.

There were few words upon parting, for Yves and Isabelle had not left anything unsaid between them in the years they had spent as family. There were no confessions of things kept hidden or expressions of affection that had been retained. From what she had heard of the English and their penchant for keeping their feelings constrained, she felt a moment of explosive gratitude that she had been raised here, in a place where she was allowed to know herself, even if it had been the result of so much early tragedy.

Watching her father ride away with his chain of horses, crown of daisies still in his fair hair, had given her a few residual hiccups of emotion as she scrubbed the tears from her cheeks with the heel of her hand. She couldn't help but smile at the vision he made, and told herself she would never forget this moment as she embarked on the great unknown.

Peter and Mathias had joined her on the hill after a time, as though they had discussed between them to first give her privacy and then offer their support. Neither man spoke, but both stood by, simply offering their presence as a pillar of strength until Isabelle felt ready to turn around and declare that it was time to go.

∽

It would only take a day or two to reach Marseille from Aix. Mathias had suggested a period of rest, as the remainder of the journey was so short, but Isabelle was eager to reach their destination, and so they caught a coach headed southward into the night and stopped at an inn well into the evening hours.

It had been a quiet ride, crammed into the coach's interior as they were with a clutch of tightly packed strangers.

Despite having her father's blessing mere hours beforehand, Isabelle could not shake the feeling that she was doing something very, very wrong. It felt as though she might be caught out at any moment, by any of these sour-faced strangers on all sides. Surely they would see her expression and raise a pointed finger, labeling her a runaway or worse and dragging her back home in disgrace. Of course, the reality of the experience was that the others in the carriage were focused only on themselves and the burden of surviving the rumbling and heat of the journey.

More than once, she wished she had ridden Hortensia, who was tethered to the coach with their belongings and Goliath, trotting along happily in the wake of the carriage. At least out there, she'd have access to a nice breeze and pretty scenery and enough elbow room to get lost in her thoughts. Within the coach, every time she began to nod off, they hit another bump in the road or a fellow passenger had to stretch and jostle everyone, and so on.

The arrival at a coaching inn might as well have been a divine gift, sent directly from heaven in answer to her prayers for reprieve.

"I feel as though I will never be completely clean again," Isabelle said with a grimace, reaching across the donkey's saddle as she retrieved a bag of her things to bring inside for the night. "I do not think I've ever realized how disgusting we are as a species."

"Best not to dwell upon it," Mathias replied jovially. "Such awareness ruins everything."

"I hate to say it, but he has a point," Peter said, his expression thoughtful as he took her bag from her to sling over his shoulder alongside his own. "What he just said is a sentiment often shared by those who study medicine at Oxford. It is one of the reasons the field did not interest me."

"Best to leave some intrigue to the human form, hm?" Isabelle teased, only to realize from the way he hesitated, drawing in his breath, that her words could be construed as fairly suggestive. She hurried ahead, more pleased with the idea that he thought her flirtation deliberate than not.

The inn was a brick and mortar structure situated on a grassy decline. The building had all of its windows thrown open to allow for circulation of the warm summer air throughout its sparsely decorated central room. With the sky as cloudy as it was, there was not much in the way of moonlight to illuminate the space, which instead relied on the dull glimmer of a scattering of candles throughout a long dining hall and the reception foyer, leaving each cluster of tables in the dining area afloat in its own aura of light.

Peter approached the matron and requested two rooms, taking it upon himself to negotiate the price. The exchange made Mathias's smile wither away, and he cut an accusatory glance to Isabelle, whose heart had skipped a beat at his words, and perhaps she had given herself away with a grin or a small bounce on her toes. Those words marked the first moment that they would pretend to be wed, and for that brief stolen pocket of time, others would think she was his and he was hers.

Of course, Peter would not share a room with Isabelle tonight. He would share with Mathias, and all things would be done properly. Still, it was a bit of a thrill to imagine otherwise, especially when he looked so self-assured, haggling over price with his dark hair falling over his brow, unmoving on a reasonable deal, despite his foreigner's accent.

Once he had struck a deal and departed up the stairs to deposit their bags, Isabelle took Mathias's arm and allowed herself to be led into the dining hall, where she observed her companion's slight frown with open curiosity. He was the last person she would have expected to be so dour about the subterfuge, especially given how harmless it was.

"Have I done something to offend you, Mr. Dempierre?" she asked, pleased to see her clarity and directness gave him a start.

He turned his wide, amber eyes onto her with something like alarm and shook his head vehemently. "Of course not," he said a little too loudly. "No! Why would you ask such a question?"

She gave him a wan smile, separating from him to take her seat, allowing her silence to speak for her.

He heaved a sigh, a begrudging half smile twisting its way onto his lips, awakening one of his dimples as he gave her a sheepish glance. "It isn't you I'm worried about," he insisted. "I promised your father, your cousin, and your brother that I'd keep you safe and secure throughout this journey, and Mr. Applegate's obvious infatuation with you is not helping matters. Do you think I enjoy being cast into the role of chaperone? Why, it's against my very nature!"

"You assume Mr. Applegate is the party who would be responsible for a scandal," she said, raising her eyebrows. "My father ought to have warned you about how difficult it has always been to discipline me into docility."

Mathias chuckled at that, his hands relaxing on the table. "Miss Monetier, I have met wild, rebellious women, and I find it difficult to believe you are amongst their ranks. None of those girls would make daisy crowns for their fathers."

"There is a wide berth between docility and rebellion," Isabelle said, cocking her head to the side. "Freedom does not necessarily denote poor behavior. After all, you yourself seem to have a wild streak. How will you manage having a daughter who inherits your nature?"

"Perish the thought!" Mathias said with open horror.

"What thought?" asked Peter Applegate as he approached, happily relieved of their luggage. He slid into the chair next to Mathias just in time for a barmaid to bring out glasses of watered-down red wine and three bowls of today's stew, which had gone a bit tepid at this hour.

Mathias reached for his spoon with an open look of distaste. "Nothing of consequence," he said. "Miss Monetier is attempting to frighten me away from ever having a family."

"I am doing no such thing!" Isabelle scoffed. "Mr. Dempierre is afraid that he might have a child who behaves the same way he does, which ought to be a moment of introspection, don't you think?"

"Not a child," he corrected, "a daughter. Little girls do not behave like little boys. They are sweet and mild."

Identical sputters of amusement came from both Peter and Isabelle, which only made Mathias flush further.

"Was your sister Gigi sweet and mild when she was small?" Peter asked curiously, seemingly not at all put off by the lackluster fare, which he had dug into with gusto. "Nell certainly wasn't, nor were any of my other sisters."

Mathias considered this, his frown deepening, which was all the answer they needed for the table to ignite with laughter. Never one to resist joviality, Mathias Dempierre gave in to the amusement, giving a self-deprecating laugh as he reached for his wine. "You are right," he allowed, inclining his head in defeat to Isabelle. "Little girls are terrifying."

Peter removed his spectacles, rubbing at the bridge of his nose where they'd left an indent throughout the day. He blinked several times, his gray-blue eyes adjusting to the sparse light, and left them there, folded next to his bowl. Without his spectacles, Isabelle noticed his long fringe of dark eyelashes and the subtle circles under his eyes from their days of demanding travel. The shadows cut harshly over their faces, sitting as they were between a pocket of light and dark, but she found the effect quite striking on the lines of his face.

He had such a lovely, deep voice, and even in his exhaustion there was something about him that made her want to find an excuse to touch him, perhaps to smooth his hair into place or straighten his wrinkled collar. She leaned on her hand, forcing her attention to her food so that she would not be caught in her train of thought.

"I'm surprised to hear you talk of such things at all," he said to Mathias. "I believe you told Mme. Olivier just some days ago that you were already wed to your ship."

"Ah, she is a fine companion," Mathias answered wistfully, "but alas, it seems that the traditional route of marriage and children eventually catches up to all men. It is only women who have the option to reject it entirely, having only to avoid or decline any offers until a certain age, and then live out her life in freedom, picking up some charming trade or another. Like your spinster aunt."

"My aunt publishes prints of prominent people behaving in embarrassing ways," Peter replied with obvious amusement. "That's hardly quaint."

"Prints?" Isabelle asked, intrigued. "Like paintings?"

"Illustrations, the types you'd find in a newspaper," Peter explained with a shake of his head. "Some of them are quite shocking and ribald, but she has an enthusiastic clientele in London and it has effectively made most of the *ton* fear her wrath. My father is one of her artists. That is how he met my mother, who was, at the time, working in Aunt Zelda's shop on Bond Street."

"That is a fascinating vocation! Has she drawn anyone you know?"

"Oh, yes," Peter said with a fatigued chuckle. "Your brother Nathaniel has been depicted at least twice. She has a particular vendetta against a professor of mine, which has caused me significant strain. A lovely viscountess, whose home I visited last autumn, was also once a popular subject, as she had the misfortune of having two fiancés die before they could wed, giving her a rather morbid reputation as a deadly debutante. When she finally did marry a man who survived the engagement, it was by eloping with her cousin's intended, which of course rattled up the gossip sheets yet again."

"Oh. Well, that is unfortunate," Isabelle said with a frown. "I suppose all people are drawn to gossip. What a horrible thing to have done to her cousin!"

Peter grinned, a realization spreading across his handsome face. "Come to think of it," he said, "her cousin was also supposed to marry your brother, but he ran off with Nell instead. In both cases, the prospective bride seemed relieved, and she is married now, quite happily, to a man who dotes upon her."

"Good God," Isabelle replied, too gobsmacked by these dramatics to formulate a more coherent answer. "That poor woman. Your sister must be nothing like you!"

"Do not judge Nell too harshly for her elopement," Peter said earnestly. "It was a chaotic decision that was honestly and truly for the best, in the end. They are very happy together."

"Nell is a lovely, kind woman," Mathias added, though it was clear from his scandalized expression that he hadn't known this story either. "She must have had compelling reasons for doing such a thing. You would never think it of her."

"Hm," Isabelle pondered, turning her eyes mischievously back to Mathias. "Her father likely thinks her sweet and mild, perchance?"

"Oh, for God's sake," Mathias moaned, squeezing his eyes shut. "I know nothing of the world at all!"

∼

Isabelle slept fitfully, secure in the decision they had made as a group to ride horses rather than take a carriage the rest of the way to Marseille. Compared to the first leg of their journey, this one would be much shorter, likely less than a full day, with hot meals and soft beds waiting for them at the Olivier house.

She had worried over Goliath, being left in the stables for the night, but when she had gone to give him scraps from dinner, she had found the little dog curled into the belly of the sleeping donkey that he had spent several days pestering. Their differences had evidently been overcome, with each one snoring contentedly into the other's fur.

"We can sell the horses when we get to Marseille," Mathias

had reasoned, after being thoroughly bested by the man who made the sale. "Perhaps the Oliviers will even want them, knowing they travel well alongside Hortensia."

Hortensia gave a flat bray at that, as though not to encourage these wild ideas, while Goliath panted happily from his perch in the saddlebag, paws hanging over the flap and long, pink tongue lolling from the side of his toothy grin.

After some needling from the joined persuasive forces of Isabelle and Mathias, Peter indulged them in another tale of Robin Hood, this time with Little John as the center of the action, rescuing the hero from the imprisonment of a wicked monk. After this story, the two men bickered back and forth over which character each resembled more, with Mathias insisting that Peter was the most like Little John, while Peter acerbically suggested that Mathias himself was most like the evil sheriff, who plagued the merry men in every tale.

Mathias countered that if he must be a villain, he was far more like Guy of Gisborne than the Sheriff of Nottingham, particularly when it came to tempting the romantic preference of the beautiful Maid Marian. This raised the necessity for another story, both to explain this character to Isabelle, and to embellish his negative traits at length in an effort to needle Mathias.

By the end of the second tale, Isabelle suggested that of the three of them, she was the most like Robin Hood. Of course, while they protested on the basis of her sex, she pointed out that she was more likely to navigate life in a secluded forest than either of the two men, who had lived their lives in cities. She was then included heartily into the argument, which veered towards skills with weaponry, charm, and style and, in the end, had no resolution whatsoever, dissolving into laughter instead of grumbles.

They stopped twice to rest, choosing grassy meadows rather than coaching inns, where the soft ground and wrapped food from the saddle bags served just as well as any offering of the road, with spectacular views of the countryside besides. When they came close enough to see the first signs of the outskirts of Marseille, Isabelle felt a twist of anxious anticipation begin to build in her chest.

She found herself toying with the locket around her neck, her thumbnail fussing with the little piece of protruding metal that escaped from the seam. When she realized it had begun to loosen, she forced herself to stop, fearful of damaging this priceless thing she had only just come into possession of.

Something in her feared being able to ask questions about her mother, of being confronted with the first true encounter of this other life she was being given. She glanced at Peter Applegate, wishing in the moment that they could be truly alone to talk. If only there were some errand to send Mathias on so that they might sit together for a while and she could tell him about these fears, she was certain it might ease her mind.

She liked Mathias well enough, but she rather wagered he would be very uncomfortable with such an emotional confession, and besides, she did not have the same rapport with him that she'd developed with the stranger in the forest. One can be honest in the deep wood in a way rarely acceptable in the open.

He turned his head, as though he could feel her eyes upon him, and met her gaze with a little smile, which she attempted to return. From the way he raised his eyebrows, his expression sobering, it seemed to her that he knew immediately that something was amiss. She found her hand going back to the locket, her thumb settling on the loosened bit of metal before she had consciously thought to do it.

How had she formed such a habit so quickly? She stopped her fumbling, but kept her hand circled around the stone, finding its weight comforting somehow.

"Dempierre," Peter called ahead to Mathias. "Might we stop a moment? I am lightheaded from the heat."

"We are very close," Mathias told him, but was already coming to a halt, wheeling his horse around to cut off Hortensia's steady plod. "Are you well?"

"I am fine, just a bit too much sun," Peter lied, sliding down from his saddle and stepping over to assist Isabelle from her own. His firm, dry hand closing over her own was immediately an effective distraction from her worries, causing a flutter in her chest that had nothing at all to do with their nearness to port.

She slid off her horse, landing dangerously close to him, their noses almost brushing, before he stepped away with a polite clearing of his throat, and a telltale smile floating near the corners of his lips.

"Sit over here," she instructed, putting on her sternest caretaker voice as she led him to a large tree with a good amount of shade and instructed him to sit. "Mathias, are any of the canteens full?"

"Yes, but the water is warm by now," he answered with a furrowed brow. "We passed a stream some ways back. Give me a moment and I shall retrieve fresh water."

"Thank you," the other two said in unison, perhaps sharing a mirrored feeling of guilt over the deception as Mathias stomped off into the clearing with more than a little urgency.

Peter in particular looked a little shocked, watching the other man hurry to his aid. But he shook off whatever thoughts he was having and turned his attention to Isabelle.

"What ails you?" he whispered, those deep gray eyes filled with concern.

"I think I am frightened." She winced as she said it, wishing there were a better word for what she was feeling. She knelt next to him on the grass, twisting her hands in her lap with embarrassment. Perhaps stopping to talk about this was a mistake. Even edging near the topic at the core of her worry was making her heart race and her head spin.

When he reached out and took those hands, enclosing them in his own, she remembered to breathe, focusing on deep, steady breaths that would bring the toppled world back into steady shape around her.

"Frightened of what?" he asked softly. "The journey?"

"No. I mean, yes, but not the travel itself," she said, squeezing her eyes shut in an attempt to pluck the right words from the muddle of emotion. She took another careful breath and then spoke again. "For the next hour or so, this is all still a construct of my own fantasy. My dead parents, my powerful English brother, and my uncertain but possibly adventurous future. Once I meet Mme. Olivier, once I can ask questions to someone who has answers for them, it all becomes much more real. Peter, I do not know if I can bear for it to be real. I do not know if I want my questions answered, deep down, in the truest part of my soul."

He nodded in understanding, squeezing her hands in a way that was a reassuring reminder that she was still planted on solid earth. "You do not have to ask Mme. Olivier any questions at all," he told her, a statement which hit her as a surprising truth. "It is perfectly understandable if you wish to meet your brother and have his tales be the first you hear."

She drew her lip between her teeth, considering this, picturing the unknown woman on the other side of the city in the distance as a figure larger than life, brimming with secrets that could further shatter all Isabelle knew and held dear. It was objectively overdramatic, but she could not shake it.

"What if I disappoint them?" she whispered, her throat thick with fear. "What if I am so much less than Mary Atlas was and wished me to be? I am not refined, nor respectably educated. I don't even have a proper dress to wear to dinner."

"Isabelle," he said, his voice deep and soothing, sharp with sincerity, as he stroked the top of her hand. "Your upbringing and talents are irrelevant to how you will be received by those who have mourned your absence. You could be the dullest miss imaginable and all would still be ecstatic that you simply survived and grew and found your way back to them. The fact that you are so much more than a bland, predictable young woman is marvelous. All that you are is an additional gift, which will only further delight those who thought you lost forever. You have nothing at all to fear."

She sniffed, blinking away panicked tears that had begun to gather near her lashes. His words were comforting, but the fear in her chest only pounded more insistently when confronted with reasonable challenges to its manufactured anxieties. "Just because you like me, it doesn't mean others will," she argued. "The only wealthy person I even know is Charles, and he finds so much about me lacking."

"He wished to marry you," Peter reminded her. "He wished for you to be the bride he introduced to all of Paris. And he is only one man, you know. People see value in many different things. I have spent time in the company of both your brother in England and Mme. Olivier here in France, and I am confident that both will adore the woman you have become. You must see how fond both Mathias and I have grown of you in just the short time we've known one another, and we are as different as men can be."

She did not think they were so different at all, but she knew now was not the time to say such a thing, especially to a man who would contest it with fervor and likely at length.

Instead, she gave a strained laugh, dashing the wetness away from her lashes with the tip of her finger and taking a deep and bracing breath. "Thank you, Peter. I am ... I am very fond of you too," she said, hesitating only because she did not wish to imply that the way she felt for her two companions was equal.

Fondness, yes, but it was not the same sort at all.

She hadn't spent the last week lobbing admiring glances

back and forth with Mathias, after all. She hadn't kissed Mathias in a dark, wooded glade in the dead of night, either. She didn't fluster when Mathias touched her hand or shiver when he spoke, or find herself lost in the stories he told. She gazed at Peter, remembering the way he'd held her that night, the way his fingers had dug so firmly into the flesh of her hips, the way his warm, strong body had felt encircling her own, and she found herself quite breathless.

The way he held her gaze was almost as though he could see those memories playing behind her eyes, as though he knew exactly what she was thinking and feeling. A knowing twist of his lips sent her heart pounding as his grip on her hands suddenly felt significantly warmer and more dangerous.

She found herself leaning into the comfort of his nearness, fingers and toes tingling as reason seemed to fade into instinct.

It was Mathias stomping back through the brush with a full canteen in hand that broke the spell, sending Isabelle hastily to her feet. She stepped away from Peter before their interaction might be observed by their disapproving guardian, and this time, when she looked at the horizon, she knew that the rushing of blood in her veins had nothing to do with fear.

CHAPTER 12

The sun had begun to set by the time they reached the city gates of Marseille. From there, it was a matter of navigating the evening market crowds, milling about on the thoroughfare between the center of the city and the residential outskirts, which slowed down the party significantly.

Peter had taken hold of Hortensia's reins, worried she would be spooked by the chaos, but their little donkey seemed far less shaken by the throng of people than the horses, and had shown them the best direction to open air at least twice. He felt a strange pride in her competency, having traveled for so long at her side, and murmured gentle praise to her when he was reasonably certain that Mathias and Isabelle could not hear him.

Isabelle had taken her dog into her lap for the final leg of their journey by land, and the donkey seemed to have grown rather fond of the little creature, frequently craning her neck and adjusting her step to keep him in her sights.

Peter knew how she felt. It was difficult not to look the same way at every available opportunity.

Had he been imagining the looks she'd given him? The poor girl was in a state of upheaval, her life shattered into a series of question marks, and so he knew he should not even think it, but it was impossible not to wonder. Earlier, under that tree on the outskirts of the city, he had thought for a moment that she was going to kiss him. He had *wanted* her to kiss him. After all, with all the contextual barricades about them now, he certainly didn't know if it would ever be proper for him to do so again.

She had confided in him, though, and there was meaning in that. She told him things she did not wish to tell Mathias, no matter how often he made her laugh or held her attention.

Yes, jealousy was an ugly emotion. He knew that. So was impatience, and he had never been particularly good at quashing that one either.

Admittedly, his prior episodes into the sin of envy were more frequently to do with academic rivals than romantic ones.

He glanced at Mathias with a little chuckle. Guy of Gisborne indeed!

Once they had passed the old port, which was dotted with restaurants lighting their candles for the evening, the roads cleared considerably. Was it a lucky happenstance that the Oliviers lived so close to the port? Peter guessed it was not. From the road, he could not make out the *Harpy's* sails from the muddle of boats clustered together for at least a league out.

Here on the street, the trio was able to draw closer together, with Isabelle indicating a short stop to watch the last of the sunlight dip below the horizon.

"Do you see that island there, some ways off?" Mathias asked her, leaning close and pointing until she nodded. "Chateau d'If," he explained, "a fortress and a prison, and recently, a formidable wartime tomb. Rather inconsiderate of them, wouldn't you say? Building something so impossible to escape."

"Little John could devise a means of escape," she decided, squaring her shoulders. "Will Scarlet would make quick work of it."

"Not Robin Hood?" Mathias asked, surprised.

"Robin Hood always seems to need rescue from Little John," Isabelle said with a shrug. "I think perhaps he is not truly the hero after all, only the self-proclaimed master."

"I beg your pardon!" Mathias gasped, wheeling around to follow her at a passive-aggressive canter.

This proclamation made Peter smile, and he did not mind falling behind again as they wove their way through the cobblestone streets in search of the Olivier townhouse under the slow fade of summer's dusk.

Mathias held his hand up, his horse slowing to a stop, and turned over his shoulder to beckon Peter closer. "Something is wrong," he said grimly, motioning ahead towards the familiar row of townhouses that marked their destination.

Peter furrowed his brow, noting the gap in the lit windows of the boulevard, where one townhouse was conspicuously dark, a thing only achieved by a place being entirely empty.

"We should approach from the rear, I think," Peter said grimly, glancing at Isabelle to ensure she was not overly disturbed.

She was upright and alert, her eyes focused ahead on the darkened house with a frown. "I agree," she said, "and I think we ought to approach on foot."

It took some maneuvering, finding a secure place to leave the animals, near enough to approach the house. It was indeed the Olivier domicile that had gone dark, its shutters closed tight. Mathias was undeterred, making short work of the locked door at the rear of the house and leading them in through the abandoned and pristine kitchens, where copper pots hung silently on the wall, into long and empty hallways, and into a sitting room set for afternoon tea.

"What in the blazes...?" Mathias muttered, snatching a lamp from a hallway table and taking a moment to light it.

Peter blinked away the shock to his eyes as the flame climbed high and spread an illuminating glow around the room. It did not look as though it were absented intentionally. None of the furniture was covered, and teacups stained with the dregs of evaporated afternoon repast were discarded on the table.

"The strongbox," Peter said, unease clogging his throat. "Our papers are in the strongbox."

Mathias cursed sharply, turning on his heel and making haste out of this room and into the next, his companions following close on his heels until he stopped dead in the doorway of the study, heaving a deep, agonized groan that answered Peter's questions before he had a need to ask them.

He stepped around him, taking the lantern from Mathias's limp fingers and approaching the strongbox, which was hanging open, its contents available for anyone who happened past. Despite being able to clearly see there were not enough documents stacked inside for their papers to still remain, he found himself experiencing that pang of dashed hope once he was close enough to know for certain.

All that was left was a handwritten letter and a small bag of coin.

"It's written to you," Peter said, glancing over the cramped and looping words in Pauline Olivier's handwriting to Isabelle and Mathias, hovering in the doorway.

"Just tell me what it says," Mathias replied, his face slack with disbelief. "I do not trust myself to read at the moment."

Peter glanced over the letter, a meandering, detailed account of the events that had transpired after they had set off for Serre Chevalier in search of Isabelle. It was perhaps a story Mathias would have more appreciation for at a later date, but in this moment, Peter was certain that only the relative gist was of importance.

"They went to the *Harpy* to collect cargo," Peter relayed, narrowing his eyes in suspicion. "You did not tell me you had additional cargo."

"Why would I have?" Mathias returned, exasperated. "It was irrelevant to our mission."

"Well, it went poorly," Peter said tightly. "The *Harpy* is under observation by authorities, and the Oliviers stole our counterfeited travel papers to beat a hasty exit for themselves. Pauline is apologetic, to a point, but insists we must understand the situation they found themselves in and the rare opportunity of having such documents in their possession."

"They were allowed to return home after being caught with contraband?" Isabelle asked incredulously.

"In exchange for assisting in capturing me," Mathias said, his voice a horrified rasp. "As I told Applegate some days ago, I am not particularly well loved by the port authority in Marseille."

"How in the devil are we going to get out of France, then?" Isabelle moaned, leaning against the wall with a hand to her brow. "They have the *Harpy* and presumably your crew."

"They didn't take the crew," Peter told her, raising his brows. "It is a trap for Mathias, after all. The crew are being watched and are contained to the ship, but they are not imprisoned. I am to warn you that they have been promised their freedom if they keep their silence until you are in custody."

"Good. That is good," Mathias said, oblivious to the noises of disagreement made by the others. He began to pace, rubbing his thumb and forefinger over his eyes with enough vigor that Peter thought he might be attempting to physically extract an idea from his mind. "That means they want to catch me in the act, but I don't have any illegal goods with me this time!"

"Except for me, Dempierre," Isabelle reminded him flatly.

"No, no," he said shaking his head, "we still have the marriage documents."

"But not permission to sail between warring nations," Peter

reminded him. "What about your friend on the docks, who helped us dock the night we arrived? Could you bribe him again?"

"I doubt it. Offering me cover in darkness is a fair sight different than assisting me opposite his entire regiment, ready and waiting for my appearance." He dragged his hands through his hair, gritting his teeth together in frustration. "We are going to have to fight or connive our way out."

"I prefer conniving," Isabelle said quickly. "I'd rather not get imprisoned or impaled."

"Agreed," Peter put in, giving Mathias a stern look. "Consider what you are suggesting."

Mathias waved him off, still pacing, nervous energy radiating off him. "I know a man who will buy the horses," he said. "You two stay put, and I will return with enough coin to perhaps buy our way out of here. We will deal with the Oliviers and their betrayal when we return to England."

"Please do not lose my dog," Isabelle called after him. "He is with the ass."

He did not answer, the intensity of his bootfalls only increasing as an indication that he had heard her, but that sound vanished almost as suddenly as Mathias himself had. They did not hear the kitchen door open nor shut, for Mathias was a practiced hand at the art of sneaking about.

Against all odds, though perhaps in the least ideal circumstances, Isabelle and Peter were finally alone again.

It took several hours to piece together something resembling a realistic plan.

While Mathias had been seeing to the horseflesh, Isabelle had been scouring the house for anything useful, while Peter spread out in the study with maps of the pier and shipping docks on hand.

They kept to the rear of the house, not wishing to alert anyone who might have been watching the home from outside that anyone was within. After all, it was likely that the authorities had noticed the flight of Pauline and Gerard Olivier by now. The letter hadn't been dated, but it was best to take no risks.

Mathias returned, looking more rattled than Peter thought him capable, his expression tight and tense. Evidently, his contact had agreed to purchase the three horses, but did not have a use for Hortensia.

"What are we going to do with a donkey?!" he demanded, his eyes wild. "I can't just leave her tied up here to starve to death, or wandering the streets to be eaten by some vagrant!"

"We'll take her with us," Isabelle said with a shrug, as though transporting a donkey across the Atlantic Ocean were the simplest matter in the world. "You have cargo space, presumably? You are a smuggler, after all."

"You want me to sneak a donkey across Vieux Port under the threat of an alert guard?" Mathias had railed, throwing his hands in the air. Truly, it was alarming seeing him shaken by anything at all.

"No," she said, taking him by the shoulders and pushing him

onto a couch, opposite where Peter had been working at the desk in the study. "I will. You will simply have to ensure that I know which ship is yours for the first stage of our plan."

"What will we do with her in London?" he asked, though he did seem somewhat calmed by the implication that there was a solution in the works. "No one in London needs a donkey."

"Mathias, one crisis at a time." Peter sighed, rubbing at his eyes beneath his glasses. He had worked in poor light before, but never under such duress. He felt as though his eyes would wither and drop out of his head if he had to do this for much longer. "If the Oliviers went to England, perhaps they will want her back, anyhow."

"We found clothes in the servants' quarters," Isabelle said briskly, clearly uninterested in either panic or fatigue. She tossed a bundle of garments at Mathias, who seemed to notice in that moment that both of his companions had changed into the drab, gray uniforms of the serving class.

The fit was not ideal, of course, but it was well enough to provide them with temporary invisibility in Marseille. Peter's shirt was missing two buttons up top, which they had compensated for with a bit of loose fabric tied around his neck. Isabelle's apron had a rather large patch on it that was coming away at the seams, so she simply ripped it off and declared the hole in the fabric less conspicuous than a poor patch job. She had also gathered her hair into a coil under one of the lacy caps favored by French serving maids. It was an effect Peter found extremely fetching, though he kept that thought to himself.

"I will take Hortensia to the dock," Isabelle said, once

Mathias had returned in his servant's garb. She was perched on the chair opposite the desk and beckoned him over to take a look at the maps Peter had laid out. "Because your men have likely been unable to resupply while at port, we have packed away some rations to ensure we do not run out of food at sea. There was a generous new supply of summer preserves and some bread and cheese that will hold up for at least a few days. It is actually great luck that Hortensia is still with us, as our things would have required multiple trips otherwise."

"Smart," Mathias said, patting her on the shoulder. "The *Harpy* is a leisure class cutter, at least on the outside. She has three sails, the middle of which is blue. You might not be able to make out the color in the dark, however. If they had left her in the same place we docked her, it would be an easy matter, but I am willing to wager that she has been moved."

"She has," Peter confirmed, turning the map around and pointing to a series of triangles drawn onto the harbor. "In the letter, Pauline mentions that she is under the watch of a guard tower, of which there are three. It cannot be the two that are on either side of the merchant loop, so she must be in this rear shipyard, where local pleasure boats are kept for long periods of time."

"We considered waiting until morning, and perhaps gaining cover as the fishermen embarked for the day, but Peter rightfully has pointed out that the fishing vessels would not be a concern for the authority, and are likely not docked in the same area." Isabelle took a deep breath and blew it out with her cheeks inflated. "We are going to have to hope the darkness of night is enough to preserve us."

"If Isabelle or I are caught, we may pretend to be a married pair of servants, left adrift in the flight of the Oliviers," Peter explained. "I have the papers showing that, at least, and the French version will protect my identity, though of course I can't do anything about my accent. If you are caught, is there a chance that they will know you by looks alone?"

"Oh, yes," Mathias said, significantly cheerier than he had been only a few moments prior. "If they capture me, get on board and order the crew to sail back to London immediately. I can negotiate my own release from here, if necessary. Obviously, I would prefer to avoid it."

"You said not three hours ago that the prison here is inescapable!" Isabelle protested. "We cannot leave you behind."

"We may have to," Peter said, surprised to find that the idea did genuinely disturb him. "But let's hope it is not a choice we are forced to make, hm? Mathias, we need you to tell us the times that the guard changes. You knew their rotation when we arrived here, so hopefully it has not changed."

And so, heads together in the light of a single lamp, in the study of an empty house, the three planned their daring escape.

CHAPTER 13

Isabelle held the lantern in front of her, high and steady as she led a very nervous Hortensia over the brine-soaked planks of wood that made up the eastern dock. She hummed to herself, partially to quell the anxious fluttering within her, and partially to calm the animals in her care. She thought too that a humming woman seemed more likely to linger and take her time about her tasks than one who was silent.

One by one, she read the names of the ships as she passed them, looking for the large and embellished letter H that would lead her into the name she wanted.

"Harpy," she whispered, "Harpy, harpy, harpy."

Hortensia huffed, using her snout to nudge her mistress more than once in an impatient discomfort with their current surroundings, but Isabelle knew she could not rush, lest she have to double back again and extend their plight even further.

The click of her heels on the wooden planks seemed

conspicuously loud, for one did not often wear riding boots under a servant's frock. She hummed with determination, telling herself that no one other than herself would even think to notice such a thing, even as the first pink tendrils of dawn began to creep over the horizon.

Finally, and to her great relief, she saw the ship she was looking for, a slender and sleek vessel, positioned in good vantage to the guard tower looming over her shoulder. She saw that the loading plank was lowered onto the dock, which had likely been done as a hindrance to escape, but would accommodate their last-minute donkey-smuggling needs very well.

She brought Hortensia onto the ramp, with much coaxing and tugging, and finally managed to get her into the ship's storage cabin, a pitch-dark cavern with a hay-strewn floor. Goliath was squirming inside the cushioned saddlebag he had come to favor, and gave a sharp yap of relief once Isabelle had hung the lantern and come to free him.

Of course, shushing a dog rarely has any effect whatsoever, but it did save her the trouble of waking the crew ...

~

IN DRAB, ill-fitting gray, with a cap pulled down low on his brow, and shoulders hunched in the humble posture of the working class, Peter thought Mathias completely unrecognizable. If only he would stop checking that damned pocket watch he'd taken from the study, they would be shockingly inconspicuous.

Luckily for the pair, the eastern docks were widely built and cluttered. The guard tower was a significant obstacle, but in a neater arrangement, they would have had a much more difficult job of remaining unseen. For all his bluster, Dempierre was light on his feet, and the two of them were able to move slowly and noiselessly through the bulk of the pathway, towards the beacon light Isabelle had lit.

"You know," Mathias said under his breath, "this is going to make me an even larger target than I was before."

"Oh, undoubtedly," Peter agreed. "Infamous, if you will."

"Hm." Mathias was quiet for a moment, as though he were turning this word around in his head, inspecting it like a gemstone. "Infamous," he repeated, with obvious glee. "Yes, I suppose so!"

They huddled down a distance from the beacon light, listening carefully to the commotion of raised voices coming from either side of the ship.

"Please, *monsieur!*" Isabelle cried, her voice a convincing mask of hysteria. "You must save me! My master will wonder where I have gone!"

Two guards stood on the dock, staring up at the bow of the ship, where she was being held at the end of a musket by the ship's cook, trembling in an impressive imitation of terror.

The men were shouting back and forth at one another, each making frenzied, angry demands for the exchange of this innocent parlor maid who had been captured by brigands working for a notorious smuggler. Once the commotion had been noted from the guard tower and a trio of additional bodies were hurrying down to assist their comrade, each a dot in the distance of lantern light, Mathias and Peter began to move again, parting ways where the dock forked.

Mathias vanished from Peter's view, drawing the flintlock pistol he had commandeered from the Olivier house from his coat. A few moments later, the telltale pop of the false shot fired into the air alerted the guards to Mathias's presence opposite his vessel, and the price of his passage in return for this poor, frightened maid.

The shouting of the men was a good indication that all attention was now focused on Mathias, giving Peter the freedom he needed to sprint the rest of the way to the starboard side of the ship, where the crew had lowered a rope ladder into the water. It would take a quick dive and a bit of physical finesse, but he was confident he could get on board in time.

A second shot ringing out, however, gave him immediate pause. They had not planned for a second shot.

There was a frenzied exchange of fire and the telltale ring of blades being drawn as increasingly frenetic shouting echoed from without. Peter hesitated, remembering that they had planned in the case of Mathias's capture, but he could not bring himself to dive in. He tried to be discreet, inching back towards the curve in the dock, if only to get a look at what was happening.

It was not good. Mathias had his pistol drawn, pointed in front of him at two of the guards, as the other three moved to surround him.

"Little John!" called a voice from above, just faint enough to be drowned out by the commotion down below.

Isabelle was hanging over the railing, two swords in a sling of fabric in her hands. "Here! Quickly!"

"Throw them!" Peter cried, gesturing to the dock floor.

They clattered to the ground in an instant, quicker than Peter had time to consider his actions, and before he knew what was happening he was dashing towards Mathias, a sword in each hand. The guards did not see him coming until he was close enough to reach Mathias, diving haphazardly into the circle of guards.

Mathias accepted the sword with a flourish, holding his pistol steady as he added this second deadly weapon to the mix. It was still not an equal fight, to be certain, but for just a moment it felt less hopeless.

"We will kill the girl!" one of the crewmen shouted from the deck. "Let him pass!"

"And who is this, hm?" the guard with stripes on his uniform asked, eyeing Peter. "Another accomplice, Dempierre? And the girl too, I think."

The *Harpy* groaned, her sails snapping to life as the crew dragged them into place. It was clear now that they intended to depart with Isabelle in tow, else throw her into the water. The ramp was still down to the cargo compartment, panicked braying punctuated with yaps of a dog sounding from within.

"You think?" Mathias mocked, his stance strong despite his taunting tone. "Quite a risk to take, Dumand. You do not strike me as a gambler."

The man's lip curled, his eyes flicking up to the deck once more where Isabelle stood gripping the railing, flanked by the threatening forms of the crew. "She is just a maid," he said with a shrug, and then to his men, "Take them."

The third fire of the pistol gave away the unfortunate truth. It was not loaded with anything but powder. Mathias tossed it to the ground and made a leap towards the guard named Dumand, his blade catching the other's with an ear-splitting clash.

The surprise of a man vaulting into the air after their leader gave the others enough of a pause for Peter to weave his way backward, attempting to clear a path for Mathias to the loading ramp, which was pulling away from the dock inch by alarming inch. He caught the swing of one blade with practiced instinct, giving him a clear shot of the other man's chest, which he used to boot him into the water.

The splash drew two more, while the third rushed to the aid of the fallen man. When he bent over to offer his hand, Mathias took the opportunity to back into him, knocking the pair of them into each other in the sea water.

Dumand appeared a man possessed, furious beyond what one would imagine his post demanded of him. His swings at Mathias were brutal and lethally aimed, his face contorted in rage.

Peter had two men bearing down upon him, a thing he had only ever practiced at the very end of his tenure with his teacher at Oxford, and truly only for fun. He stomped one of his feet onto the ramp of the ship, as though the sheer force of his will alone could hold it in place, parrying and dodging frankly ill-refined attacks from the guards, who clearly were not trained in nor regularly expecting to be confronted with swordplay.

"Mathias!" he shouted, impatience fraying at his words as he ducked from a metallic swing and used a riposte to knock one of his opponents from their balance, sending him tumbling onto the planks of wood with what looked like a painful landing. "Leave him. We must go!"

The final guardsman tossed his sword down and went running off towards the guard tower. It was unclear whether he was fleeing the fight or in search of more men, but either way, it was their window.

Mathias was backing as quickly as he could towards the ramp of the ship, where Peter stood, arm outstretched, urging him to hurry. Dumand was bearing down on him with an unrelenting energy, twice coming close enough to landing a blow that Peter could hear the ripping of Mathias's clothes.

A sudden *thunk* and shattering of glass dropped Dumand from pressing forward to collapse on the ground, dazed and surrounded by what appeared to be a disproportionate amount of congealed blood.

"Run!" Isabelle called frantically from above, another jar of preserves held over her head like a missile. "Run, you idiots!"

That was all it took. Peter grasped Mathias by the hand and pulled him onto the ramp just as it separated from the dock. The two of them went tumbling onto their backs within the ship as Dumand clambered to his hands and knees, screaming obscenities at the retreating vessel.

One of the swords was still on the dock, and Dumand picked it up and flung it at them with a force that might very well have sent it far enough to strike, if he had been able to aim properly. It spurred them into action, grabbing the white lines of rope that attached to the now waterlogged ramp, dragging in the Mediterranean waters as the ship sped away from land.

It took their last dregs of energy to pull the ramp wall up into place, after which they both collapsed onto their backs, heaving oxygen in and out of their lungs with the appreciation of men who had just been confronted with their own mortality, comforted by the anxious nickering of a donkey and the yapping of a dog, which signified their return to safety.

CHAPTER 14

*T*he great, reeling surge of the ship taking on wind and leaving the Marseille dock had knocked Isabelle flat on her back. It was a position she was gruffly told by a crewman to maintain until they were well and truly out of sight of the harbor.

It was just as well, she thought, laying a hand to her stomach as another wave tossed the *Harpy* into the air and then brought it back down again. She wasn't sure how well she'd be doing if she were standing. This was, after all, her first time on a boat. It was an opportunity to watch the sky turn pink and orange as the sun made the rest of its journey into the morning sky, the last hint of the northern star winking out of view until evening came again.

By the time she realized that they had been at sea long enough for her to safely rise, the crewmen appeared to have long forgotten about her and the brilliant ruse they'd performed together. She pushed herself to sitting, wincing as she adjusted one of the pins in her hair that was anchoring the maid's frill to her crown. She stayed this way until the movement felt normal, and then used the railing to pull herself to standing, gasping in great breaths of sea air as the endless span of the ocean unfurled in front of her.

It was truly paralyzing, the sheer expanse of it. Another time she would have been content to stand here until the sun had set again, stricken with awe at the beauty of this world, so much of which she had not yet discovered. As it was, she hadn't slept in over a day, and judging from the speed of the blood pumping through her veins, it would be a good while before she could possibly rest again.

She retraced the steps she'd taken from the cargo hold to the deck, much more carefully this time, holding to the walls every time it seemed the ground would pitch itself directly out from under her. She wondered how poor Hortensia and Goliath were handling this, terranean creatures that they were, and if Peter and Mathias had escaped their confrontation unscathed.

Watching them in combat had been as thrilling as it was terrifying. Peter moved like a dancer, his body lithe and agile, but strong enough when he needed it to shove more than one of the guards into the murky water of the port. At another time, in another context, she would have enjoyed watching him at this business a great deal more. The sharp light of dawn had glinted off his blade, his feet light and quick, and his face determined as he'd warded off their foes.

She would remember it forever.

As for Mathias, she had feared that the dark gentlemen with whom he clearly shared a past would run him through. Hurling a jar of preserves into the fray was perhaps not the most elegant way to assist her friends, but she was proud that she had, in her own small way, contributed to a victory.

She paused just short of the doorway to the cargo hold, straining her ears for some indication of what she might find behind it. Alas, it was a thick and sturdy door, and she would have no information until she straightened her spine and opened the damn thing. All she could do was pray there was a minimum of injury to her friends.

She used her shoulder to urge the heavy door open, just in time to hear a cry of pain and an alarmed bray from Hortensia. She shoved herself the rest of the way through, weaving around a shelf of rations to find Peter standing over Mathias's doubled-over body, a large stick in his hand. When he caught sight of her, he attempted to whip the thing behind his back, evidently unaware that it was several inches taller than he when held this way.

"What in the devil?" Isabelle demanded, looking from man to man. "How are you already back to bickering again!"

"We ... weren't," Mathias managed, wheezing in a breath between the two words. He was apparently laughing, though she could not hear it with so little air in his lungs to give it sound. "Weren't," he said again for effect, as Peter hastened forward to assist him to his feet, the stick he'd held clattering to the floor.

"It isn't what it looks like," Peter assured her, averting his eyes as he used the bulk of his weight to heave Mathias to his feet.

"I have spent a not insignificant amount of time caring for the village children over the years," Isabelle replied, her eyes narrowed and hands on her hips. "And one thing I have learned is that it is *always* what it looks like. For God's sake, Mathias, sit down!"

"Good, yes," Mathias agreed, using Peter's grip to leverage himself around the other man and onto an empty crate. He braced his hands on his knees and drew in a few deep breaths, sabotaging his own attempts to recover with what was almost a giddy sort of persistent laughter. "Sometimes," he said between giggles, "it is *worse* than it looks."

"It isn't!" Peter protested, looking an awful lot like an actor at center stage in this moment, between the other two. "We admired one another's form on the dock, and Mathias asked me to show him the disarming move I used when caught between two opponents."

"I think he broke my rib!" Mathias said cheerfully, if not in a voice uncharacteristically thin. His eyes were wide and glistening like a little boy who had just seen his first horse.

"Well, of all the stupidity I might have imagined, injuring one another after narrowly escaping an earlier injury is perhaps beyond even the powers of my imagination," she huffed, crossing her arms over her chest.

"We're also a little bit drunk," Peter added, in a tone that suggested he thought this might make things better. "We tapped a barrel of wine. Would you like some?"

Isabelle blinked at him for a moment as he stood awkwardly between her and his injured compatriot with a hopeful, if sheepish smile. Indeed, now she could see two wooden goblets on the ground, one fallen to its side with a stain of red dregs on the wood below. She closed her eyes for a moment, at last distracted from the way the ground was constantly moving beneath her, and told herself that this was truly not a bad outcome, all things considered.

"Oh, all right, then, give me a cup," she said with a sigh, looking around for something she might seat herself upon and settling on a pile of woolen blankets. "When in Rome, I suppose."

"Fabulous!" Mathias grinned at her. "I will have some more, too, Applegate, if you don't mind."

"I don't," Peter replied with a chuckle. "I did just cripple you. My apologies, by the way."

"Nonsense, nonsense," Mathias insisted, his dimpled cheeks stretched in a wide grin. "I'll master the damned move before we get to England. Be certain of that."

"It will be an exchange of techniques," Peter agreed, handing each of them a cup of wine before returning to pour his own. "I've never seen someone move with such calm and consideration in combat, and I've only ever watched sparring. How you kept a cool head while that man was attempting to remove yours is truly a thing to admire."

"Yes, who *was* that man, Mathias?" Isabelle asked, drawing her legs up under her skirt and curling them to the side as she settled in to enjoy these early-morning libations. "He seemed rather angry with you, specifically."

"Yes, well, I have been smuggling in and out of his port for the better part of his career, I suppose." Mathias grinned, scratching sheepishly behind his ear. "That type of thing doesn't foster friendship."

"Smuggling what?" she asked, aware suddenly of how fine

the wine in her wooden cup tasted. "Is this wine even yours?"

"It is fair payment for the Oliviers stealing our boarding papers, I'd say," Peter muttered, shaking his head. "I still can't believe they did it."

"Yes, it does present a bit of a conundrum, I'm afraid," Mathias replied, his breath seemingly returned to him. "We won't be able to dock in London without them, so back to Dover it is. We can send a missive to Nate in London when we arrive and have him come meet us at Meridian House. He won't be happy about it, but it does spare us all from high Season nonsense, doesn't it?"

Peter frowned. "I was hoping to see my sister before she goes into confinement," he confessed. "I haven't seen her face-to-face in half a year at least."

"Women don't go into confinement anymore!" Isabelle sputtered, forcing herself to swallow her wine before she released something between a cough and a chuckle. "It isn't the sixteenth century!"

"Well, I don't know anything about it!" Peter replied, his ears turning pink at the tips. "My mother always seemed to vanish before one of my siblings arrived, and ... and I suppose my only reference to such things is in historical texts. That is to say, men are not ... well, not generally present ... for ..."

"Steady on, Applegate," Mathias said directly into his cup. "We know what you meant."

There was a lingering moment of silence, accompanied by Hortensia snorting around for something to eat and the creaking of the boat as it floated on the waves. Isabelle busied herself with draining her wine, lest her impulse to laugh some more come bubbling to the surface.

"I suppose I should address the crew," Mathias said on a sigh, his emptied cup clattering down next to him. "Would bloody well prefer more to drink, though."

"They seemed perfectly competent without orders," Isabelle said, pushing herself off her crate to take a turn serving the drinks. "Perhaps you can safely dawdle a bit longer, though I rather think we all should indulge in naps sometime soon. Assuming, of course, that it is possible to fall asleep in a room that never stops moving."

"Ugh," Peter muttered, shaking his head, "I'd forgotten about the hammocks."

"Worry not, my dear, you will take the bed for the duration of this journey," Mathias assured her. "Though I find the hammocks perfectly comfortable, myself. You will adjust to the movement sooner than you know, and then find the stability of the ground strange for a bit once we're back on dry land."

"As though I won't be disoriented enough," she said, handing him his refilled cup. "Perhaps it's for the best that I will have a day or two in England to prepare before meeting my brother? I have no idea what I will say to him."

"Oh, I wouldn't worry about that," Peter said. "Nathaniel built a career on being the person who presides over the conversation."

She tapped her fingernail against her cup, an anxious flutter going through her chest. She imagined simply presenting herself for assessment in a room of blank-faced English relations, allowing them to circle her, plucking at her clothes and counting the freckles on her nose with dour frowns.

More wine, she thought. Wine would drown out the future, for at least a little bit.

⁓

By lunchtime, the three of them had thoroughly partaken of the smuggled wine, and were seated in a circle on the floor of the cargo hold, eating hardtack and cheese in an attempt to get their bearings back.

Isabelle had taken great relish in removing the pins from her hair and tossing the ruffled cap away, never to be reclaimed. She'd started to ache from the severity of the style and felt a true sympathy for women in service who must wear their hair this way for all of their lives. As she'd run her fingers through her thick and messy hair, shaking it loose around her face and shoulders, she had caught Peter Applegate watching the entire transformation with an intensity that made her stomach drop.

His eyes had turned stormy here in the low-lit cargo hold, his face bright with the warmth of the wine. The way he had looked at her had made her hesitate, suddenly self-conscious and awkward in her movements, when she would have given anything in the world to be bold enough to hold his gaze and continue, utterly cool and unflappable. She imagined the sophisticates he had known, brushing shoulders with nobles in London, would have managed the ruse with exacting skill.

He had noticed the change, however, and had given her half

a smile and a sheepish shrug of apology before respectfully averting his gaze. It was the perfect acknowledgement of the situation, something that felt like a private amusement rather than an embarrassment of inexperienced flirtation, and Isabelle thought, afterward, that it had felt as though an entire conversation had taken place there in the silence, with no one else any the wiser.

The wine, Mathias had revealed to them, was bought with simple sacks of gold guineas. Goods from France brought a tidy profit when sold on the other side of the Channel, especially spirits and textiles. This Silver Leaf Society, which Isabelle's mother had reportedly been a part of, built their riches with simple smuggling exchanges, and then used the proceeds to finance the movement of people across the border in the direction of their choosing.

The *Harpy* was built for leisure sailing and had been modified into something that could discreetly transport simple goods. Isabelle gathered that she was one of very few, if not the only, person that had ever been smuggled in place of contraband.

"Why a harpy?" Peter had asked, sprawled with his back against a beam and his hand on Goliath's head. "Strange choice."

Mathias had wrenched a ring from his finger and tossed it at the other man, landing it directly into his cup of wine with a resounding plop.

"Oops," he had said, though he looked rather smug with himself as Peter fished it out, wiping the red liquid onto the hem of his borrowed servant's shirt. "Apologies."

Peter pushed the ring onto his own finger, holding up his

hand to examine the signet. He was evidently unaware of how amusing the image he presented was, squinting at it and adjusting his spectacles onto the tip of his nose as he held his fingers wide like a fawning bride-to-be. "Some sort of bird?" he guessed, after a moment. "A hawk?"

"It's the Dempierre family crest," Mathias explained. "Thoroughly destroyed outside of that ring, as were most things belonging to the gentry when the world changed. We keep the idea of a family crest alive in our own little ways. Mother with her feathered masquerade, Gigi with her pet parakeets, and I have the *Harpy,* a creature that is divided in half by two different worlds, just like I am."

"What about your father?" Isabelle asked, reaching out to take the ring from Peter for her own inspection.

Mathias snorted. "Father has never truly stepped over the line from the past to the present. He lives in the clouds, denying that anything at all has changed. I suppose it's easier for him. He isn't a deep thinker."

"Deep-thinking fathers are harder to outsmart," Isabelle said with a quirk of her lips, tossing the ring back to its owner. "Trust me on that."

"His mother is cunning enough for the both of them," Peter put in. "Not in an obvious way like my Aunt Zelda, but soothing and charming until you realize you're doing her bidding of your own accord."

"The trick is to just never do anything at all," Mathias said with a grin. "Or so I thought it was, until I realized that she'd manipulated me into staying *out* of trouble."

"My parents let us run wild from the start," Peter said wistfully, his deep voice a little louder and more assured with the influence of the wine. He laughed, a free burst of amusement, free of any of his customary reservation or self-scrutinization. "We had the whole of Winchester to play in, and very little oversight. We must have terrorized the locals. My parents were much more interested in one another than any of their children. Strangely, in the end, it created a sense of responsibility in us, where we were writing and imposing rules on ourselves in the absence of authority."

"Clearly not very strict ones," Isabelle teased, smiling at the look of befuddled outrage that flickered across his face. "You are now an active member of a criminal enterprise, are you not? Counterfeiting and smuggling and the like."

"The counterfeiting was for naught," he replied glumly. "We've lost the half of my documents that created the need for the half we've retained. Guineas and the port in Dover could have done my job for me."

"Well, I certainly appreciate your presence," Mathias replied. "It's a far sight superior to spending the next few months in Chateau d'If."

"They were protection on the road to Marseille, as well," Isabelle reminded him. "If my cousin had decided to make life difficult or one of the innkeepers had been suspicious of impropriety, they were the only shield we had."

He gave a great sigh, leaning his head back against the wooden beam, his eyelids flickering shut as the culmination of fatigue and alcohol seemed to overtake him. "I suppose you are right," he muttered, stifling a yawn which quickly transferred from Goliath to Mathias to Isabelle.

"I could always legitimize the marriage, if that would

comfort you, Applegate," Mathias teased. "We are, after all, at sea on my vessel."

"My dear Mathias, I rather suspect any legal proceedings you oversaw would be considered suspect," Isabelle replied with a laugh, hoping her amusement would disguise the flush of blood that had rushed to her cheeks at that prospect. "You should add your crest to the false documents, though. I imagine you have very little call to use a signet as it is intended."

Peter scoffed. "I bet he has an entire room littered with bits of paper and wax that he's pushed that ring into."

"Maybe I do!" Mathias replied jovially. "It's not unlike that necklace Isabelle's wearing, though, is it? Simply a link to the past. These things are precious to us silly mortals."

She felt her hand go automatically to her throat, her fingers encircling the dark blue stone. She had been fiddling with it so much that she had feared she'd knocked something out of order. The protrusion now jiggled when she fussed at it with her fingernail, and she had been attempting to stop.

Perhaps she could get it repaired in England.

"I'm just going to sleep on the floor," Peter decided on another extended yawn, peeking at the other two with one eye, shrouded by his lashes. "The hammock will wait."

"We should all sleep," Mathias agreed, pushing himself to his feet and offering a hand to Isabelle. "Let me show you your quarters."

She took the hand and brushed the wrinkles from her skirt, glancing down at Peter, who already seemed to be breathing in a steady rhythm. "Are we going to just leave him there?"

she whispered, raising her eyebrows. "He can't truly sleep there, can he?"

"I'll bring him a blanket," Mathias promised, ushering her towards the door. "He is a high-strung fellow, but he sleeps like the dead. Perhaps we all will today. Remind me to get him drunk more often."

Isabelle cast one more glance over her shoulder, noting that her dog had chosen to curl into the recess of Peter's arm rather than follow his mistress to the deck. The frames of Peter's spectacles were askew, his face resting on his arm, and he truly did seem to already be completely lost to oblivion.

She gave a little chuckle, following Mathias to her own promise of long-awaited slumber, and she thought to herself that it was a shame that everyone already knew those marriage papers were counterfeit, for she would be rather happy if they were real.

CHAPTER 15

*P*eter wasn't sure how long he slept. What he was certain of was that the only thing that forced him back into the land of the waking was the inconvenient need to hydrate himself after so much wine. By the time he forced himself to blink his eyes open, he had been lamenting this inconvenient necessity for some time already.

He realized that he was covered with a scratchy wool blanket in a rather garish red and purple dye pattern and that Isabelle's little dog was still snoring next to him. Goliath had nestled into his shoulder and fallen asleep on his back, all four paws limp in the air while his tongue lolled out of the side of his mouth.

It almost tempted him to stay put for a while longer, but alas, he was perhaps the most parched he'd ever felt in his entire life.

The instant he stood, he became aware of the movement of the ship beneath his feet again, stumbling forward and reaching out with both hands to steady himself on one of the beams supporting the cargo hold. It took him a moment to spot his spectacles, which had been taken off him and folded neatly on top of the empty barrel of wine.

Had Isabelle done that? He wasn't sure if imagining her doing such a thing was thrilling or mortifying.

Whoever had done it hadn't been fast enough. One of the temples looked like it had been bent under the weight of his sleeping head on the floor. It was no matter. He had repaired worse and slumped off to sleep in many less opportune poses, often right on top of wet ink and paper, uncomfortably close to low-burning candles.

He made his way onto the deck only to find it mostly deserted, a low glimmer of indigo light indicating that he had either slept for a modest handful of hours or an exorbitant bucketful. Was the sun rising or setting? It was impossible to tell with nothing but open sea around him.

He found Isabelle and Mathias in the galley, drinking cups of tea on either side of an abandoned game of dice. Upon his entrance, Isabelle groaned in frustration, while Mathias clapped excitedly, his face blossoming into a wide, dimpled smile. It was confusing enough to root him to the spot until an explanation came forth.

"You've just lost me a wager," Isabelle said finally, using one of her slippered feet to nudge an empty chair back from the table for Peter's use.

"I said you'd awaken by sunup, and Monetier said you'd not sleep through the night, for certain. It was sensible to assume night was the safer bet, but I know better. You sleep like the dead," Mathias gloated, taking a delicate sip from a rather large and clunky mug.

"The sun is still rising," Peter said, taking the seat and reaching for one of the empty mugs, "or setting, I suppose."

"Rising," Isabelle confirmed with a haughty sniff. "We discussed the terms of twilight. The win still goes to Mathias. How on Earth could you have been comfortable for so long down there?!"

"'Comfortable' isn't the word I'd use, necessarily," Peter replied, unable to stop a self-deprecating chuckle. "Sleep is more of an overpowering beast that tackles me from time to time than some desired reprieve I must court and nurture to enjoy."

"Many people would envy that," Mathias said. "Not I, but many other people."

Now that he'd had a moment to settle into the land of the waking again, Peter did take note that his traveling companions looked refreshed and had changed out of their servants' garb. Isabelle was wearing the same red skirt she'd had on the night they'd met, with her customary wide leather belt and plaited white blouse. Her hair was damp and braided over her shoulder as he was accustomed to seeing it.

Mathias was back in his lackadaisical shirtsleeves and breeches, clean shaven and bright-eyed.

Both looked refreshed from a night of rest, whereas Peter was certain he appeared like something resembling a haggard old forest crone.

The ship's cook stumbled in, mumbling something about the amount of eggs they had left, and vanished into the galley pit where his cooking tools were. It gave Peter an opportunity to excuse himself and run to the crew cabin. He quickly changed into his own clothes, ran a comb through his hair and a wet rag over his face, eager to restore himself to something presentable before the shafts of sunlight began to really illuminate his features to the others.

He felt more himself when he returned to a steaming plate of breakfast, and listened happily as Isabelle explained to him the game she had been teaching Mathias , holding the scuffed bone out to him as she detailed rules and how to break them.

∼

THE AFTERNOON UNFURLED in a blast of brilliant sunlight in a cloudless sky. Waves peaked in glittering white exploded into shards of light against the *Harpy*'s bow as she carved her way north, slashing prisms into the ocean as she went.

Isabelle had insisted on being shown the whole of the vessel and instructed in the basics of how it operates, lest the sea toss all the men out and leave her on her own to navigate back to dry land, and Mathias had complied with this request, saying he needed to inspect the state of things anyhow. Peter, however, had declined an invitation to join them, opting instead to find a nice spot on the deck to enjoy the warmth of the day and to fix his mutilated spectacles.

He had been gifted a small kit of artisan tools for this purpose when he was a teenager, after enough trips for professional repair had rendered such an investment frugal and sensible. Indeed, it had saved him a great deal of time and money over the years to simply fix simple problems himself, and it was a relief that he would not have to spend the rest of the journey to England with lopsided vision.

In the absence of a formal workspace, he had opted to use one of the white plates from the galley as his surface, which was working well if not for the way the tiny screws and such rolled about as the ship bobbed in the water. He was so focused on the tiny pieces and his manipulation of them that he hadn't even noticed Isabelle settling herself down next to him, observing his work.

When she spoke, he damn near jumped out of his skin.

"What funny little tools," she had said, grinning at the way he startled. "They look like things that go in a doll's house."

He had adjusted his posture so that she may look over his shoulder as he worked, which she did close enough to make his hands less steady, her breath stirring the hair at his ear. She rested her chin on his shoulder, seemingly unconcerned with being seen like this, and remained silent, as though she didn't want to disturb him overly much, only enough to amuse herself.

"They are a jeweler's tools," he explained, satisfied that the final screw had been returned to the mechanism securely enough to allow himself to breathe again. He slid the spectacles back onto the bridge of his nose, checking the level of the stems on his ears, and was satisfied. They no longer sat at an angle.

"Oh?" she said, scooting backward so that he might turn to face her, though her eyes were fixed on the little leather box and the items within. "You seem skilled with them."

"I've had a lot of practice," he demurred with a crooked little smile, though her pretty hazel eyes had not budged from his tool kit.

She was toying with the dark blue stone around her neck, the gears in her mind turning loudly enough that he could swear he could hear them. "Do you think you could use those tools to get my locket open?"

He hesitated, looking at the trinket in her hand, warm from lying against her soft skin in the sunlight. "I would hate to damage it."

"It is already damaged," she said, a little breathless with excitement as she moved to remove it from around her neck. "I insist we try. Could you help me remove it? I have not mastered the clasp yet, I'm afraid."

He did not have a chance to answer before she turned her back to him, using her fingers to pull a few tiny strands of hair at her nape to the side as she presented the slender column of her neck to him. He was struck by the smell of her, sweet skin recently bathed in seawater and flowers. He blinked rapidly, holding his breath in an effort to steady his thoughts as he worked the little hook from its eyelet, releasing the necklace into her palm.

"The protrusion is loose," she said, gathering the chain into her hand and holding it out to him. "I've been fussing with it like a loose tooth, so it is likely better to have your tools urging the thing free than my brute force. I am just curious about what was inside, and if anything remains."

He shifted in the sunlight, turning the stone pendant over in his hand and examining the seam of it. He cleared his throat, reminding himself to focus, and in an effort to distract himself from her nearness, asked, "Did you enjoy your tour of the boat?"

"I did," she replied, though in doing so she scooted closer to him to see what he was doing. "I learned what a bait and tackle is."

"You shall have to enlighten me," Peter replied with a wry smile, "for I have no idea what that might be."

His thumb slid over the protruding bit of metal that stuck out from the seam. She was right: it was loose and wobbled in either direction fairly easily. Something within prevented it from going any farther, but perhaps if he could dislodge it, the locket would open up to reveal its interior.

A dab of oil on one of his finer-pointed tools set it to farther movement, though only in one direction. He pulled it with tentative force, working more oil into the seam as he realized that whatever this protrusion was, it likely took up the whole of the cavity of the locket.

"Isabelle," he said softly, turning it to its side to show her what he was seeing, the metal gleam flashing in the sun. "I do not think this locket opens in the way we are imagining. Look here."

"Oh, how strange," she breathed, pressing herself into his side as he urged the mechanism back into functionality, bit by bit. "The protrusion was not damaged," she realized, "it was a handle. A very tiny handle!"

"I have never seen anything quite like this," he marveled, hooking his thumbnail over the smooth little lump and giving it one final tug. There was a delicate sound of metal scraping metal, the protest of motion after so long sitting idle, but the locket unfolded like a switchblade, revealing a detailed slat of metal that had been tucked inside, between the dark blue stone and its metal casing.

"It's a key," she said, wide eyed. "Peter, it's a key!"

"It does appear to be, yes," he replied softly, holding it out to her by its stone base. Looking at it unfurled like this, it seemed a wonder that they hadn't known what it was from the start. It looked more natural as a key than it had as a locket, somehow, anchored by its glittering chain. "I wonder what it opens."

"I wonder if whatever it opens even still exists," she said, reaching out to take it with a trepidation like it might burn her. "It seems my mother was built of layered mystery, with every new reveal only leading to more questions."

"I have rather gotten that impression as well," Peter agreed, transfixed by the awe in her face as she cradled the necklace in her hands. "You resemble her, you know."

She blinked, giving her head a little shake as though she'd just been roused from a dream. Her eyes swam with emotion, the golden highlights in the hazel gleaming beneath her tears. "How do you know that?" she asked, drawing a deep breath in through her nostrils in an attempt to calm herself, though her voice carried a raw edge. "You knew her?"

"No, but I have seen her portrait," he answered as gently as he could, suddenly concerned that he was trespassing on a moment that Isabelle wished to experience alone. "There is a painting of your family at Meridian House. I saw it before setting sail for France. You are in it, though only just a babe in arms."

"I am glad to know such a thing exists," she replied, meeting his eye with what felt like a silent plea for anchor in this sea of awakened feeling. She put her hands out, taking hold of his with the locket in between them. "I wish very much to see what they looked like. Is my brother very like me in appearance?"

He considered her, tilting his head and attempting to conjure Nathaniel to mind. "His hair is lighter," he told her, "and his eyes darker. You have similar cheeks and jaws, though. I think it will be clear to anyone who sees you together that you share blood."

"But I am prettier, yes?" she said with a little twist of her lips. "Tell me I am prettier."

"I prefer you to him, on my honor," Peter replied solemnly. "Though admittedly, Nathaniel has never kissed me nor lured me into secluded woods."

She tittered, batting her lashes and giving his hand a squeeze, the imprint of her mother's secret key between them. "Nor has he evaded capture by the law and set sail with you to adventures unknown. Even if he is prettier than I, surely I am more exciting."

"You are, without a doubt, the most exciting woman I've ever met," he replied, unable to resist leaning into her aura, settled so close together as they already were. "I would follow you anywhere."

She bit her lip, turning those pretty hazel eyes up to meet his. "Do you think that if I kiss you again, Mathias will appear and switch me over the hands?"

"Perhaps," Peter replied, a shiver running through him at her nearness and the crackle of suggestion in her whisper. "It is best if I shoulder the risk, then, wouldn't you say?"

"It would be the chivalrous thing to do," she agreed, but leaned in all the same, making the true initiator of this kiss a question that could never be answered.

He had forgotten how soft her lips were, and how quickly all rational thought fled him when she was this close. He lifted his free hand to cup her cheek, indulging in the taste of her and the sweetness of a craving finally satisfied. So overpowering was the sensation that he did not worry that they sat in broad daylight, nor that any member of the crew could observe them freely. Any risk seemed worth it in this moment.

She released the necklace into his grasp, trusting him to keep it safe so that she might wrap her arms around his neck and lose herself as well. It was a burden he happily carried, closing his fingers around the precious trinket and remembering to breathe as her body pressed against his own, their kiss deepening with Isabelle coming very close to simply sitting in his lap.

When she broke away, her breath coming warm and heavy, eyes wide and sparkling, Peter thought he felt the world reel just a little, well beyond the movement of the waves beneath them. She was intoxicating, and his mind was as free of the persistent chatter of thoughts just now as it was in his most rigorous training with his sword. He stroked the errant strands of hair that fell around her face, and gazed at her with a sort of transfixed wonder.

It was difficult not to wish they were somewhere more secluded, not to imagine what it might be like to strip the clothing from one another and experience the feeling of skin on skin. He had never wanted someone like this before, had never felt so utterly driven to touch another person at every given moment. Perhaps it was for the best that they were on the deck, exposed to a degree, for he could easily see himself behaving dishonorably if given the chance.

Her cheeks were pink and her breathing shallow. He could not guarantee that her desires were as carnal as his own, but he rather suspected that if they had more privacy, neither of them could be trusted to uphold the rules of polite society. He hoped not, anyhow.

She turned back around, sweeping that thick auburn braid over her shoulder. She shivered when he draped the necklace back around her pretty throat and sighed when he lingered at the clasp so that he might enjoy the sensation of the skin there for just a moment longer.

When she turned back to him, her lips moist and parted, and eyes shining bright with mischief, she did so while also inching away, as if to provide them both some space to regain their heads.

"You should take a tour of the *Harpy* too, sometime," she said, averting her gaze from him to stare out into the sun-drenched sea. "I imagine you'll have no idea how to navigate to the captain's quarters until you do."

CHAPTER 16

By the third night, it had become apparent to Isabelle that there would be no clandestine knock at her door.

It certainly wasn't that she had failed to make the invitation explicit enough. Peter was an intelligent man, and after she had said what she said, he had kissed her once more, pulling her firmly into his lap, where proof of his interest in the proposition was apparent.

So why had he decided against it? Either it was a misplaced sense of morality at work or she was not as tempting as she hoped.

He wasn't avoiding her during the daylight hours, at least. They had even exchanged amused whispers during one of Isabelle's sessions of sailing curiosity when the ship's cook launched into an argument with Mathias about whether the *Harpy* could justifiably be described as a "sloop."

In the days since, they had used every available opportunity to suggest that Mathias was acting like a sloop, despite the fact that neither knew what the word meant, simply because it was so effective at making the unflappable ship's captain sputter with indignation.

So, it wasn't to say that the trip had lost its charm. She was still having a grand time, and the endless freedom of the sea was invigorating in a way she had never experienced at the bottom of her little sugar bowl in Serre Chevalier valley. Who knew that the world was so very, very open? Who knew there were places unprotected by the stern sentry of a thousand mountain peaks?

The truth was that part of her thrill came from fear. Every morning, before she fed Hortensia and Goliath and before she went to the galley and poured her first cup of tea, she walked to the bow and stared off as far as her natural gaze would allow, looking for any sight of land. As long as sea stretched eternal, she was safe. As long as there was nothing but ocean, she was Isabelle Monetier and she knew precisely what that meant.

At least, she had a pretty good idea. Admittedly, her codex of adventures had expanded significantly in recent days, but it had all felt natural enough. It had felt like the same old Isabelle.

What would she do when England appeared? Who would she be then? If she gave herself willingly to Peter now, before she became something new and unknown, she could be certain it was right and honest. She had decided back in the Olivier home, planning their escape together, that this was what she wanted.

She wanted him. Isabelle Monetier wanted Peter Applegate.

Who could say what she would want when that was no longer the sum total of who she was? What would Alice Atlas want? *Whom* would she want?

She wandered the deck outside of the captain's quarters, her bare feet padding along the well-scrubbed floors while her night rail fluttered around her ankles. She enjoyed the utter silence, save for the sloshing of water and creaking of wood, and ran her fingers along the cool, beveled carvings in the railing. The stars were a blanket of light across the sky, with barely a sliver of a moon challenging their splendor. She tilted her head back and counted the Seven Sisters locked in their eternal hunt across the cosmos.

At least it was only one sibling she'd discovered. What on earth would she have done with seven?

She smiled to herself, remembering how she and Babette had pretended to be sisters as children, but in private, confessed to one another that they were happy to be their fathers' only child. It was the selfishness of children, for what little girl didn't want her father's attention all to herself?

Yes, they had decided. Pretend sisters were much better. They never fought.

She laughed, taking in a deep breath, filling her lungs with the happiness of that memory and the stillness of the present moment.

The breeze smelled the way one might imagine the scent of moonlight, clean and salty with mysterious notes of sweetness hidden beneath. Her hair was loose down her back, and the way it caught in the wind felt almost like the fingers of Poseidon, raking themselves through her tresses, wrapping curls around his fingers to rest wayward on her cheeks.

She closed her eyes, breathing in deeply, and that is how she knew when he appeared.

His scent had become as familiar to her as breathing, and it mingled so naturally with the moonlight smell that she thought its bouquet must have been lacking before. She didn't open her eyes right away, for fear that he might flee, and instead waited until she could sense the warmth of his body, resting against the sturdy railing of the ship next to her.

She smiled, a realization crashing over her like a warm ocean wave, and when she opened her eyes, she found him watching her, his face thoughtful and rapt. "You came every night," she realized. "You just couldn't bring yourself to knock on the door."

He returned her smile, a light shrug and a sigh confirming her suspicions, and leaned the warmth of his body into her side as he gazed up with her into the night sky. "Did you know," he said softly, "that if you travel far enough south, the stars change? Every constellation is different somewhere, tonight."

"Even the Northern Star?" she asked curiously, letting her eyes skim over the warm fur along the back of Ursa Major in search of it.

"Yes, even Polaris," he confirmed. He looked at her rather than the sky, shadows playing across their faces as the light from the *Harpy*'s lanterns swung to and fro. "Far from here, astronomers and cartographers and sailors and young children gazing at the sky have the Southern Cross instead. I have never seen it, of course, but there are drawings and maps in some of the books at Oxford. Imagine it. Six hundred years ago, a thousand, kings and bishops and Crusaders traveled far enough from home to see the very sky change. Many returned home and wrote that their pilgrimage did not change them so much as they expected. Can you fathom undergoing such a journey and feeling you came away unchanged?"

"No," she replied earnestly, turning her bright hazel eyes up to meet his own, which were veiled with the reflection of starlight in his spectacles. "I cannot."

"Even the moon is different past the invisible belt of the equator. It is still our moon, still blue and bright, but it waxes and wanes as a mirror image," he continued, twining his fingers around hers on the carved edge of the railing. "Yet, those men from a different time insist that the earth felt just as steady beneath their feet, no matter where on the planet they stood."

"Perhaps they never spent time at sea," Isabelle suggested with a nudge of her shoulder, her heart racing as she wrapped her fingers through his, leaning against the steady column of his body as the lazy drift of the night sea surrounded them. "Perhaps you cannot be reborn until there is no earth at all beneath your feet."

He smiled at her, a soft and affectionate smile that made her feel that safety that she had earlier associated with the endless horizon. He reached forward, brushing her hair from her brow, and spoke in a low voice, one meant only for her. "I have thought of it often in the last days. I have thought about those men and how it must take more than moving the heavens above them and the earth beneath them to change who they were. No one can take who you are away from you, Isabelle Monetier."

"Who am I, Peter Applegate?" she whispered back, uncertain of the answer herself.

He chuckled, shaking his head and grazing her cheek with the pad of his thumb. "I could no better summarize you than I can picture that other night sky. You are a woman who chose a little dog and named him for a giant. You fell in love with a pile of rocks in the forest, older than civilization itself. You saw them for what they meant instead of what they are and then shared that secret and all of its magic with a stranger. You can cook your own eggs and can weave flowers into crowns and kiss a man in such a way that he forgets everything but you and how much he wants you to kiss him again."

She forgot to breathe for a moment, her lips parting in surprise. "Peter ..." she began, though she hadn't the faintest idea what she should say in response.

"I am in love with you, Isabelle," he said, his voice still gentle, but his tone steadfast and strong, brokering no uncertainty on the matter. "I know the last thing you need right now is another complication thrown into your life, and I am not asking you to make any decisions or to return my love. I am telling you that I love you so that when we arrive in England, you will know there is someone standing behind you who will support your choices, no matter what they may be. And then, with your leave, and when it is more appropriate, I will ask you to consider marrying me."

She was frozen, but on fire at the same time. Words and feelings caught thick in her throat, refusing to emerge as coherent thought. Love? Did she love him too? Could she love him before really knowing who she was? Marriage? Marriage!

A month ago, Isabelle had truly considered living her life without a husband. Many women did and were perfectly happy. Her father was happy without a spouse. She would have never predicted a single proposal in the works, aimed in her direction, and here was a second one, this one far more tempting than the last.

"Why didn't you knock on my door?" she finally managed, through her breathlessness. "If you feel as you said you do, why not be with me?"

He hesitated, an amused look of surprise replacing his serious visage. "I tried," he confessed. "I raised my hand and made a fist and simply couldn't go farther than that. I'm afraid I've spent a lifetime being told of the consequences of compromising a maiden out of wedlock."

"I never said I was a maiden," she replied with a raise of her eyebrows. "Do you think you are the first man I've kissed in a moonlit forest?"

"I had not considered it," he replied, blinking in surprise, but sounding more embarrassed by his assumptions than horrified by the prospect of her impurity. "I can only hope that I was the most skilled of the forest men."

She grinned, shoving him playfully with the heel of her hand and then pulling him back towards her by his shirt. "You are the only one, you fool. I was just teasing. Come here."

He kissed her with the curve of a smile on his lips, sinking his fingers into her hair and tasting the desire on her lips without demand nor expectation. She knew she could stand here and kiss him all night and he would never push her for more, would never demand she return his love or answer his proposal. Peter Applegate was happy just so long as she continued to live and breathe, it seemed.

Was that love? Selflessness?

How, then, could she love him back when she wanted so very much from him? She would lock the two of them away together, alone, for days on weeks on months if she had the choice. She would hide from the world with Peter Applegate and never feel lacking. Isolation had never been so appealing before.

"What if," she whispered against his lips, her lashes fluttering as he stroked the base of her neck, his hands still tangled in her hair, "what if you did not have to knock, because the door was already open?"

He groaned, pressing his forehead into hers, balling his hand into a fist of her hair and gently urging her head back so that he might taste the column of her throat. "You are making it very difficult to behave honorably," he rasped, his voice a growling whisper that spoke to the secrets she desperately wished to uncover.

"What is more honorable than acting on love?" she whispered in return, nudging him backward in the direction of the captain's cabin. Her skin was alight with sensation, warmth radiating from the path of his lips on her throat. She pressed her cheek into his hair, breathing him in, reveling in the scent of sun and sea, of parchment and masculinity, all bound up in one moment of intoxication.

He did not resist her, following the steps she took towards the elevated door, without breaking from their kiss. Once they crossed the threshold into the cabin, he seemed to experience a snap of urgency, kicking the door shut behind them and lifting her into his arms for the remaining few footsteps to the bed.

He climbed onto the coverlet atop of her, the weight of him pressing her down into the mattress as his hands explored the sides of her body.

"This garment is barely anything at all," he muttered, breaking away from their kisses only to enjoy the sight of her sprawled beneath him in naught but a thin, white shift, which had gone nearly translucent in the contained candlelight.

She lay still while his hands traveled tentatively over the curves of her waist and hips, brushing the tops of her thighs while his breath hitched in his lungs. She instinctively knew that he would not touch her further without encouragement of some sort, whether it be pushing him past his breaking point or taking the reins herself.

She slid one of her hands over his, dragging his palm up the soft flesh of her belly, cupping it around her breast. Unbound and scantily covered, she knew there was little left to the imagination, garment or no. She sucked in her breath, arching her back as he slid his thumb over the sensitive peak of her nipple, teasing at it until it hardened for him, plastered in detail against the fabric of her shift.

It emboldened him, his kisses traveling farther down her body, following the path set by his hands. His kisses were feather soft over her chest, teasing and lingering over one breast and then the other. His elegant hands were as nimble and exacting in this as they were in his pursuits of restoration, just as expert and artistic. He was making a study of her body, she thought. He was mastering it.

It made her want to touch him as well, to explore him the same way. She traced her fingers over the lines of his shoulders, over the breadth of his back and the skin that revealed itself as she tugged on his shirt, delighting at the way his muscles flexed and his breath changed as her fingers met bare skin at the dimpled base of his hips.

He grumbled something, perhaps a curse, and returned to her mouth with a hard, almost reprimanding kiss before sitting back on his heels and pulling his shirt over his head. He took his spectacles off and folded them, tossing them onto the bedside table and running his hands through his dark hair with impatience.

He was almost certainly oblivious to the view he presented, finely muscled and ruffled as he was, his gray-blue eyes dark with desire and his body taut as a bowstring. He was like a storm cloud, gathering itself into a dark rumble before unleashing its passion on the earth below.

She could not resist reaching up and trailing her fingers over the flat planes of his stomach, watching with fascination as his body tensed and flexed beneath her touch, as though something beyond his intellect had taken control of all communication. She felt dizzy with the simple truth of it, this beautiful man towering over her, half dressed while she lay sprawled on a bed, hair loose and wild around her on the pillows.

She pushed herself backward, bracing against the headboard until she was on her knees, eye to eye with him, close enough to claim another kiss if she so desired. She leaned into it, allowing the pull between them to take its root, but she did not close the gap between them entirely.

Instead, she began to gather the hem of her night rail into her fists, her heart racing as his eyes dropped to watch, drawing in a sharp breath as he licked his lips in anticipation. She inched forward, her hips almost touching his, and drew the fabric up high enough to transfer it into his hands, their lips close enough to brush, if only barely.

She stroked the tops of his hands as he took hold of the gown, watching the intensity in his face as he began to lift it higher, over her bare thighs and the swell of her hips, over the forbidden crux of her desire, and the soft curve of her navel. She lifted her arms over her head, holding her breath as he exposed the rest of her, cool air caressing her ribs and breasts, her heart caught in her throat as the gown made its final departure from her form, spilling her hair back around her like Aphrodite emerging from the sea foam.

His jaw tightened, his body seeming to tense as he took her in, uncovered like this. He touched her with his eyes first, as though he wished to draw out the experience for as long as possible. Perhaps he truly was the embodiment of a storm, for Isabelle was certain she felt electricity snapping around her, running its fingers down her spine.

She did not wish to wait. She was not as patient as she thought she would be, and Peter was not as impatient as she had expected, having come to know him. She gripped him by the shoulders, urging him onto his back as she mirrored the attentions he had showered on her.

She tasted the column of his throat. She ran her hands over his chest and stomach, hesitating only a moment at the waistband of his trousers, a flash of nervousness rippling through her that she stamped down, burying it beneath desire. She touched the root of him first through the cloth, her breath coming quicker as the reality of his arousal pressed into her hand. She had known, in theory, what to expect, of course. But feeling the weight and size of it was another thing entirely.

She jerked at the ties holding his trousers together, impatience flaring through her body like great clouds of heat.

He intervened, she knew, though coherent thoughts were becoming less and less likely by the second. Somehow, without dislodging her from sitting astride him, he rid himself of the troublesome trousers, and pulled her down, skin to skin, to kiss her again, hot and demanding and overwhelming.

He gripped her bottom with one of his hands, urging her leg to wrap around his hip as he rotated them, side by side, facing one another. He locked his eyes on hers as he touched her, his fingers tracing the curve of her leg and dropping in tantalizing slowness to the place between her legs, surely hot as embers by now, and aching to be touched. He seemed to sense this, but made no move to rush to his intended task.

She had to bite down on her lip to keep from crying out when he touched her, his caresses firm and slick from her own desire. He was gentle, easing her into what it might mean to be touched there, to be penetrated. He eased his fingers inside her, keeping a keen watch on her face for any signs of discomfort or perhaps to simply enjoy the awestruck pleasure she was experiencing by his hand.

If she could have held his gaze through it all, she would have, but it was impossible. She was suspended in sensation, afloat within it, overwhelmed. Her eyes fluttered shut, her back arching as the storm clouds she pictured building in Peter cracked their thunder and fury over her, pushing her closer and closer to the brink of losing herself entirely.

She could hear her own voice, strained and gasping for air. She was aware that her hands were gripped around Peter's biceps, her fingertips digging into the firm muscle there, but it felt so far away. They did not feel like her hands nor her breaths. She was elsewhere, above herself, winding into a pure beam of white light.

When the sensation crested, it was as though that light she had envisioned burst, scattering all across the universe like the night sky above. Every inch of her shone and glittered, captured in a web of starlight.

He was kissing her, kissing her face, the corners of her lips, her nose, the crest of her ear. She held tight to him as he positioned his body against hers, pulled himself closer, until there was no longer any distinction between her body and his. She felt him enter her, felt the two of them meld into one being, and it was as though the most primal sensation of satisfaction was at war with the euphoric disconnection of what she had just experienced.

She clung to him, reveling in all that was new, drowning in the sounds of his own pleasure, and the knowledge that she was the one providing it. She wound herself around him, allowing him to dictate the pace and fervor of their joining, rocking herself against the rhythm he created.

When he climaxed, he did so with a sound of such blissful relief, dragging her mouth back to his and pumping his hips into hers with the most indulgent final strokes, each one lingering in its perfection.

They held onto one another with the same abandon, the same closeness, for some time afterward, while they chased after their breath together.

He had showered her face with kisses again, vanishing only momentarily to fetch her a glass of water and to draw the blankets up over her body. She was already dozing, already being pulled towards the most perfect oblivion, but she sipped her water, and held his wrist when he made to gather his things.

"Stay," she said softly, and felt his body go slack with agreement and perhaps also relief.

He gave a nod of assent and crawled into the bed with her, sharing a sip of water from her glass. When she extinguished the flame in her lantern, she found herself pulled backward, into the curve of his body.

She thought, in some last flicker of sentience as her mind launched itself towards dreams, that he told her that he loved her, one more time.

CHAPTER 17

*P*eter kept expecting panic. He waited patiently for that voice to arrive and demand *Oh God, what have I done?* Logically, he knew he should be agonizing over his choices, but he could not seem to bring himself to feel any regret. Nor could he stop himself from returning to her bed every night for the remainder of their journey.

It was the first and only time in his life that he slept gradually and woke with light and sound, feeling refreshed rather than beaten by the brute force of his own slumber. She still rose first, of course, conditioned by a lifetime on a farm, but she woke him by brushing his hair from his face and curling her warm body into his, speaking softly until he began to rouse.

She would tell him of her dreams. He would awaken to descriptions of sugar-spun villages or Goliath the size of a bear, and though he could never remember his own dreams in such detail, he would share the nonsensical snippets that came to mind, if only to make her smile.

If Mathias had caught wise, he did not deign to mention it. Perhaps he considered the conversation they had shared in Aix about this very prospect the extent of his obligation to participate.

They had begun to train together after breakfast, stripping down to their breeches under the blazing hot summer sun as they ran drills and exchanged techniques that had obviously originated from very different philosophies of combat. Isabelle would sometimes watch, but more frequently retreated into the cargo hold to spend time with the dog and donkey or pester the sailing crew for more information about the operation of a sea vessel.

Peter thought they tolerated her curiosity a fair sight better than they might have if she weren't a pretty girl with an infectious charm. He had never seen any of them smile on the trip south, but as they neared England, he'd caught them whistling to themselves, speaking without prompting, and handing their precious lines over to Isabelle so that she might practice her knots.

He had never in his life been happier. Even the niggling dread of this enchanted time coming soon to an end could not deter him or cast a shadow.

In the late afternoon, the three of them lingered over their suppers, often drawn into friendly debate or a game of cards or dice. Occasionally, another tale of Robin Hood would be prompted and Peter would oblige, talking as the sun set about highwaymen and princes and good and evil.

Once the Channel appeared and they began to navigate their way into it, there was a quiet solemnity that settled over the ship. It wasn't sad, necessarily, but being flanked by

France on one side and England on the other was a reminder that they had been disconnected from the real world, and all of the complications and associations that came with it.

He found Isabelle more frequently at the railing, facing the glimmer of white in the distance where Dover awaited them. She had no interest in discussing what was to come in these final hours, and much preferred the escapism they found with one another instead, be it in physical embrace or long, meandering conversation.

Almost as though the universe understood the emotions on board, as they neared the coves at the base of the cliffs of Dover, their cloudless summer sky began to darken, and a mist of rain began to fall. The *Harpy* glistened with its coat of fine rain as Mathias took on his captain's mantle and began to direct them to the cove beneath Meridian House, a secret place that must be approached with caution.

Isabelle kept her back to Calais, its shore visible throughout their approach. Perhaps she did not wish to face the view of a place where her life had diverted. Perhaps she did not wish to think of her parents, whose bodies rested somewhere beneath the waves. She clutched at her locket, unable to escape them completely, and held her shoulders back and her head high as they floated into their final destination, and at long last, the *Harpy* met dry land.

∼

Unloading the boat was significantly more complicated than they had anticipated, planning instead to dock in London on a Thames cargo dock.

The smugglers' cave that had been the foundation stone beneath the Silver Leaf Society had unfortunately undergone two solid decades of abandonment and neglect. Reclaiming Meridian House with the return of Nathaniel Atlas to his ancestral home had opened the dock for use again, but the Atlases had put the majority of their efforts into restoring the manor itself, rather than the illicit operation that once existed underground.

When Peter had arrived at Meridian in the spring to begin planning this venture, he had spent a great deal of time poking around in the cove. The Dempierres had already begun transporting out some of the salvageable wealth, which had been lost beneath the earth for twenty years. Its resurgence gave the Silver Leaf financial resources that it had not enjoyed for some time, sparking a new flurry of assignments that would liberate a great many people from both sides of a never-ending war.

Nell had told him in her letters that many things had been disposed of by necessity due to rot and erosion, particularly a cache of extremely fine French textiles. The sadness in her words over such waste had been palpable, for Nell had always treasured beautiful things.

In any event, wandering around a secret cavern filled with curiosities had been a fair sight less awkward than haunting his sister's empty house while awaiting departure. He only hoped that popping up out of the lawn without any warning or expectation would not cause any unnecessary complications.

Isabelle's expression was unreadable, for she had thrown herself into assisting in the mooring of the boat and the undocking process with the competence of a seasoned sailor. She did not struggle to carry crates onto the dock, nor to respond to brusquely shouted orders over the increasing howl of the rain.

Mathias instructed the crew to stay put until they had a determined plan of exit, and ushered them into the mouth of the cave, where, mercifully, dry torches and tinder were stacked and waiting. They walked through the cool stone corridors in silence, with only the drip of water and their footsteps joining the sound of the crackle of torch flame.

Mathias inhaled deeply enough for the three of them when they reached the antechamber, with a ladder propped up against the wall, which would lead them up and into the unknown. He lodged the torch into a slot on the wall and turned to Isabelle with a wry smile and an encouraging extension of his hand. "Come along," he said, helping her onto the first rung. "Mind your head and just press upward when you reach the hatch."

Isabelle frowned, glancing over her shoulder. "Are you certain one of you shouldn't go first?"

"Ladies first, always," Mathias replied with a wink. "You had better start adjusting to all sorts of nonsense rules. Welcome to England."

"Ladies first," she repeated in a mutter, beginning her ascent.

"But we are right behind you," Peter added quickly, his heart beginning to pound as he watched her climb, suspended in the air again, with no earth under her feet. "We'll be right behind you all the way."

Mathias clapped him on the shoulder in silent agreement and then gave him a little shove to follow.

From above, gusts of misty rain and shafts of gray-white sunlight hinted at the end of their journey. Peter climbed, resolute and determined not to feel discouraged by this turn in the road. He set his jaw, reminding himself that he was here for Isabelle, no matter what happened or how she decided her life would continue from here. He would champion her choices, even if it meant losing her.

The hatch above flapped open with little more than a tap of polite askance from Isabelle, flooding the three of them with stark daylight and the arrival of the future they had been anticipating. It arrived without elegance or decorum, the three of them muddy and sprawled on the Meridian House green, catching their breath before whatever would come next.

CHAPTER 18

It wasn't how Isabelle would have chosen to present herself, given an option.

They had taken a moment, lying in the grass under the mist of rain, near a half-constructed gazebo, before Mathias took the lead in rising to his feet. He helped both of them up from their positions around the hatch door and turned his face up to the rain with a heavy sigh.

"Guess that's it, then?" he said, sounding like he almost didn't believe it. "We should head up to the house."

"House" was not the word Isabelle would have used for the imposing manor on the hill. It loomed in front of them like a mythical beast awaiting its prey, and every step towards it she took felt shakier than the one before. Perhaps it did not look so sinister when the sky was clear and blue, or perhaps she was seeing things, as anyone under a great deal of emotional stress might be prone to do.

When they reached the front door, Isabelle froze in place,

refusing to be the one who rang the bell. Her teeth had begun to chatter, and she was certain that at any moment her heart would exert itself one beat too far and stop dead. It was almost a disappointment that she kept living through every agonizing second.

A butler answered the door, immediately aghast at their dirty and disheveled appearance. It was lucky that he recognized Peter, though his exclamation of "Mr. Applegate!" did sound rather reproachful. He ushered the three of them into a large, warm antechamber and bustled off, leaving them alone.

"Now where's he gone to?" Isabelle demanded, flabbergasted by the entire affair.

"Likely to find some chambermaids and usher us off to bathtubs," Mathias said cheerfully. "I don't think anyone is here other than the staff."

"Shouldn't be," Peter said, though he was squinting around the wings of the room, suspicious that no one had appeared yet. "Unless they've returned from London early?"

The click of heels on the stairs above them drew their attention, the three of them turning in tandem like dirt-smeared urchins, jumpy at passersby. Down the stairs walked the most beautiful woman Isabelle had ever seen in her entire life. Slender as a willow, with a crown of ice-gold curls and perfect alabaster skin, she floated towards them with an expression of curiosity on her pretty face.

"Peter!" she cried, upon coming close enough to recognize him, and she vaulted herself forward, crossing the antechamber to throw her arms around Peter Applegate.

Was this his sister? Could this possibly be Nell, whom he had described as shy and bookish? It didn't seem possible.

"Glory?" he replied in muffled surprise. "What on earth?!"

Isabelle's rapidly beating heart stopped cold, a resounding thump echoing off her ribs. This was *not* his sister. This was some other impossibly beautiful woman currently cradled in Peter Applegate's arms with the intimate familiarity of a lover.

"Nell was ordered to bed rest, but you were so late returning that Nathaniel was afraid to leave London." Her voice was breathy with emotion, and she pulled back, holding him by the shoulders and fixing him with a stern expression. "Of course, I offered to come stay with her until he could leave. Where have you been? We expected you weeks ago!"

"Nell's here?" he replied dumbly.

"She's resting, and I will not have you disturbing her. Poor thing struggles to sleep at all since she's gotten so humongous. Hello," she added, looking behind Peter at the other two people in the room. She dropped her grip of his shoulders and put on a dazzling, pearl-white smile. "I am Lady Gloriana Somers, a childhood friend of Nell's and a new recruit to the Silver Leaf Society. You must be Miss Monetier, and I posit that *you* are Lord Mathias Dempierre, yes?"

"*Lord?*" Isabelle echoed incredulously, turning narrowed eyes onto Mathias.

"It is a matter of some debate," Mathias replied with a shrug. "I am pleased to make your acquaintance, Lady Somers. Did my sister return to Dover with Mrs. Atlas?"

"She did not," Lady Somers replied with a tilt of her head. "She is rather enjoying London, from what I saw, and is staying with Zelda Smith for the remainder of the Season."

Mathias laughed outright at that. "Oh, I'm sure my mother is simply thrilled with that development!"

"Miss Monetier, you must be exhausted!" Gloriana said, floating over to Isabelle's side and taking her arm. "I am most curious about your journey here and all the adventures you must have had along the way."

"Glory?" came a sleepy voice from the top of the stairs, drawing the group once again 'round in curiosity.

"Nell, darling, Peter's come home!" Gloriana announced, rushing back up the stairs to assist her friend in her descent.

From the banister, a very petite woman with an impressively round, pregnant belly appeared, wrapped in a dark blue dressing gown. *This* was obviously Peter's sister. She had his coloring, with dark brown hair piled on top of her head in a messy bun and a pair of spectacles perched on her upturned nose over gray-blue eyes. She was clearly moving faster than her friend thought appropriate, for she kept tsk-tsking under her breath as Nell made her way down the stairs.

"Oh, Peter, we were so worried!" she breathed, rushing forward to take his face in her hands. "Mathias, what kept you? Why have you come here instead of London? And where is ..." She drifted off, her eyes finding Isabelle where she had backed into a shadow, only a small ways away from the others.

Nell locked eyes with her, her lips parted in surprise, and

she took a step forward, holding out one of her slender hands. "Alice?"

"Isabelle," both Mathias and Peter corrected, their voices overlapping in perfect time.

"Yes, of course. Isabelle," Nell corrected, ducking her head apologetically. "I cannot believe you are here!"

"Neither can I," Isabelle replied, giving a shaky laugh and extending her hand to shake the other woman's. "I have heard much about you, Nell Applegate. It is a pleasure to see you in the flesh. I only wish I were a bit more presentable for the occasion."

"Oh," Nell replied, her dark brows coming together as she glanced over her shoulder at her brother, seemingly just now realizing how dirty they were. "What in the world? Did you come up through the cove? In the rain?"

"We did," Mathias confirmed. "We thought you'd have had news of our delay by now, or hasn't Pauline Olivier been in touch?"

Nell shook her head, genuine confusion on her face. "The Olivier woman who lives in Marseille?" she asked.

"Not anymore," Peter replied. "She stole our passage papers. We assumed she'd have docked in London by now and made contact with the Silver Leaf network."

"We've had no contact," Nell said on a whisper. "Glory?"

"No, nothing to my knowledge either," the beautiful woman replied with a lift of her platinum brows. "What has happened?"

The three travelers exchanged glances, a silent roll of the dice on who would have to recount their misadventure in Marseille, which Peter evidently lost, for he was the one who spoke.

"Might we send some men down to the harbor to unload our things first?" he asked, taking his sister's hand. "We should like to be clean and dry before we tell the tale, and someone ought to head out to fetch Nathaniel as well, wouldn't you say?"

"Yes," Nell replied, blinking as though surprised by her own thoughtlessness. "Oh, yes. I am sorry. Please, follow me."

She turned and led them towards the staircase, ringing a bell that hung from the wall over the archway as she went. "We are still outfitting our guest suites, but we will see you all washed and fed before I demand aught else. Mathias, shall I send a man to *La Falaise* to alert them of your return?"

"No, please do not," he replied with a lopsided grin. "I'll see my mother when I'm good and ready."

Isabelle followed in silence, her eyes large and full of wonder as she took in the columns and embellishments of this house. Mathias would see his mother when he was good and ready, she thought, reaching for the locket around her neck. Was her own mother watching, from somewhere beyond the veil?

Did Mary Atlas know that her daughter had returned to Meridian House?

Had baby Alice finally come home?

Isabelle had been told not to hurry, that food and conversation would wait until she was washed and dried and felt human again. Still, she could not make herself linger in the tub, and pulling on dry, albeit wrinkled clothes was an absolute relief. She had washed the dirt and sand from her hair and braided the wet tresses over her shoulder, hoping that this was acceptably presentable by the standards of these two ladies, who were finer dressed and mannered than anyone Isabelle had ever had occasion to meet.

Her hands shook as she buttoned her blouse, and she shivered as she pushed herself from the washroom into the grand halls of the house again. It was so dark as evening set in, with only the rooms in use fully lit, and the halls illuminated with only sparse flames from lanterns that dotted the walls.

She felt plain and stocky, with no stays to wear under her garments or fine materials to add to her allure. She wondered if she looked like a silly farm girl to those women, with broad, plain features and unfashionable clothes. She regretted her wet hair now, as she made her way back to the staircase.

"Snooping around?" came Mathias Dempierre's voice, soft and amused from the shadows to her right. He chuckled at her startled hiccup.

"No, not yet," she replied with more bravado than she felt. "Was I supposed to wait for someone to come fetch me?"

"Probably so," he said with a grin, and offered her his arm. "Let's go down to the sitting room and wait for the others, shall we? Poor Nell looks like an autumn pumpkin. I feel terrible for rousing her."

"She is lovely," Isabelle replied quietly. "They both are."

Mathias nodded in agreement, seemingly oblivious to any implication that Isabelle was not their equal. It warmed her a little, put some more confidence in her steps as they rounded a corner and made their way into a wood-paneled room. He turned up the flame in the lantern next to the door, spilling golden light over the space within.

Isabelle stood frozen, her gaze caught by the very large family portrait hanging above the fireplace, its oil finish glinting against the candlelight.

"Ah," Mathias said with a click of his tongue. "I should have warned you about that. Apologies."

She waved her hand, unable to form the words to either admonish or forgive him just now. In fact, it was as though Mathias himself had slipped away, leaving her alone in a space where there was nothing but herself and this portrait.

Peter had been right: she did resemble her mother. The woman in the painting was holding an infant, still in swaddling, her face turned down affectionately to admire her baby.

Me.

She had Isabelle's jaw and her nose. Her hair was lighter, a warm mahogany color, and her lips were rounder, less punctuated into a cupid's bow.

Her eyes slid over to the husband, a tall man with auburn hair, whose hand rested on the shoulder of a young and very serious little boy. She saw herself here too. There were the lips she saw in the mirror, and the eyes. He was almost smiling, an unusual expression for an adult man in such a portrait, to be sure. He seemed happy, she thought. Welcoming.

The little boy was ramrod straight, gripping a military medal in his hands. *This must be Nathaniel*, she thought, taking a mindless step forward. Eyes like her own gazed back at her from this little boy, captured in time, gazing out at a future he never could have predicted.

She wanted to touch him, her hand reaching out, though of course she was not tall enough to reach the painting from the floor. She couldn't help it, standing there with an arm slightly extended, fascinated with the renderings of these people she'd only imagined right here, in front of her.

"Are you all right?" Mathias asked finally, a note of genuine uncertainty in his voice.

When she turned around, tears glistening in her eyes, he flinched, as though he was seeing the result of his own blundering. "I am truly sorry," he said again. "I was not thinking."

She shook her head, sniffing on the strangest urge to laugh as she dashed the tears from her eyes with a finger. "Do not be sorry," she told him. "Nothing can prepare someone for all of this."

"Perhaps a painting first, and then the real thing is easier, hm?" Mathias suggested, gesturing to the couch so they might sit together. "Nate isn't nearly so serious in person," he assured her. "He's good with people. Charming. You will like him."

"Hopefully the feeling is mutual," she said, still nursing a few residual hiccups of emotion, dabbing at her eyes impatiently. "Oh, goodness, get yourself together, Isabelle."

Mathias gave a light chuckle, reaching out to squeeze her hand. "I'm already at capacity worrying about Applegate. Don't make me worry about you, too, now. You're the strong one."

"What?" she said, shaking her head in surprise. "What's to worry about with Peter?"

Mathias held her gaze, his mouth a flat line that brought his dimples into relief. It was such an exasperated, deadpan look that Isabelle couldn't help but blush. Had they truly been so obvious?

"Men like Peter have dalliances all the time!" she said defensively. "I'm sure *you* have had a great many. Why should you be concerned for him and not me?"

"Peter isn't like us," Mathias replied softly. "You have so much ahead of you, so much to manage, that maybe you can't see it. The poor sod is completely drowned in his infatuation and he will never recover from it, no matter what you do next. I warned him not to do this. He doesn't listen."

"You *warned* him?" she repeated, narrowing her eyes. "Against me?"

"Yes!" Mathias said, dropping her hand and throwing his own in the air. "I should have asked you before we ever boarded the *Harpy* what your intentions were with him. He has a tender heart, Isabelle, and he does not deserve to have it broken."

She opened her mouth, but could not formulate a reply, only able to release a stilted sound of affront at this accusation.

She shook her head, sucking in a deep breath through her nose, and pointed her finger at Mathias. "How dare you imply I'd do such a thing!" she snapped. "I have never given you cause to think me cruel or uncaring."

"You've never given me cause to think you are serious about your little flirtation either," he quipped, raising his chin in defiance. "You have clearly been enjoying yourself, but if life took the two of you in different directions, you would survive the heartbreak, and we both know it. I'm not sure he will."

She locked her jaw, leaning towards him and hissing, "I would never harm Peter. Never! I love him!"

She cut herself off, having surprised herself just as much as Mathias. There was a punctuated beat of quiet between them, both frozen in shock.

She swallowed her silence, dropping her hands into her lap, and looked at Mathias with her eyes wide and blinking. "I love him," she said again, in genuine awe.

"Oh, thank God," Mathias said with a sigh, looking as though the weight of the world had just rolled off his shoulders. "Thank God for that. Have you told him?"

"No, I—" She stopped, snapping her mouth shut as voices approached in the hallway. She tossed Mathias a look and he motioned that his lips were firmly closed on the matter as they awaited their hosts and all the questions that would follow.

Her own questions, both those she had for the world and the ones she had just realized she needed to ask herself, would have to wait.

CHAPTER 19

That first night without her was harder than he could have anticipated.

Peter spent the hours twisted in his sheets, wishing he knew which door she was behind so he could just go to her. He had never seen her looking so lost and afraid as she had tonight in the drawing room. She had avoided his gaze the whole night, her voice sounding hollow rather than certain as he was accustomed. She had looked pale and small, swallowed by the alien trappings of the room around her.

He persuaded Nell to retrieve Goliath from the stables and have him brought to her room tonight, so that she might have some familiar comfort in this strange new place that asked so much of her. Goliath would stand vigil over Isabelle, even if Peter could not.

Evidently the donkey had protested very vocally at having her companion taken away. Peter silently empathized with Hortensia's distress. He wanted his companion back too.

By the time he woke, there was already a cold bath in his

room and a cold plate of breakfast next to his bed. He sighed, knowing Nell would have much to say on that matter when he made his way downstairs. He used the cold bathwater but decided he would rather wait until the next meal than attempt to stomach the congealed remains of what was likely a tasty offering, several hours ago.

He took his time getting dressed, hoping to appear somewhat more together today than he had in the wake of their arrival. His hair was due for a trimming, but combed back neatly enough, and he always felt better after a fresh shave. He polished the frames of his spectacles and made sure the glass was free of smudges. He chose a waistcoat from the trunk that was one of his nicer pieces of clothing—something he hadn't brought to France for fear of losing or damaging it.

Judging from the position of the sun, it was still early afternoon, and perhaps in this instance, he had earned his lie-in, on account of the journey he'd just undergone.

Meridian House seemed brighter with Nell here. The staff seemed more alive, the rooms felt warmer, even the light seemed brighter than it had for the weeks Peter had stayed here alone prior to his journey. He supposed he had been a lackluster guest as well, with only the occasional visit from the Coopers and Dempierres to keep him company.

The thought of being so isolated seemed strange to him now. Unbearable, even. And that was how he had spent the bulk of his adulthood, wasn't it? He would have said with complete confidence, only a mere month ago, that he preferred his own company to that of others, and here he was, brightening noticeably at the sound of voices at the base of the stairs, heaving a sigh of relief at the appearance of other humans, reminding him that he was not alone.

"There you are!" Nell had cried, rising from her perch on the drawing room sofa with a half-knitted blanket in her lap. "I was about to fetch a bowl of water like Mama used to if you didn't rise soon!"

"Please never do that," he said solemnly, kissing her cheek and motioning that she should leverage her very pregnant self back onto the cushions. "Sleep is a sacred thing."

Nell scoffed, picking her knitting back up, a soft lilac blanket, small enough for a newborn. Like everything else Nell did, the blanket was crafted with exacting perfection. "Do you want me to ring for some food? You've missed luncheon too."

"Food would be lovely, yes," he said with a sigh of relief. "Where is everyone else?"

"Gloriana took Isabelle and their dogs on a walk of the grounds after we ate. Lord Mathias has gone to see his mother and find out if she has heard anything from the Oliviers. I sent word to the Cooper House, and Susan will be joining us at dinner. I am hoping that Kit returns from London with Nathaniel."

"Glory has a dog?" Peter asked with a grin, attempting to picture it. "Now that is unexpected."

Nell's lips twisted into a conspiratorial smile, and she leaned forward so that she would not speak too loudly. "Wait until you see him!" she said with a laugh. "He is the most awkward little thing, still gangly and adolescent, and a mutt to boot! Still, she dotes over him, all the same."

"I stopped expecting predictable behavior from her after what happened at Somerton," Peter replied with a chuckle of his own. "Though I imagine ownership of a mutt was more her husband's idea than hers."

"Evidently not," she insisted, amusement glinting in her eyes. "Sheldon Bywater's big hound dog had a ... well, an unplanned litter earlier this year, and Glory volunteered to be the first to take one of the puppies. Alex had no choice but to agree. From what I understand, the entire Somers clan now has Echo's puppies in their stead."

"We never had pets," Peter said wistfully. "Though we had plenty of tiny siblings to fill that void, I suppose."

"You have a donkey now, don't you?" Nell held up a finger before he could reply, pausing their conversation to wave over a servant to fetch them something to eat and drink. She did this with the natural comfort of someone who has always had servants to call upon, rather than a girl who had mended her own clothes not half a year ago.

The way she leveraged her body with its strange and large burden was fascinating to watch. She had always been such a tiny thing, and right now she seemed to have doubled in size. This baby might well be a giant for all the mass it had added to his sister.

"You are staring," she chided, though her reproach was not harsh. "Would you like to feel the baby?"

"Feel it?" he asked, dumbstruck, but she was already leaning forward, reaching for his hand.

"Mm, just here. You can feel the child move."

She pressed his hand into her stomach, significantly more

firmly than Peter ever would have attempted on his own. He opened his mouth to ask what to feel for but she shushed him, a grin growing on her face as the life within her moved, unmistakable and shockingly strong.

It felt as though the baby had rolled completely over, its little limbs beating against the confines of its mother's body. The strength of it, the proof of real and solid life, took him by so much surprise that it hurt his chest, filling him with an emotion he could not quite name.

There was a child inside Nell. A child that was half his sister. Where he had felt mere curiosity before, there was a sudden wave of endearment. He had just met new family, small and hidden as it may have been.

"Oh Peter," she whispered, dropping her grip on his hand and reaching up to touch his cheek.

It wasn't until her fingers wiped the wetness from his cheeks that he realized he had shed tears.

"Oh," he sniffed, embarrassed, and leaned back so that he might clear his face of emotion. "I am sorry, Nell. I don't know what came over me."

But it was too late. She was teary-eyed now, too, pressing her lips together so that she would not lose herself to her feelings. She reached out and gripped his hand, squeezing it hard, and for a moment, they just sat together, like they had always done, when words were not necessary to understand one another.

"I have missed you so much," he finally said, his voice thinner than it ought to have been and the urge to spill more tears hovering dangerously close to the surface. "I have wondered if I lost you when you married. I have even envied this child, I think, in the back of my mind. Before, we only belonged to each other. Life was simpler as children."

She made a little sound, like he had struck some blow, somewhere in her heart. "Peter, you will *never* lose me," she said, gripping his hand as though she would never let it go again. "Never. I have a husband, and soon I will have a child, but you are my brother. You are my *twin*. Nothing can ever replace that. Nothing can ever change it."

He nodded, wrapping his other hand around the one he held, managing a sheepish smile amidst his trembling emotions. "Likewise," he said softly. "I know that now. I knew it, I mean. I have realized recently that many people may enter one's heart, because it expands to allow the extra room rather than expelling those already in residence. My heart grew in France and I thought it already near to bursting, but just now, feeling that kick, I think it perhaps doubled in size."

She blinked at him, her eyes wide with surprise. "Peter," she said softly, "are you in love?"

"God help me," he replied with a little laugh. "I absolutely am."

"Sir Francis, you must slow down!" Gloriana Somers called to her puppy, a long-legged hound mix that had scrambled off the side of their path and into a patch of soggy grass. "Honestly, he is impossible," she complained, shooting a jealous look at the way Goliath trotted obediently by Isabelle's feet.

"My dog is only behaving this way because he has a new audience," Isabelle assured the other woman. "He has a reputation back home for diving off into the wilds for days at a time and only coming home when he gets hungry."

"I will believe you, even if you are only protecting my feelings," Gloriana sniffed, indulging in a properly childish pout as they turned the corner on the path that would lead them back to Meridian House. "Perhaps Sir Francis will grow into good behavior. His mother is *much* better behaved!" She said the last bit louder than necessary, as though the admonishment would reach the dog's ears and cow him into obedience.

It made Isabelle laugh. She liked this woman more than she would have expected at first sight. Her delicate beauty and impeccable manners had framed Gloriana as exactly the type of frosty English miss that she'd always heard about on the other side of the war—rigid and emotionless and oh so very boring.

That wasn't the case at all. Both Nell and Glory had been delightfully warm and fun-loving during this first day on English soil. They had not pelted her overmuch with personal questions nor demanded she change into more suitable clothes or prepare for the arrival of her brother. Rather, they had asked her about her journey and her home, while openly sharing stories of their own lives, commiserating over the impatience of long trips and indulging in nostalgic idealization of the places where they had grown up, including the boarding school where they had become such good friends.

Isabelle was even impressed by Gloriana's stamina, and the speed and distance she was able to cover in her frothy and restricting clothes without becoming short of breath or requiring a rest. The hills were not steep, but they were plentiful along the trail they'd taken. This woman might spend her life in balls and drawing rooms, but she was clearly no layabout.

"It is a beautiful house, isn't it?" Glory said with a happy sigh, watching the manor come into sight over the hill. "I could never have managed what Nell has done with it. It's only one of the many reasons I am certain that things concluded as they were always meant to. She has brought out a side to Nathaniel I have never seen before."

"What has she done with it?" Isabelle asked curiously.

"Oh, she has renovated it," Glory said, widening her pale blue eyes. "If I had ended up marrying Nathaniel and he'd attempted to dump me off in an empty house that hadn't been dusted in twenty years, you can bet your last shilling I'd have lost my mind. Look at it now, though. It is a home."

"Wait a moment," Isabelle said, stopping and holding up her hands. She gaped at the other woman in abject disbelief, staring at this stunning creature, glowing like a calla lily against the summer grass. "*You* are the woman he was going to marry? He ran off on *you*?"

"He wasn't the first to do so either," she replied with mischief in her smile. "You should not judge your brother too harshly. In both incidents, I was relieved at the departure of my prospective bridegroom. In the case of Nathaniel, I was already deeply in love with the man I did marry when Nell and Nathaniel made their escape together."

"Still! Surely it was a deep betrayal, and yet you're here not even a year later, with Nell, as though nothing happened?"

"It was for the best," the other woman said with a shrug and a toss of her platinum curls. "Nell and I reconciled almost immediately, and I insisted that Alex and Nathaniel learn to tolerate one another. I was not going to lose her. It is not often that you find true friends in life. You must do all you can to retain them. Trust me on that."

"I only have one friend like that," Isabelle confessed, thinking of Babette and that last day that they'd picnicked on the floor of her bedroom. She could see her friend's laughing face, her dark curls brightened with shafts of sunlight from the high window above. "I would likely forgive her anything too."

"Only one?" Glory scoffed, shaking her head. "The boys who brought you here clearly dote on you as well. Or perhaps one of them is more than a friend?"

Isabelle hesitated, color rushing to her cheeks before she could think to turn her face away.

"Ah, delightful," Glory said, clapping her hands together. "Lord Mathias is very dashing."

"Mathias?" Isabelle choked, torn between amusement and horror. "Good Lord, no."

"Oh." The other woman stopped walking, turning to study Isabelle with a sudden keen interest. "Not Mathias. You must pardon the assumption. I'm afraid I rather have a predisposition to a certain type of man. Are you saying that you've grown ... erm, *fond,* of Peter instead?"

"I haven't said anything of the sort," Isabelle protested, though she was certain the panic in her voice gave her away completely. She rushed to speak more, to distract from this accidental revelation, "But you are right. They have both been true friends. We were like Robin Hood's merry men, working together all the way from the mountains to the sea to this place, on the other side of the world."

Gloriana was looking at her oddly, somewhere between amused and sympathetic, her head tilted to the side. "Isabelle, my dear," she began carefully, "I promise I will not speak a word of this to anyone. However, you should know, you will never meet a better man than Peter Applegate. There is no one kinder, gentler, nor more sincere. I have never met any man quite as brilliant and dedicated and filled with curiosity about the world. I have known him since I was only a girl, and I will attest on my honor to the goodness of his soul."

Isabelle did not have the opportunity to answer, for as quickly as Lady Gloriana Somers had taken on this air of concern, she seemed to snap back into the cheerful new friend that had stood in her place some moments before.

"Let us hurry back to the house," she said brightly. "I should like to change before dinner."

CHAPTER 20

*D*inner at Meridian House that night had felt to Peter very much like a rehearsal for what was to come.

So far, Isabelle had only been confronted by those whom the law and the bonds of friendship might deem as "family." First, there was Nell, of course, who was always kind and gracious, but had never known the parents Isabelle had lost.

When Susan Cooper stepped into the dining room that night, she had frozen so suddenly that one foot was still raised in the air, preparing to step in front of the other. Her eyes had fallen immediately to Isabelle, her hands coming up to cover her mouth. "Good gracious," she said several times. "Good gracious."

Nell had interceded, pushing herself awkwardly to stand and hurrying over to take Mrs. Cooper's hand and lead her to a chair. "Isabelle," she said as gently as she could, "this is Susan Cooper. She is your aunt by marriage to Archibald Cooper, your mother's brother."

Isabelle, for her part, looked just as transfixed at this other woman, this aunt who had just entered her life. "And is he coming as well?" she finally managed, turning questioning eyes to Nell.

"My Archie passed away some years ago," Susan explained, though her voice was shaky with emotion. "Oh, he would have fainted dead away at the sight of you, my dear. You are the very spit of Mary. I held you as a baby, you know."

"I didn't know," Isabelle had replied with a warm smile. "But I am very happy to learn of it now."

Dinner had progressed from that point with the usual questions. Isabelle talked about Yves and the valley, about her pets and her home and the journey to come here, while Susan told stories of Walter and Mary Atlas, occasionally including the antics of her husband, when they fit into the humor of a story. Peter knew that his life had been a tragedy, and thought it kind that Susan avoided his end while sharing his life.

"We have a son," she told Isabelle, "your cousin, Christopher. We call him Kit."

"Nell has told me," Isabelle replied, excitement giving itself away as she learned more and more. "He sounds a shrewd and determined man, and a devoted son. I would love to see his orchards when he returns from the city."

Peter had felt a tinge of envy there. He should have told her about Kit, at least the little he knew of the man from the time they had spent planning her retrieval. He wished to be the source of every smile he could, he thought, though of course he could not begrudge the happiness of those around the table, nor would he, ever.

"Your necklace," Susan had said, as dessert was cleared away and cups of coffee poured. "I have seen that stone before."

Isabelle brushed the polished lapis around her neck with a shy smile. "It was hers," she explained. "My mother's."

"No, I ..." Susan stared at it, seeming to drift off for a moment. "I have seen the other half of the stone," she realized, her eyes brightening. "It is embedded in a small keepsake box, one of the few things we managed to take from the house when it was abandoned. It was a gift that Archie made for Mary, a wedding gift. He was a talented woodworker, you know. I will bring it to you, if you wish?"

"Is it locked?" Peter found himself asking, and immediately regretting as all of the women at the table turned to look at him in synchronized curiosity.

Susan blinked at him, and gave a slow nod. "As a matter of fact, it is," she said. "Though I'm sure we can find a way to get it open."

"I have the key," Isabelle said, wonder in her voice as she gripped the pendant at her throat, her eyes darting to Peter, who shared her secret knowledge of said key. "I would love to discover what is inside."

"Of course, of course," Susan said, nodding. "I have an assortment of the Atlas family's things that I ought to return anyway, now that Meridian is alive again. Eleanor, would it be an imposition? I can wait if you'd rather."

"No, bring as much as you are able, please," Nell said immediately. "Nathaniel will be eager to explore these things as well, I'm sure."

"What could be in the box, do you think?" Isabelle said aloud, her eyes dreamy and unfocused.

"Jewelry perhaps?" suggested Gloriana.

"A journal," guessed Nell.

"Perhaps mementos of her children," Susan suggested.

Peter wondered what he would lock away in a box, if given the opportunity. He wondered if he had erred to not keep a journal, especially of the adventure he had just had. What mementos of that story could fit into a box? Not his sword, of course, nor his servant's garb. Hortensia was far too large, and his volumes of Robin Hood far too rare and priceless, back at the university.

And of course there was Isabelle, he thought, looking at her through the firelight as she smiled and laughed and asked questions that, finally, someone could answer.

He did not need a journal, he thought, nor a chest of treasures to remind him of what had been. He would only ever need Isabelle herself. Only her.

And he would be content for the rest of his days.

∼

When his bedroom door clicked open in the night, he knew without moving that she had found her way back to him. He did not move, just in case it was a dream. If it was a dream, he could not risk it ending.

She crawled into the bed with him, silent as a cat, and sighed, staring up at the ceiling and reaching for his hand.

Her grip was warm and soft, her fingers twining their way through his. She spoke in a whisper, reminding him of how forbidden this moment truly was.

"Let me tell you what I dreamed," she began, the same words she spoke to him every morning on the *Harpy*. "I dreamed that I opened the box, alone, next to the sea. Inside were these ... these papers." She stopped, her voice gone thick for a moment.

"Papers?" he prompted, matching the tone of her secretive whisper.

"Papers proving that I was not the true child of the Atlases either," she continued. "And then I ran to tell you and found you at the altar on the Meridian lawn. You were getting married to Gloriana."

Peter was quiet for a moment, uncertain how to react. He settled on responding factually first. "Gloriana is already married," he reminded her.

"Yes, I know that," she responded impatiently. "And I know she loves you as a brother. Dreams are not always rational, are they, Peter Applegate? Or perhaps yours are."

"I rarely remember mine," Peter admitted. "Though this moment, right now, could easily be one."

"It isn't."

He sighed, rubbing his thumb along the back of her hand where it was clasped with his. "You know they are your parents, as well. Even if you didn't look so much like them, it is irrefutable."

She nodded, the movement subtle in the dark, accompanied

only by the sound of her hair moving on the pillow. "I did not expect all of this to be so ... so easy, Peter. I did not think they would all be so warm and happy to see me. I do not know what I was preparing for, but it was not this reception we've received."

Peter's brow furrowed, and he rolled onto his side to face her, making out what he could of her profile in the night. "Why would you think otherwise?"

She shrugged, seemingly unable to answer, but did not let go of his hand.

"You are worried that Nathaniel will be the difficult one?" he guessed, running his free hand over the softness of her arm, hoping he could reassure her. "I promise you, he will be easiest of all."

"Because he was trained to charm," Isabelle recited, remembering the stories of her politician brother and his many talents. "How will I know what is real?"

Peter pondered this, pulling her closer to him and allowing her to sink into the warmth of his body, to borrow his strength where he could lend it. "Your cousin Charles is also a politician of sorts," he said. "He must put on a certain visage to navigate court and the military, yes?"

"Yes." She nodded. "But he is not like that with us. You saw how he changed that morning, when he thought you were a messenger from Paris, and then realized you were not."

"Nathaniel is only a person, just like Charles," Peter said, though privately he had never seen Nathaniel appear vulnerable in any way. "Talk to Nell if you are uncertain.

She wears all of her true feelings on her sleeve. You never have to doubt if she is telling you true."

"Just like you," she said, her voice giving away a tiny smile alongside the smallest nudge of her elbow. "You must be happy to see her."

"Yes," Peter said immediately. "I missed her very, very much."

It was hard not to press her with questions about the two of them, about what it meant that she had come to his room when they were in a house full of people, servants and hosts alike, who might catch them. It was hard not to tell her that he had told his sister how he felt. Perhaps he should not have done that, but he had never kept anything from Nell. Never.

"I like her," Isabelle told him. "I like everyone. I didn't expect that either."

"I had not realized you were such a pessimist," he teased, hoping that another little smile would tug at the corners of her lips. Unable to resist the lure of at least one small confession, he said with a deeper voice, "I wish you could stay here until morning."

She shivered, burrowing herself closer to him, the warmth of her body and its sweet scent providing a muddling elixir of temptation. "Me too," she said. "Though I am not sure I will ever sleep well in such a large house."

He nodded, thinking of his little loft in Oxford. "I visited a grand manor last year and stayed for several weeks. The entire time, I kept thinking of the cottages in the nearby township and how much I'd prefer them to a room in that massive cavern of a house."

"What is Oxford like?" she asked, lifting herself up to rest on his chest, her hair falling in a curtain around them. "Do you spend all of your days lost in study?"

"Sometimes. Those are the best days," he confessed. "The city itself is a jewel, with historical sites and beautiful buildings no matter where you turn. I used to wander it in the winter, when no one was outside, and stare up at spires and walls mortared with centuries of stories to tell."

She sighed, as though the dreamy appeal of doing such a thing would have captured her too. He wished they were in Oxford now, so that he might take her hand and lead her onto the streets, taking her to every place that ever sparked his imagination.

"I am surprised that you are not stuck at the university at all times. Mathias made it sound like something bordering slavery."

He shook his head, chuckling at the dramatics of their friend. "I have been kicked off the campus more frequently than held to it. Libraries close; rooms need to be locked, and so on. The university is a fair sight more conducive to a day of study than a poorly lit room in a boarding house."

"I should like to see it," she said.

"I would love to show it to you," he replied with feeling. "Lately, my time cannot be completely consumed by manuscripts and manifestos. At this point in my study, I am also expected to teach the greener students, and so I am relegated to that twice a week in return for assistance with room and board. This arrangement often serves as a bridge, should I wish to dedicate my career to educating."

"Is that what you want?" she asked. "To teach?"

"Maybe. It has its appeals." He sighed, having asked himself this same question many, many times. "It is hard to say what one wants to do with his entire life."

She giggled at that, shaking her head so that her hair brushed his chest. "I know that is true better than most, wouldn't you say? I think that few decisions are forever, and vocation is certainly one of the more flexible aspects of your identity, no?"

"I suppose you're right."

"Of course I am. What do you teach, Professor?" she teased, and though it was playful, something about her calling him that stirred his blood.

He stroked her hair and pulled her down for a light kiss, pleased to make out the curve of a smile on her face in the dark. "Historical context," he answered, "basics of restoration and preservation, and an assortment of other foundational concepts. I enjoy it more than I thought I would, so long as the students are the sort who wish to hear what I'm saying."

"Am I a good student?" she asked sweetly, tracing her fingers over his chest.

The question jolted through him in a surge of desire, conjuring memories of their nights on the *Harpy* and her eagerness to learn. "Very good," he said, strain in his voice.

"You are such a surprise to me, Peter Applegate. I have

always imagined students in pubs, planning revolutions and seducing unsuspecting maidens," she said.

"Pubs sometimes," he confessed wryly. "Maidens, rarely."

"I have always suspected," she said, "that you have had many lovers before me."

He could not suppress a laugh, pressing his lips together in an attempt to stifle the amusement, lest she think him a cad. "Why on God's earth would you think that?"

"Because," she said, her own voice darker than it had been before, "you are very adept at pleasure."

He took a breath, attempting to swallow down the arousal rising in him at such a statement. "I am pleased to know you think so," he managed, wondering if he ought to scoot away before she felt just how pleased he was.

"You use your hands, your fingers." She sighed, rolling onto her back and stretching like a cat, arching her back as she remembered their time together. "Your lips and tongue ..." she continued, her voice gone ragged.

"Is that what you want?" he asked her, whispering close to her ear, nudging his nose into her hair and nipping at the soft lobe so close to his teeth. His hands were already moving, already seeking out the part in her thighs, craving the warmth and slickness of her sweet body and the way it reacted to his touch. "Do you want me to put my mouth on you again?"

She moaned, as softly as she could, spreading her legs so that he might touch her however he wished; might plunge his fingers into her and drag her to climax, just as a girl might deserve for crawling into a man's bed in the night.

"I want the rest of you," she murmured, her hips already moving against his fingers, begging him for things she could not put into words. "I want to taste you too."

"Ah, Christ," he muttered, pressing his arousal into the softness of her thigh. "You shouldn't say things like that."

"Why not?" she asked, her words scraping against the pleasure he was giving her, the distraction of the way he explored her most private area, the way he touched her knowing what would drive her past the peak. "It is what I want," she insisted, her hand coming down to take hold of him the way he had done to her. "Why shouldn't I want that?"

"You are a good girl," he reminded her, though he could not resist thrusting his hips as she had done, giving in to the dizzying want of the moment. "Good girls do not do things like that."

"Then I am not so good," she whispered, stroking the length of him with a confident and knee-weakening perfection to her grip. "Do good girls do what I am doing right now, Peter?"

He did not know how to answer that. In fact, his ability to speak at all was becoming rapidly compromised.

"You can tell me I am naughty," she said to him, sliding herself off the attentions of his fingers in order to push herself to her knees. She tugged the blankets down around him, revealing just how hard she'd made him with her touch. "Wicked, wanton, debauched."

"Libertine?" he suggested, his voice husky as she stripped

him of his clothes, running her warm hands over his bare thighs, her fingertips over his aching cock.

"Libertine, yes," she replied, dropping herself down to do as she had promised, dragging soft, lingering kisses along the length of his shaft, confidence seemingly building as she made her way higher. Her tongue emerged, and when he cursed, drawing in a sharp breath of shock, she seemed to take this as a sign that licking him was an effective means of pleasure.

The lapping of her tongue would kill him for certain, he thought. The way she gripped the very base of him while she tasted something so forbidden would drive him mad. The way she took as much of him as she could into her sweet mouth would render him incapable of speech, ever again.

"You are delicious," she told him. "Perfect."

"Isabelle," he choked.

"Mm, hush," she said, dragging her night rail over her head, just as she'd done that first time, at sea. This time, she did not let him take control, did not rely upon him to decide what pace they went.

She lingered over her curiosity, ensuring he was thoroughly tasted and slick enough to slide into her at a moment's notice. She climbed astride him, a pose he had only ever imagined, and used her hand to guide him into her, a careful but indulgent stroke to the hilt, where she pressed her legs wide to accommodate every inch of him.

She leaned forward, bracing her hands against his chest and rotating her hips, throwing her hair back and arching her back as she tested different motions, different sensations within her that she might enjoy from this position of power. He was, of course, powerless to stop her, mesmerized by the vision of her astride him like some warrior queen.

He couldn't resist reaching up to touch her, to stroke the movement of her breasts, to take hold of her hips and guide her in a rocking motion that made them both forget to breathe. He knew he could not stand this for much longer, but damned if he didn't wish it would go on forever.

"Keep doing that," she told him, bearing down as he guided her hips. "Yes, just like that. Oh, Peter."

It was his name in her mouth that drove him to the brink, his fingers digging into the soft flesh of her waist, his hips speeding of their own accord, driving into her as his mind scattered and buzzed, his body aflame with the impossible pleasure of it.

She very nearly cried out, bringing her fist to her mouth in an effort to stifle the roar of her climax. Her hips stayed on rhythm the way he wanted, the way he craved. He drove into her wildly until he exploded, a dam of desire bursting into primal satisfaction. He dragged her down to claim her mouth with his own as he continued to pump his seed into her, stifling his own pleasure with her lips and their sweetness.

He held her still, unable to stop kissing her, even after he was spent. By the time he released her, it was only because he could no longer breathe, no longer think. From the gauze-thin breathlessness of her own gasping for air, it seemed she felt the same.

He did not know when he caught his breath, for he seemed

to slip into slumber before it ever happened. He slept in peace, with her by his side.

He did not wake when she climbed out of bed and slipped out of the room, but he knew, even in sleep, when she was gone.

CHAPTER 21

Isabelle had spent the entire day avoiding Peter.

It hadn't been difficult, for he was not a man to impose when unwanted, and likely only thought she wished time to reflect on all of the mementos that were brought to the house that day by Susan Cooper.

Aunt Susan? No, it didn't feel right just yet.

Mrs. Cooper had arrived at breakfast and had her man deposit two trunks full of things in the Meridian House ballroom, where Nell and Isabelle were invited to go through them at their leisure. When she joined them at the table, she did so with the dark wooden box, embedded with the other half of the dark blue stone that made up Isabelle's pendant. It was smaller than the one in her dream, only about the span of two hands wide, and far less ornate.

This had been crafted by a man with sensible aesthetics and a talent for shaping wood.

Uncle Archie.

Yes, that one felt more natural, if only because she'd never have to use it.

It was indeed locked tight, and when she held it, she could feel Peter's eyes on her, curious, questioning, and above all concerned. She would reassure him if she knew how. Instead, she had quickly excused herself and gone to the bedroom they'd given her, where she had sat cross-legged on the bed for nearly an hour, staring down at the box that matched her necklace.

She had not opened it. She thought perhaps she should wait for the brother she'd never known. She thought perhaps that if she did wait, that doing this together might endear her to him. And she thought that if she did open the box, she would not be able to resist running to Peter to tell him what she'd found inside.

She simply wasn't ready to speak to him. Not just yet.

She wanted to get all of the words right in her mind before she attempted to say them. Should she lead with apology or affection? Proposal or penance? Whatever she was going to say, she needed to figure it out, before something half cooked and damning came out of her mouth at some inopportune moment and ruined her chances at a happy life forever.

He'd ridden off to Dover with Mathias to see to a few errands in the afternoon, managing to catch her eye once and give her a knowing smile, his eyes scraping over the body he had so thoroughly enjoyed just hours ago. He'd donned his hat and swept out the door, oblivious to the way he'd temporarily crippled her. That smile had made her toes curl. In fact, for most of the morning, she had been able to think of little else but the previous evening and how easy it had been to slip into his bed unseen.

She couldn't quite put words to the problem she was having. She had told him back on the *Harpy* that she had to meet all of these people, to see this place, to discover who she was before she could love him back, before she could commit to a life with him. But here she was, three nights in England, with her mother's secret lockbox mere steps away, and she was no more certain of how this had changed her than she had been on that fateful morning back in her childhood home, when she'd stared in the mirror and wondered who was looking back at her.

She had gone for a long walk with Goliath and Hortensia once he'd left, and when she returned, she had asked if she might retire early, and eat dinner in her room—a request the sweet and mild Nell would never deny. She had been hiding in that room ever since, waiting until the sky was dark and sleep would take her.

Like most other things, sleep did not come willingly when demanded, and Isabelle found herself instead staring out at nothingness as the hours ticked past, uncertain if she wished to sneak through the manor again tonight or continue to hide until morning.

She had managed to evade him all day, trying to decide what to say, but tonight she wanted to do anything but talk. She wanted the escape again, the comfort and simplicity of being with him. It was selfish, a pure and simple need that she could not take again without giving something of herself in return.

The truth of the matter was that it was not simple anymore. Perhaps it never had been.

She sighed and threw her legs over the side of the bed. If she could not go to Peter, perhaps she could go down to the ballroom and look at the things in the trunks again. She and Nell had curiously picked through some of it, though most of the things she'd found had seemed to be more items of value, protected from a decaying home, than sentimental relics, hiding insight into her parents' lives.

Nell, of course, was just as ignorant as she of what these things might have meant, and they had decided that waiting for Nathaniel would likely be the more sensible course of action.

Nathaniel. He was more than just an idea now. Everyone around her knew him, had spoken to and spent time with him, had formed opinions of his spirit, with only Isabelle left to imagine who and what he might be.

For years afterward, she would wonder if her thoughts that night somehow summoned her brother home faster than he might otherwise have traveled. She would wonder if perhaps the sheer strength of her desire had altered the flow of time, and brought him to her.

She pulled a dressing gown around her night rail and tied it at her waist, rubbing her arms for warmth. She stepped out into the hall, prepared to snap herself out of this silly fugue, only to end up halting dead in her tracks at the unmistakable sound of an arriving presence.

Servants spoke in hushed tones, of course, but she could hear the door open and close several times and the authoritative ring of a man's voice as he answered questions and asked after his wife.

She quickly extinguished her candle, stepping backward into the recess of the wall so that she would not be spotted as servants bustled past. She did not know why she was hiding, but it was too late to reveal herself now without looking ridiculous. Besides, it gave her a chance to eavesdrop before making herself known.

She could only see his shadow from here, impossibly tall and jumping from wall to wall as lanterns were lit and his arrival attended to. She could hear his boots on the polished floor and the flap of his coat as he removed it. So engrossed in these details was Isabelle that she nearly leapt out of her skin as Nell passed her by, one hand supporting her swollen belly and the other reaching for the banister so that she might descend as quickly as possible to greet her husband.

"Nathaniel?" she called, somewhere between a shout and a whisper. "Nathaniel, is that you?"

"Hello, my dear," he said, his shadow swallowing little Eleanor as she reached the bottom of the staircase. Isabelle leaned forward, and saw him lean down to kiss her in greeting, though his features were obscured from the distance and lack of light. "I rode as fast as I could."

"Is Kit with you? Have you even slept?" She paused, evidently reading an answer in his face. "Nathaniel, it is dangerous to ride without sleeping!"

He chuckled, pulling her into a warm embrace and clicking his tongue. "Kit is following with our things. It will take him a day or two. I gave firm instructions at Marylebone that your aunt should be alerted to the *Harpy*'s return no sooner than three days from now. I can only deal with one thing at a time."

"Probably wise. Mathias has kept Therese away as well, while we've waited for you."

There was a pause, though Isabelle was unsure if they were simply speaking too low for her to hear. Then, Nathaniel's voice cut into the air once again, asking plaintively, "Where is she?"

"Asleep," Nell said. "And I will not wake her. Poor dear was feeling ill and has had a tumult of a month, as you know. It can wait until morning."

"Can it?" he asked, the frown evident in his voice. "Ambushing her at breakfast hardly seems the thing to do."

"We will talk about it in the morning," Nell replied firmly. "You need to sleep, and so does she. You can save all the questions you have for Isabelle herself."

"Isabelle," he repeated, a certain nervousness in his tone. "Not Alice. Must remember that."

"Yes," Nell agreed. "You must. Now see to whatever you must and come to bed, all right? I'll be waiting."

"I won't be long," he promised her, and she turned to walk back up the stairs again.

It happened so quickly that Isabelle forgot to slip back into the shadows, meaning her sister-in-law saw her at the head of the stairs as soon as she had ascended a few steps. Both women froze, with Nell's gray eyes meeting Isabelle's, wide and curious.

Caught, there was no reason to flee. Indeed, Isabelle couldn't seem to move at all.

Nell paused for only a moment, an expression of understanding blossoming on her face, and continued to climb until she had reached the landing. "He is right, you know," she said to her. "Breakfast would be a far less personal time to meet. If you are feeling better, perhaps you might go greet him now."

Isabelle tried to swallow, her throat suddenly dry. She scrambled for something to say, but found Nell's lantern pushed into her hands and the other woman floating away before she so much as had time to truly wrap her thoughts around this suggestion.

If Nell had strong opinions on what Isabelle should do, she was not going to push them, nor was she going to stay and spy on private conversation as Isabelle had just done to her.

It seemed, as Peter said, that the only path worth taking was the one that went forward.

She squared her shoulders and approached the staircase, taking the steps one at a time, so that her legs would not shake as she went. When she reached the bottom, she sank onto the bottom steps and used them as a seat. She was unable to force herself to go any further. That was how he found her when he returned to the antechamber, seated on the stairs with a lantern at her feet and her hair wild around her shoulders.

She was able to observe him first, coming back in from the outside and brushing the mist of a late-evening rain from his hair. He was handsome, she thought, tall and elegant. He had been riding for a day straight, but somehow still looked as though he were ready to greet polite company, even as he stamped the mud off his boots. His hair was the same mahogany brown she'd seen in the portrait in the drawing room, and she imagined that when she got close enough, she would see that his eyes were a little bit darker than her own.

She was frozen in place, waiting for him to see her, waiting for his reaction.

He turned his eyes up to where she sat, clearly thinking at first that she was Nell, judging from the smile on his face. The smile fell away as fast as it had appeared, his eyes locking onto hers and his posture stilling, as though he had to remind himself to keep breathing for a moment.

They simply looked at one another for a moment, finding the familiar in one another's faces.

It was Isabelle, pushing herself unsteadily to her feet, that broke the spell, spurring Nate into action. She opened her mouth, intending to perhaps extend a hand for him to shake or to introduce herself by name, but he crossed the room in three wide steps and wrapped his arms around her in an embrace so primal that it precluded any need to speak, and so ferocious it could only be sincere.

She held him tentatively at first, but the reality of who this was and what he meant hit her hard enough that she might otherwise have been knocked to the ground. She gripped him back, her breath suddenly locking in her throat. She squeezed her eyes shut and held him as hard as she could. She listened to the sound of his breathing and felt the beating of his heart, and found herself quite at a loss to stop the flood of emotion that spilled out of her.

He cupped his hand over the back of her head, holding her

cheek to his chest, and she gripped him 'round the middle, certain that she could only remain standing because she was holding onto him.

She wasn't quite weeping, but she trembled, and tears were spilling from her eyes. He pulled her back and held her face, smiling so widely at her through the mist of his own tears, and he said, "My sister. My baby sister."

She nodded, reaching forward to touch his face too, her hands trembling and her voice still caught beneath the riptide of feeling that had overtaken her. When she finally could make a sound, it was something like laughter, wondrous, incredulous laughter, and they embraced once more.

"Isabelle," he said, once they had finally caught their breath. "My name is Nathaniel."

∼

They rang for tea and sat in the drawing room, beneath the portrait of their parents. It did not matter that it was closer to sunrise than sunset and that neither had slept, nor did it matter that their first attempts at conversation were uncertain and awkward, more often fading into embarrassed laughter than coherent thought.

After all, where does one even begin after a lifetime apart?

"You traveled well? I trust Mathias and Peter saw to your needs."

She had given a delicate cough at that, and averted her eyes. "Yes, they were very attentive," she said, snatching a biscuit from the tray to avoid having to elaborate further. After she'd chewed and swallowed, she met his eye and said with an apologetic smile, "It was an unexpected journey, in many ways."

From there, they volunteered information, rather than requesting it. Nathaniel talked of his education and his career, while Isabelle recounted key moments from her own life, with a heavy emphasis on how good a father she'd had, despite it all.

"Is that our mother's necklace?" he suddenly asked, after over an hour of conversation. He was seemingly awestruck to have noticed it around her neck, his teacup halfway to his lips.

She raised her hand to touch it, realizing she had forgotten to remove it during her long night of confinement in the bedroom. "Yes," she said softly. "My father ... my French father kept it for me."

"I had forgotten it existed until this very moment," he said, clearly amazed with the spark in his memory. "I have forgotten so much."

"Less than I have, I'd wager," she said with a weak smile and an apologetic shrug at his look of mortification.

She strung the chain through her fingers and pulled the clasp around to the front to unhook it, allowing the necklace to pool in her hand. She held it out to her brother, transferring it into his hand, and asked, "Do you know what is inside the locket?"

He nodded, memories piecing together behind the hazel shadows of his eyes as he opened his palm and looked down at the blue stone. "A key," he said in a voice full of wonder, "to a little wooden box. She would never tell me what was inside."

"It is upstairs," she said, her heart racing. "It is in my bedroom. I was waiting for your return to open it. Your ... our aunt Susan has kept it all this time. Shall I fetch it?"

He seemed speechless, managing only a faint nod, which was all she needed. She flew up the stairs and back down again, the box clasped in her hands, and set it on the coffee table between them, staring down at it like it might burst into flame at any given moment. Nathaniel looked at it much the same way.

"I'll do it," she said, holding her hand out to take the necklace back, which he had already unfolded into its key shape. She held it firmly between her thumb and forefinger and slid it into the little keyhole, which likely needed a good oiling after so many years of neglect. All the same, the mechanism turned easily, the top of the box giving a slight jump of freedom when the latch gave way.

She held her breath, pushing the lid back as both she and her brother leaned in over the top of the box. Inside were a stack of letters tied with a thin, pink ribbon, and a little paper envelope with the scribble of an address on it. She reached for the envelope, while Nate took the stack of letters, slipping the topmost one from the ribbon and unfolding it carefully near the lantern at his side.

"Dearest Mary," he read, "it has been nearly a year since you brought our daughter into the world, and almost ten since you had our son. I could never have predicted in those days that my love for you could be any stronger. It did not seem possible. It still does not seem possible, and yet, I find my affections stronger with the rising of every new sun."

"Love letters," Isabelle said with wonder, tipping the envelope over into the palm of her hand, where a ring slipped out along with a written receipt. She held the ring out to her brother, puzzling over a receipt for far less than the ring could have possibly been worth.

"That's my father's," Nathaniel said immediately. "Our father's. He was always denting it doing one thing or another, and mother was always having it repaired for him. She'd say 'take it off while you're working, Walter,' and he'd scoff and say he only took it off when he absolutely had to."

He chuckled, turning it over in his hand. "I had forgotten about that too. He used to pester Uncle Archie to teach him woodworking and he was absolutely hopeless at it."

"There are two trunks' worth of items that are like to spark all manner of memories in you," Isabelle told him. "It seems Mrs. Cooper has been keeping many things safe over the years, and yesterday she finally returned them to this house."

He frowned, handing the ring back to her and glancing over his shoulder at the portrait. "Yes, I know," he said with a sigh. "I should have asked her what she'd kept when I returned to Meridian House last year, but I was afraid of having those memories stirred up. I was afraid of the pain."

Isabelle nodded, understanding all too well what it meant to be afraid of facing the past. "It must have been horrible for you, being orphaned so young."

"I never thought of myself as an orphan," he said earnestly. "I had my aunt and uncle and I had Kit. I also had Uncle Archie's ravings and conspiracies about what had happened to my family, and with those I drowned my sorrow with anger and plans for revenge. What a spectacular waste of my youth."

"What did you think happened to them?"

He set the letter back on top of the pile and rubbed his eyes, shaking his head in distress at his own mistakes. "You must first understand that Archie was not well, and that I ought to have known better, if not as a lad, then certainly as a man. It is only that there was just enough truth in his delusions to make me believe him, even when no one else did."

"If he told you it was murder, then he was not lying," Isabelle said softly. "It was."

"He misled me as to who was responsible for the murders, and why," Nathaniel explained. "I spent my life trying to discover and infiltrate the Silver Leaf Society, believing they had executed my parents and infant sister as punishment for treasonous work against the Crown. If I had stayed here, lived my life in Kent, I imagine I would not have been kept in the dark for nearly so long."

"We were both misled," she said, "but neither of our lives were wasted, Nathaniel. Look at all you've become. You will be a father very soon."

At that, his face split into a smile, hinging somewhere between bashfulness and pride. "Isn't that something?" he said, and truly seemed to believe it.

"How did you know that you wanted to spend your life with Nell?" Isabelle asked, tilting her head curiously as she eyed the letters between her parents. "How does anyone know for sure?"

"We had been married for some time, when I realized," he confessed. "We were headed to a dinner party and she was wrapped in spectacular finery, the most beautiful thing I'd ever seen, and just before we were to leave, she bent over and put her spectacles on so that she could check a list of tasks she'd written out for her maid." He laughed, taking a deep and wistful breath. "Something about that particular moment just broke the glass around my heart, I suppose. I can still see it so clearly."

"You married her before you loved her?" Isabelle asked, incredulous. "Instead of that angelic creature staying upstairs?"

"Ah, yes, that," he said, a sheepish blush rising on his cheek. "Miss Blakely ... that is Lady Somers and I had a businesslike courtship. Gloriana is beautiful, yes, but she is ... well, she is not Nell," he said carefully. "Things ended well for all of us in avoiding that marriage. It would have been cold and professional, structured for politics and social climbing, which is what we both thought we wanted at the time. She and I were lucky to be taught differently, and somehow we both found something more valuable in our spouses. For that, I am keenly grateful."

She looked down at the ring in her hand, its hammered metal catching the light in all the spots where a smith's hammer had repaired little dents. "I only ever seem to hear about her," Isabelle said, closing her fingers around the ring and nodding towards Mary's visage on the portrait above them. "I wish to hear of him too."

Nathaniel nodded, his expression tender. "Why don't we read some more of his letters?" he suggested. "Let him speak to you in his own voice."

"Yes," she decided, noting the sheen of pink that had begun to tint the windows, beneath their linen curtains. It was no matter. "Yes, please. Will you read them to me, Nathaniel?"

And he did.

CHAPTER 22

By the night of Isabelle Monetier's debut party, the guest of honor began to make some decisions. She could hardly have avoided it with the hubbub that had been sprouting around them in the last week, particularly the arrival of so many spectators.

Peter had watched most of her evolution from the wings of Meridian House, unwilling to interrupt this metamorphosis, no matter how badly he missed her company. He had watched her build a burgeoning bond with her brother and seen the way Nathaniel doted upon her, disbelief still occasionally shining in his eyes. She had met her cousin with far more certainty in her eyes than she'd had before, and from there the others had come.

Mathias brought his mother and sister, the latter of whom was just as blonde and dimpled as he. Zelda arrived from London with her customary commanding presence, but to Peter's surprise, she had restrained herself from attempting to take charge of the gathered few, allowing Isabelle to ask her questions and spend time with her at her own discretion.

Nell and Peter had not been so lucky, of course. Aunt Zelda was constantly checking Nell's belly and fussing over her food, lest she was occupied in correcting Peter's form during his morning drills and advising him of the best people to charm en route to a tenure when he returned to Oxford.

In a way, it was comforting, to have something of familiar life back after the journey he had taken. Hearing his aunt and Lady Dempierre snipe at one another over tea had been its own brand of amusing as well. He had never met another person who could spar with her so skillfully.

There was still no word of Pauline and Gerard Olivier, and they could only hope that their silence was better than the arrival of tragic news. The remaining Silver Leaf members insisted that she would crop up eventually, and that all would be well. Perhaps because it was comforting, Peter chose to believe this too.

Isabelle had decided that she would keep her existing name and identity. For those who knew the family, there was no need to keep her origins a secret, but it had been far too long since she had been Alice Atlas, and she had decided, at last, that it was too late to move backwards now. She had also decided that she wished to stay in England for the time being, so long as she could write to her father back home.

The party was, of course, Gloriana's idea. Though she had already returned to London to join her husband in his diplomatic duties, she had managed a fair few logistics prior to departing. Key amongst them was accompanying Isabelle to a particular modiste in Dover proper, a French exile, who could create designs that suited Isabelle and her transition into a new and alien world.

The event was held in Meridian House, in the large ballroom where Nell kept her harp. Though she was too round to play herself, she had employed skilled musicians to entertain their modest gathering, as those who had known Mary and Walter had an opportunity to meet their long-lost daughter.

Isabelle, of course, was resplendent. She was dressed in white and blue, a gown that revealed her shoulders; sunkissed, strong, and delicate, centered with her mother's lapis pendant. It was not the simple fashion favored by ladies of the *ton*, but rather its own being, constructed for one particular woman, to make her shine.

She was not a socialite and did not flit about the ballroom, mingling with everyone, champagne in hand. Rather she stood near her brother (and sometimes Kit or Mathias) and used their knowledge of the surroundings to guide her speech and manner. It was endearing to watch, if not a bit disorienting to see her thus.

He had decided he could wait forever. He could wait a month or a year or a decade, and he would happily do so if the chance of being with her, whether it be a single stolen moment or a home in the countryside. It seemed he had learned patience, at last.

"Why are you hiding over here?" came a voice from his shoulder, startling him out of what was likely overt staring.

He turned to find Mathias, leaning against the wall with his customary glass of white wine held loosely in his hand.

"I am not hiding," Peter replied indignantly. "If I wished to hide, I'd duck behind a curtain."

"Fair enough," the other man chuckled, drawing a begrudging smile out of Peter as well. "She keeps looking for you, you know, and you are never there anymore. Did something happen?"

Peter shook his head, uncertain how he could even begin to answer that question. Many things had happened. "I did not want to burden her, when she is already so overwhelmed," he said instead. "She knows I am here if she needs me."

"Does she know that?" Mathias asked with a raise of his eyebrows, his eyes darting beyond Peter to a look of evident further surprise. "It appears she does," he allowed. "The lady doth approach."

Peter felt his stomach drop, though he turned with reasonable elegance to smile at Isabelle's approach, her frothy skirts swinging around her legs.

"How are my merry men?" she asked, grinning as she approached the table. "I have missed our games of dice and story-filled dinners very much."

"Perhaps we might make them a tradition," Mathias said with a wink, taking her hand and kissing it. "If your brother would allow something so scandalous."

"Ha," she smirked, raising her glass to her lips. "If my father could not contain me, what makes you think a brother can? Nathaniel is well aware that I am a woman of her own mind. He does not seem disturbed by it."

"Well, he hasn't seen it in practice," Peter pointed out, giving her a sidelong look, full of meaning.

"Mm, that is true," she agreed, tilting her head in thought. "Come, will you walk with me in the garden, Peter Applegate? I wish to clear my head."

"Not me?" Mathias asked cheerfully.

"Not tonight," Isabelle told him with a playful laugh. "Peter?"

He cleared his throat, not wishing to give away the flutter of anxiety in his chest, and nodded, holding his elbow out for her to take. He told his heart to settle, though her scent wound around him and muddled his thoughts straightaway. They did not speak as they walked out onto the lawn, the moon full and heavy in the sky, and the sound of waves crashing in the distance mingling with the music from inside.

The Meridian gardens were still burgeoning, newly planted only a handful of months prior, but all the same, there were fragrant blooms and flickering torches along the gravel pathways. The gazebo was not yet finished, but for a moonlit stroll, the ambiance was ideal.

"I have missed you," she said, once they were far enough from the door to speak privately. She still spoke in a hushed voice, with hurried words, as though some interloper might hop out of the hedges at any given moment. "There are far too many people milling about Meridian for me to visit you at night. And far too many people watching for me to speak openly in the day. I did not want to speak until I could speak honestly, and I am sorry if I caused you distress."

He pressed his lips together, stifling the urge to smile like an idiot. It would not do to erupt in relieved and joyous dance just now. "Oh? I was not certain you had room in your thoughts for diversions."

"Peter, I frequently *only* have thoughts of your particular diversions," she said seriously, coming to a halt and tugging at his arm so that he would turn to face her. "It is what I wished to talk to you about."

She held his gaze for a moment before dropping his arm and clasping her hands together, fidgeting as she looked for the words. "I want to stay in England," she said. "For now."

"Yes, I know," he replied with an encouraging smile. "I was very happy to hear it."

She huffed, turning her head and bouncing on her heels. "I will want to visit France sometimes, and maybe even stay for months or a year. I'd love to sail again."

"That is reasonable." He was beginning to feel fidgety himself, suspecting that he was not properly reading this conversation, especially as she gave a short, frustrated sigh. "Isabelle, I am behind you, no matter what you do."

"I don't want you behind me, Peter," she snapped, her lovely hazel eyes snapping up to meet his, "I want you *beside* me."

"Beside you?" he repeated, dumbfounded. "I will stand wherever you want me to stand, Isabelle."

She gave a little laugh, shaking her hands loose and stepping away so that she might pace. The pacing seemed to calm her, giving her time to fish something out of the little beaded bag that hung on her skirt.

When she found what she was looking for, she swung around to face him again. Firmly, she reached out, grasped his hand, and turned it over by the wrist so that it opened for her. She pressed an item into his palm, hard and cool, and took a shaky, steadying breath.

He held still, allowing her to calm herself, to ground her body with his hand clasped between hers. It seemed they both felt the electric anxiety that was abundant in the garden this evening.

After a few deep breaths, she nodded, turning her eyes up to meet his, and ready to speak.

"It was my father's," she said quietly, lifting her hands away, revealing a small metal circle that she'd put into the palm of his hand. "My English father's, I mean. It was his wedding band."

He stared at it, momentarily lost for words. He tentatively picked it up, turning it around in his fingers, watching the torchlight bounce off its polished sheen.

"I had it fitted against Mathias's signet ring," she continued, her words coming faster and more agitated, her hands wringing and her eyes averted. "That ring fit you, you see. I saw that it fit you when you put it on that day in the cargo hold and inspected the crest. So, I knew the size of your finger and wanted to ensure it would fit."

"You want it to fit me?" he asked, though he was not certain if he was speaking to Isabelle or marveling at the wonder of it.

"It is an imperfect ring, Peter, one that has been dented and repaired many times. It isn't solid gold or encrusted with jewels, but it originated in a union of patience and passion ... of two people who championed one another. I thought it a poignant representation of what it is to love someone."

"Being damaged and repaired?" Peter asked curiously, ducking his head to catch her eye, so that she would turn and meet his gaze again. Was she confessing her love to him?

She nodded, looking relieved. "Yes! Yes. Resilience. Don't you see? No matter what happens, it can be fixed. It can always be fixed."

"Isabelle," he said softly, unable to stop himself from a short chuckle at her distress. "I am not certain I am following this correctly. Are you ... are you proposing to me?"

She blinked at him, disbelief and frustration so evident in her face that his chuckle evolved into a full-blown laugh. It got him a good shove to the shoulder, which he knew he deserved, and he used the opportunity to wrap his arms around her and pull her close, pressing a sweet kiss into her temple.

She huffed, turning her chin up to give him a halfhearted look of reproach.

"I was accepting *your* proposal," she protested. "From the boat!"

"I never proposed," he told her. "And you got me a ring."

"You said you were going to propose," she argued. "That is the same thing."

"Is it?" he asked, if only to irritate her further as laughter built in his chest. Whether it was laughter of happiness or relief or surprise, he could not say, only that it was born of joy. "Isabelle, I would marry you tonight if you found a willing vicar."

"Well," she said, shifting her weight, a smile breaking its way through her pique, "I thought perhaps a ship's captain might do the job. I should like to wed on open water, between one home and the other..."

"A novel idea," Peter said, raising his brows, "and did you find one who is amenable to the concept?"

"I did, as it happens," she answered. "He's a bit of a pirate, but I'm convinced there's no one better for the task. He simply has to run an errand for me first, and fetch my Papa from the valley."

He looked at her, amazed that he was lucky enough to hold a woman like this in his arms, ecstatic that she wished to hold him back. In his wildest daydreams, he never would have thought her so committed to the idea of marrying him.

"I told Nathaniel already," she added. "When I asked for the ring, he wanted to know why."

"Ah," he said, so quickly reminded that life was not always so easy as following one's wishes. "And did he tell you that you have better prospects on the horizon, now that you've come home?"

"No!" She looked up at him, aghast. "Peter! What an awful thought! Nathaniel was delighted. He told me he knew firsthand how it felt to fall in love with an Applegate twin."

Peter blinked, immediately stunned and humbled by this news. He never would have predicted Nathaniel Atlas giving his blessing. He would expect justified horror at a man like Atlas seeing his sister, so recently rescued from afar, wed to a penniless scholar. He was so shaken by it, that he had no words to express how it felt.

"But where will we live?" he protested, making the arguments that Nathaniel had not. "How will I support you?"

"I'm entitled to a very large dowry, it turns out," she said with a careless shrug. "And we will live wherever we like. We can stay in Oxford while you teach, or travel until the stars change overhead. It will not matter so long as we are together ... after you finish your studies, of course."

"My studies," he repeated dumbly, making her giggle.

"That night on the *Harpy*." She sighed, winding her arms up and around his neck, pulling him close so that the tips of their noses brushed. "You told me you loved me. I should have told you that the feeling was mutual. I agonized for weeks over how one defines love, how I could know for certain, when I should have simply allowed myself to feel it and share it and tell you what you deserved to hear.

"I realized that I was doing this nonsensical overthinking about everything. I was doubting the very essence of myself as well as my right to love you. I do not need to be defined or changed or finished to be who I am. I am not a stranger to myself, no matter what secrets I uncover. And I do not need anything other than my own heart to know how I feel.

"I feel remorse, Peter. I am remorseful that I did not tell you the truth sooner and that I've taken so long to come to my senses."

"I did not mind," he told her, enchanted by how close she was, moved by how honest she was being, dying to brush his lips against hers. "I love you still."

She kissed him, warmth and enthusiasm flavoring her lips and spreading from her kiss into his every cell. "I love you back, Peter Applegate," she whispered, grinning. "So? Will you marry me?"

He nodded, unable to suppress his own grin and the happiness that lit within him, never to be extinguished again.

"Yes," he said, "of course I will."

EPILOGUE

*T*he tide was going out.

Yves Monetier looked down at his bare toes, dug into the sand on Dover beach as another flurry of white rose petals were washed out to sea.

He never thought he would stand on this side of the Channel again, but then again, he had long ago learned that life will unwind as it pleases, regardless of his plans.

It was a small wedding party, most of whom had already begun to climb the trail back to Meridian House for the feast to follow the vows. Those left on the beach were mooring the *Harpy,* which had served as a wedding chapel, bobbing on the sapphire waves between two nations, both dear to the bride.

"Papa, are you coming?" called Isabelle, her wedding dress gathered about her knees and her eyes shielded by the flat of her hand as she called to him from farther down the foam. "There is cake!"

"I'll be right along, my love," he called back, waving her off.

She smiled at him, turning to the ready arm of her new husband, who very clearly doted on every step she took. He watched them melt into the sunlight, walking in the easy strides of two people who knew each other completely.

Yves had never planned to have a daughter, and he certainly had never considered having a son. Now, he appeared to have both, and extended family besides.

He had waited those weeks of midsummer for word from England, reassurance that she was safe and well. His surprise at the personal return of the Dempierre boy, ready for yet another challenge of human smuggling, had been a pleasant one, even if its reasons were not entirely unexpected.

He had, after all, known his daughter well enough to see all the stolen glances she had tossed at the Applegate lad some months ago. He would have had to have been blind to miss them.

Back in Serre Chevalier, the little Monetier house was being tended by Babette Boulier, who promised to water the crops and feed the chickens until the Monetiers saw fit to return. She had sent with him a letter and a ribbon for Isabelle to wear on her wedding day, so that she might have a piece of her dearest friend on such an important occasion.

She had taken Isabelle's room, of course, leaving the master chamber neatly tucked and awaiting its master, a dried wreath of daisy flowers still hanging from the headboard. He did not know when he would return. Like Isabelle, he thought he might stay in England for a while, and find out what it had to offer him.

He trudged back up the knoll with his shoes in his hand, his hair blowing in the sea breeze. From here, he could see his daughter and her husband at the head of their banquet table. The chair to her right was empty, awaiting him, while the Atlases and Applegates and Dempierres swarmed around the table, making merry and wishing well.

He settled his gaze for a time on the fair-haired widow of Archibald Cooper, who had smiled at him so warmly when he arrived. She said something to her son, who smiled brightly at her and refilled her drink as the table was overcome with laughter.

Yes. England seemed a land of opportunity.

On the horizon, as they had sailed back to port, he had seen the looming stone walls of Dover Castle, the prison he had lived beneath for three long years, a lifetime ago.

He had expected it to grip at his heart, to fill him with ice and dread. He had thought he would fear to look upon it, fear to be reminded of the man he was and the things he had suffered. But when he saw it, he felt nothing at all. It was only stone on a hill, and above the joy of arrival and promise of the future, he could not hear its whispers of the past.

He approached these people expecting to slip into his seat unseen, and simply enjoy the revelry around him. Yet, when he approached, they turned and welcomed him, pouring him a glass of champagne and inviting him into the conversation and laughter.

On top of the table, his daughter reached for his hand, squeezing it tightly with love in her eyes.

"Thank you for giving me away, Papa," she said, sweet and soft in their native French. "Thank you for everything."

"To the father of the bride," echoed Nathaniel Atlas, standing and lifting his glass while his very pregnant wife looked on in affection. "To a man who saved a life and protected a secret, who restored a family and traveled the ocean. May we all aim to his stature and be grateful for his company."

"Hear hear," Isabelle cried, lifting her glass high so that the sun sparkled in the bubbles, casting dazzling light into his eyes.

Rumbles of agreement sounded around the table as the toast was made, and Yves did not know what else to do but give an appreciative smile and nod to the host, who looked at him with so much gratitude and admiration that Yves thought his ears would burn.

Later, when the sun had set and the two men sat at an empty banquet table, they shared a final glass of wine away from the chaos of the merrymakers. As they enjoyed the quiet, Yves told Nathaniel stories of Isabelle's girlhood. He talked of skinned knees and English lessons, of rescued animals and stolen sweets, and so many evenings spent calling her home from adventures in the forest.

He attempted to explain, to the best of his ability, just what it meant to have a child, and try to express just how much she had changed him, inside and out. He did his best to describe it all and he failed, for some things are beyond the powers of speech.

In the end, he imparted the one thing he could put into words. He told Nathaniel that whether she called herself

Atlas or Monetier or Applegate, she would always be that little girl with scraped knees and endless questions too, and so it must be for all fathers.

He waited until he was alone in the twilight-drenched Meridian yards to make his way to the overlook, near a newly finished gazebo, which faced the crashing waves of the sea and the endless, endless sky.

Next to the gazebo's elegant roof and carefully crafted railing and the smell of fresh paint, there were two stone markers in the grass. They were polished and gleaming with newness, topped with flowers and carved with a simple poem honoring the passing of Mary and Walter Atlas, who left the world together, as so many lovers wish to do.

He sat with them for a while, cross-legged on the green as the sun finished its journey beneath the horizon. He spoke, not very loudly, but with feeling. He gave what explanation he could of what had happened after that fateful day on the shore of Calais, after the two of them had left this world.

He did not know whether to apologize or to thank them, and so he did both, for both feelings were just as true.

He sat with the songs of the night as they came alive, the chirp of insects and the call of birds and the sweet serenade of the ocean, which he could no longer see. He would have stayed all night, but he knew he would be missed, and so he pushed himself to his feet, dusted his trousers off, and turned his sights to the manor, pulsing with warm light.

"You would be so proud of her," he told them before he left. "You would both be so proud of our daughter."

AUTHOR'S NOTE

Thank you so much for reading! As I'm sure you noticed, this book was a little different from the others. It was special to me because it gave me the opportunity to go back in time to a beloved part of my life.

In 2009, when I was 22 years old, I moved to Isabelle's little village in the Alps to work as an au pair (nanny) to two little girls. It was the first time in my life I'd ever seen snow. I skied poorly, I learned to drive (and walk!) on ice, and I fell in love with my surroundings just like Isabelle did. I imagine her living in the very same house as me, walking the same stream trails, and eating salad made from dandelion leaves that she'd gathered herself.

Serre Chevalier today is primarily a winter vacation spot, filled with world-famous ski slopes and packed with tourists in the snow. However, I recommend you visit in the summer, when it has emptied of visitors and has blossomed into the explosively beautiful and serene paradise I remember so well.

AUTHOR'S NOTE

Kit and Gigi will be next in the Silver Leaf saga, but don't worry, Mathias will absolutely be getting a book as well. As always, it can make a world of difference for a small, indie author like me if readers take the time to leave a review. To all of you who have done this for me, or will in the future, know that you have my overwhelming gratitude.

Like I say in every book, I love to hear from my readers! If you have feedback, questions, or ever just want to say hi, you can reach me at Ava@AvaDevlin.com

Thanks again!

Ava

BONUS MATERIAL

Read through a selection of Walter Atlas's love letters to his wife Mary, a special bonus for readers of this book. Get it HERE or at AvaDevlin.com/Bride

Printed in Great Britain
by Amazon